# The Emerald Prince

## A Novel

## Kristina Stangl

ISBN: 978-1-963232-09-7

First Edition
Cover Art: TheBookVeil
Map: BigValleyPress
Library of Congress Registration Number: TXU002489058
Printed in the United States of America

# DEDICATION

iii

In dedication to my loving family. Thanks for always encouraging my wild imagination.

To my readers, thank you for following me on this ongoing and epic journey.

Lastly, if you should by chance happen to magically stumble upon an emerald green frog of your own alongside your travels, then don't be afraid to pause and say hello. You never know, they just might be a cursed prince in disguise, after all…

# Also by Kristina Stangl

## The Enchanted Forest Saga:

The Curse of the Dark Horseman

The Sleeping Knight

The Emerald Prince

## Silverheart:

Cupid's Serenade

## Sex, Lies & Politics:

The Ambassador's Wife

Wake Up, Darling

My Life is a Soap Opera

Kill Me, Kiss Me

**www.kristinastangl.com**

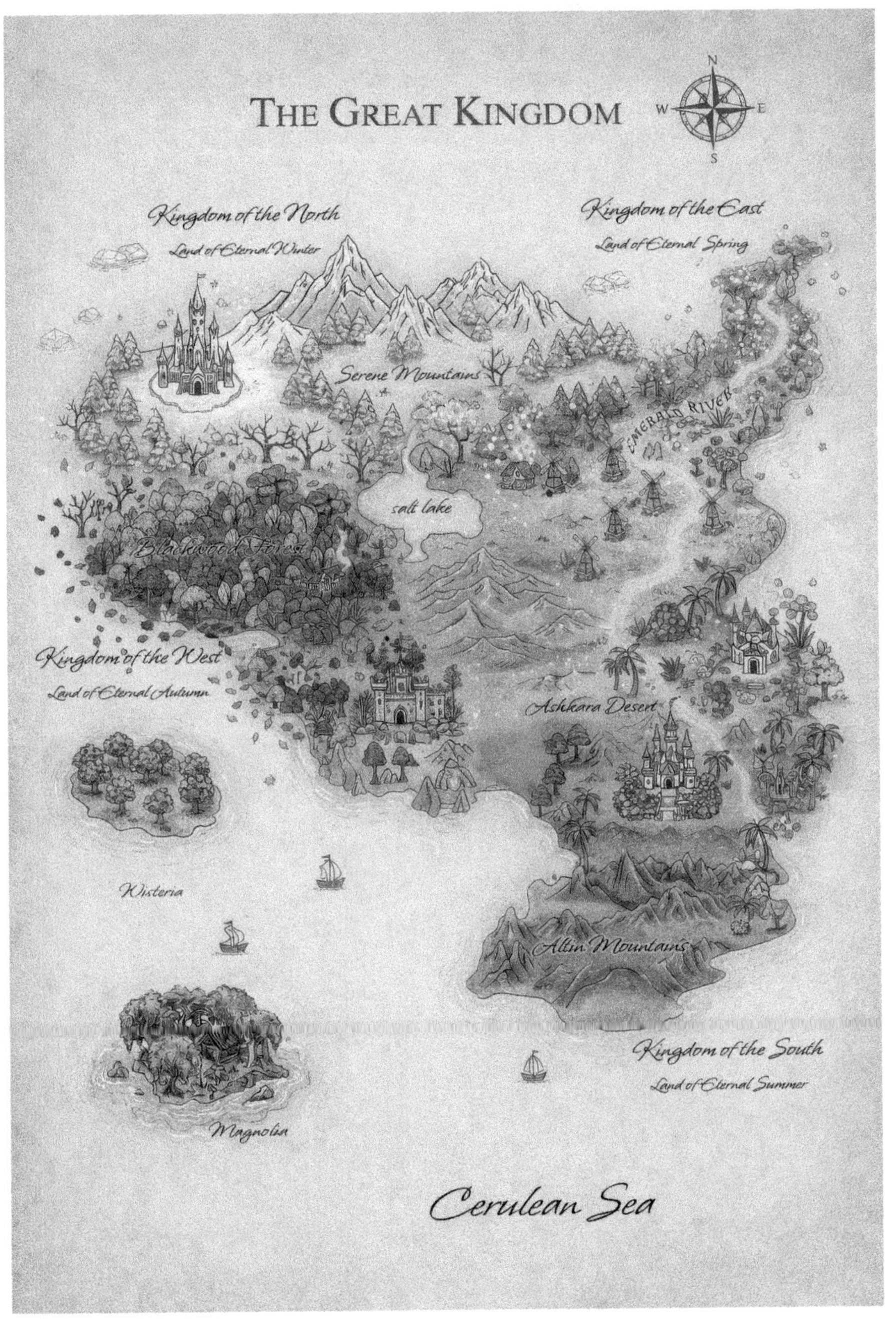
THE GREAT KINGDOM
N
W E
S
Kingdom of the North
Land of Eternal Winter
Kingdom of the East
Land of Eternal Spring
Serene Mountains
EMERALD RIVER
salt lake
Blackwood Forest
Kingdom of the West
Land of Eternal Autumn
Ashkara Desert
Wisteria
Altin Mountains
Magnolia
Kingdom of the South
Land of Eternal Summer
Cerulean Sea

# CONTENTS

# Chapter 1

## *An Enchanting Proposal*

Ever since Daphne Galloway was a young girl, she always dreamed of growing up and marrying a prince. It's why her mother, Kassie, gifted her with their family's heirlooms of tiaras, while her elder sister, Violet, was bequeath with a chest of jewelry.

After all, their mother knew that Daphne wanted to be a princess and all royals need tiaras. And so, she had a collection of ten, with her favorite being an emerald green heart-shaped stone tiara that just-so-happened to match her own emerald green eyes— a family trait of the Galloways.

But as Daphne grew into adulthood, she was starting to realize that finding, let alone marrying, a prince was going to be a real challenge. While her sister might have been so lucky to marry a prince of her own— a real knight in shining armor— Daphne didn't share the same such luck.

After Violet married King Maximus of the West and was crowned as his queen, Daphne stayed behind in merry old England at her family's ancestral estates, Galloway Manor and Wiltshire Hall, alongside with her younger brother, Adrian.

Eventually, as the years passed by, Daphne debuted into society as a young debutante in search of a respectable husband. But unfortunately, for her, Daphne's standards were far more exceedingly high for the available lot of bachelors. Many of whom, were either too plain, dull, obtuse, obnoxious, snobbish or simply put, *undesirable.*

As the daughter of Lord Henry, Earl of Galloway, Daphne was expected to secure an advantageous marriage. A union with another gentleman of nobility, with a respectable rank and title. But the problem was that none of the available bachelors in her vicinity captured her attention. None of them matched her personality. None of them were *a prince.*

Now, several years later, at the ripe age of twenty-three, Daphne found herself alone, unmarried, a soon-to-be-spinster and most importantly, *not a princess.*

And so, as Daphne sulked underneath a laurel tree located within the garden of her father's ancestral estate, Galloway Manor, she sat and pondered deeply about her future… or *lack thereof.*

Meanwhile, across from her was a small pond, which was covered with a blanket of vibrant magenta colored lily pads floating above the water. Picking up a small stone pebble from off the ground, Daphne promptly threw it into the pond and made a wish.

"If only I could meet and marry a prince," she sighed to herself.

And as the cold breeze from the traveling wind blew across her flaming red hair, Daphne tugged at her emerald green silk empire style gown, which was adorned with white ribbons and lace along its edges, and hoped for the best.

Suddenly, out-of-the-blue, to her surprise, she heard something approaching her. A splash of water, accompanied by a loud thump. A hop, perhaps. Afterwards, it was followed by a rather peculiar deep sound.

"Ribbit," it said.

Curiously, Daphne looked straight ahead and saw absolutely nothing. And so, she carried on and continued to daydream about what could never ever be…

But then, she heard that same sound, once again. Whatever it was, it simply refused to stop making noise!

"Ribbit… Daphne… ribbit…"

What the hell! Did it just say her name?

"Ribbit… Daphne… fret not… I'm here to make… ribbit… an offer…"

Looking straight ahead, Daphne still saw nothing before her. Was her mind playing tricks on her? Was she going mad?

"Daphne… I've been watching you… ribbit… for some time… ribbit …"

"Who's speaking?" she cried.

Unfortunately, Daphne saw nothing but the air. Indeed, she must have been foolishly talking to the wind!

"Ribbit… I'm here… ribbit… please look down…"

Following this direction, Daphne did just that and to her surprise, she saw a small emerald green creature staring back at her. It was round, slimy and covered in warts, along with a tiny pair of glowing yellow and button-shaped eyes. It took Daphne a full minute, before she soon recognized that this stranger was none other than a frog…. and unfortunately, for her, she always hated frogs!

"Gross!!!" she cried in disgust.

Instantly, Daphne jumped up to her feet and then, she ran as fast as she possibly could away from it. But, unfortunately, for her, the little emerald green frog was on a mission. He was simply determined to catch up with her. And so, as she ran, he followed in suit and hopped his merry way right behind her.

Relentlessly, the emerald green frog chased Daphne down the

garden, beyond the rose bushes, around the pond and eventually, circling right back to their original meeting place underneath the laurel tree.

"Daphne… ribbit… please… I just want to talk to you… ribbit…"

Out of fear, Daphne quickly climbed up the laurel tree and hid there. At least, to her, she believed that if she was off the ground, then the frog couldn't reach her. Too high enough for him to leap up towards her.

"Go away," she cried. "I don't care for frogs! Especially, ones that talk!"

Was she really speaking to a talking frog? Honestly, she must have gone crazy! Her brother, Adrian, must have snuck something into her tea this morning. Or, at the very least, tampered with her latest meal during breakfast!

"You're going to want… ribbit… to hear me… ribbit…," he croaked.

"I'm *not* coming down!" Daphne shouted in protest.

"I've been watching you… ribbit… for some time," he revealed.

"And?" she asked.

"And I rather *like you*…ribbit…"

"Oh great," she sighed aloud. "Are you saying that I can *only* attract frogs? Thanks, but this doesn't help my self-esteem!"

"Listen… ribbit… I'm under a spell… I wasn't always this way… ribbit…"

"What? Are you saying that you're cursed?" asked Daphne.

*That* certainly caught her attention.

"Yes… I am… ribbit…"

"Oh," Daphne replied in surprise. "In that case, are you asking for my help?"

"Yes… ribbit…"

A strange emerald green frog asking for her assistance. She, a young maiden. Daphne read enough fairy tales and books to know where this conversation was heading.

Her sister's favorite childhood fairy tale might have been *The Traveling Knight*, but Daphne's was always *True Love's Kiss*. Everyone who read that story knew that any spell or curse required true love's first kiss to break it.

"Wait, this doesn't somehow involve me kissing you, does it?" she asked him directly, with a raised brow.

"Yes… and… no… ribbit…"

"Ah," Daphne sighed.

Suddenly, she had a change of heart. After all, her own father, Lord Henry Galloway, was once the cursed Dark Horseman. Had it not been for her mother, Kassie, then his curse would never have been broken. Sadly, Daphne had a soft spot for those cursed.

"Unfortunately, my family has also experienced our fair share of past curses, too," she admitted with a dramatic sigh. "Alright, I'm listening."

"I know your sister… ribbit… Violet… the Queen… and her husband… Maximus… the King… ribbit…"

"You do?" Daphne asked, in astonishment. "Does this mean that you're from the Great Kingdom, too?"

"Yes… ribbit… I am…," he answered.

"Then why are you here in England? Who are you exactly?" Daphne finally asked the million-dollar question.

"I ran away… from my fiancé… ribbit… I teleported… into your world… to get away… ribbit…," he continued, "But… I'd like to make you… a proposition… ribbit… an enchanting offer…"

"And what's that?" Daphne curiously inquired.

"If you agree… to come down… from that tree… ribbit… and kiss me… then… I'll marry you… ribbit…"

"What makes you believe that I'd want to even marry you, in the first place?" she mocked him, sarcastically.

"I've been watching you… ribbit… for some time… and I'm rather fond of you…," he began, "You're patient… kind… and lovely… you'd make a fine bride… ribbit… plus… you seem to be at the perfect marriageable age… ribbit… but you have… no ring… on your finger… as for me… ribbit… I… too… need a wife… if I marry you… then I won't… have to marry my fiancé… it's a win for us both… plus I'm very rich… ribbit… I'll dress you in fine clothes… adorn you in gold and silver… along with rubies and pearls… and emerald tiaras… and make all of your dreams come true… ribbit…"

"Are you honestly proposing a marriage of convenience between yourself and I? A fair maiden married to a slimy green frog?"

"I won't be a slimy green frog for long… ribbit…," he clarified. "If you agree… to kiss me… and free me… from this curse… then you'll come to see… ribbit… I'm quite handsome… really… I'm rather a catch…"

"If I do as you say, then what becomes of your fiancé? Plus, how do you know my sister?"

"My fiancé… will have no other choice… but to move on… ribbit… after I take you as my wife… as for your sister… I've met her at court… I'm from the Kingdom of the East… the Land of Eternal Spring… ribbit…"

With his promising words, Daphne was *almost* ready to accept his enchanting offer. By now, she was most likely, never going to find a suitable match for herself in her homeland. Plus, her dreams of marrying a prince and becoming a princess was a reality practically deemed impossible at this point.

Perhaps, a marriage to a perfect stranger wouldn't be so bad, after all? Besides, if he really did turn back into a human, then maybe life with him wouldn't be so terrible. It was certainly a far better fate than staying at home and dying as a lonesome spinster, alongside with her younger brother.

Plus, he did offer to make all of her dreams come true. Truly, it was a magical proposal. Therefore, why the hell not?

"Okay, I accept your proposal. I'll marry you," Daphne reluctantly agreed, taking a huge blind leap of faith.

"Now, what shall I do next?" she asked him, as a follow-up question.

"Come down... ribbit... from that tree... and kiss me... ribbit..."

And so, Daphne did just that. As she picked up the small emerald green frog from off the ground with her trembling hands, she took in a deep breath and gathered all of her inner courage to kiss him. In the past, Daphne was never a fan of frogs and yet, here she was agreeing to marry one.

"Come on... ribbit... don't be afraid... I won't bite... ribbit... oh wait... a fly!"

Suddenly, to her absolute horror, he actually swallowed the damn creature and ate it right in front of her!

"Do you mind!" she angrily exclaimed, out of sheer frustration.

Truly, it was bad enough that she agreed to kiss a frog; let alone, kiss him right after eating a disgusting fly! Another small creature that Daphne also equally detested, right after frogs. Frogs. Flies. Perhaps, she was the real one *cursed*, after all!

"Oh sorry... ribbit...  couldn't help myself... I forgot to eat breakfast... ribbit..."

To his credit, he actually did make a genuine effort to apologize to her. Either way, Daphne just wanted to get this dreaded task over and done with. The sooner she kissed him, then the sooner this madness would all come to an abrupt end!

Closing her eyes shut, she leaned in and kissed him, right along the top of his slimy green head.

Afterwards, she slowly reopened her eyes and to her complete surprise, she saw the most handsome man standing right in front of her. In awe, she stared at the highly attractive figure, as his golden head of curly hair shined brightly against the gleaming sun. Meanwhile, his eyes were a deep shade of lapis blue, and his heart-shaped face was fair in complexion. Furthermore, he possessed a strong and sharply defined jawline, along with a pointed Grecian nose. And, within the blink of an eye, this perfect stranger stood before her and smiled from ear-to-ear.

With his body fully transformed, the charming and dashing young man— who appeared to be in his early thirties— wore a shiny black pair of leather wingtip oxford shoes, a ruffled cream blouse and a crisp emerald green cashmere suit, which was tailored to fit his tall, muscular and hourglass physique to perfection.

Additionally, he carried a white linen pocket square with an embroidered image of a little green frog resting above a pink lily pad that was tucked away within his breast pocket, and styled using a two point fold. Furthermore, alongside his ticket pocket was a golden pocket watch, which carelessly dangled off from his midnight black velvet petticoat. He was, without a doubt, regal and handsome. A true aristocrat.

"It's a pleasure to finally meet you, Daphne. My name is Prince Florian," he proudly announced, with a beaming grin.

But before she had a chance to react, he quickly grabbed a hold of her hand and said, "Come, let's get married. It's time to make you a princess."

And just like that, Daphne Galloway found herself engaged to a real-life prince!

# Chapter 2

## *The Kingdom of the East, the Land of Eternal Spring*

"The missing prince has finally returned!" the palace courtiers shouted cheerfully, upon their arrival.

As promised, Florian, the determined young prince, was on a full-scale mission to make all of Daphne's dreams come true. After all, he was a prince and she a young and fair maiden. Marriage to him would only secure her status as a princess. But most importantly, a *crown princess* at that.

However, to achieve this esteemed royal title, it required for them to journey back to his estranged kingdom. And so, by escorting his new bride-to-be through a darkened cave hidden deep within the enchanted forest, Florian and Daphne traveled through a magical portal.

Shortly, soon afterwards, the newly engaged couple stepped through a magic mirror located on the opposite end of the portal and arrived into Florian's realm, better known as the Great Kingdom. A magical world, which united four individual principalities that were each ruled by four separate monarchs. Kingdoms that included: the Kingdom of the East, the Land of Eternal Spring; the Kingdom of the North, the Land of Eternal

Winter; the Kingdom of the South, the Land of Eternal Summer; and her sister's land, the Kingdom of the West, the Land of Eternal Autumn.

"Daphne, welcome to my domain, the Kingdom of the East, the Land of Eternal Spring," Florian happily announced.

Instantly, Daphne quickly scanned her new environment. At first glance, the imperial palace was quite stunning and resembled a royal estate that was plucked straight out of a classical fairy tale. Just like the castles found within her favorite childhood storybook, the imperial palace's sparkling marbled walls were shining in the luminous shade of pearly cream— similar to a sparkling diamond star, floating high above in the night sky.

Furthermore, the windows that surrounded the palace were tall, oversized and brightly lit, providing a spectacular view of the outside gardens, which hosted a variety of flowers, all in bloom. From bold yellow sunflowers to muted pink tulips, to crimson red roses to purple irises; overall, it was a breathtaking floral oasis, designed for all visitors to admire and cherish from afar.

Meanwhile, the palace's interiors and specifically, within the current room in which they were graciously standing in, it was a place adorned with hundreds of sweet-scented pink lily flowers and aged ivy vines, which stretched across the high ceilings and wrapped around the tall porcelain columns that secured the premise. And in the center of the room was an emerald throne, fit for a king. Instantly, Daphne acknowledged that this special room must have been *the throne room.*

"My son! You've finally decided to come back home!" King Titus happily cried, as he forcefully barged in through the front doors.

Almost immediately, Daphne reverted her attention over to the king, aka her soon-to-be-future-father-in-law. At first glance, she noticed that he was a short and stout man, who was about half the size of his son in height.

Sporting a grey mustache and beard, the king also possessed a round belly, resembling a balloon. He was dressed in an emerald green velvet cape, along with a ruffled cream blouse, a black pair of trousers and a black leather pair of loafers. Additionally, he wore a floral wreath made of pink lilies above his head, which appeared to be his substitute for a formal metal crown.

Overall, he looked to be a sweet and jolly king, as reflected by his positive and welcoming attitude. However, a second later, the king's joy was soon replaced by a concerned expression, as displayed on his chubby and flushed face.

"My dear boy," the king continued, tenderly, "Why did you leave us for so long? You should have come home much earlier. We were all worried sick that something terrible might have happened to you."

"No need to worry, Father," Florian replied, soothingly. "I had… umm… well… business to attend to."

"Business? What business?" asked his father, eagerly. "What sort of business takes my sole heir, the crown prince, away to travel into another realm? Remember, Florian, you are *the* emerald prince. The bringer of spring. This kingdom cannot function nor survive without you. You're our entire future."

But before Florian had a chance to respond to his father, King Titus quickly took notice of the fair and lovely maiden standing near his son's side. Instantly, King Titus' worried expression quickly transformed into a beaming smile, which blossomed across his now satisfied face and the rest was history.

"My goodness, Florian, I see that you've finally found yourself a new bride, after all," King Titus happily smiled on.

"Yes, Father, I have," Florian proudly replied. "And as such, I'd like to proceed with the marriage ceremony as soon as possible."

"So, when you said that you had business to attend to, you really weren't joking," his father laughed on.

"Ah, if only your mother, my sweet Queen Ophelia, was still around to witness your wedding," King Titus sighed, somberly. "Your mother would have adored this upcoming ceremony so very much."

"I'm sure that Mother will be watching over us, in spirit," Florian added on.

"As you're well aware, your twin sister, Diana, is currently living up north with her husband, Orion, Duke of Starlight," the king reminded his son. "Hopefully, she'll be able to arrive in time to attend the ceremony in-person."

"We shall invite them all, including my fiancé's family as well," Florian proclaimed.

"Oh, does your lady have family living here, in the Great Kingdom?" asked the king, most curiously.

"Indeed, she does," Florian replied, as a matter-of-fact. "Her sister is Queen Violet of the West. And her brother-in-law is King Maximus of the West."

"Maximus' sister-in-law? Oh my, what a splendid match, my dear boy!" cried the king, joyfully. "With this marriage, we'll be able to unite our two great houses together, after all. What a superb union! Indeed, come to think of it, your bride does resemble her sister, the queen. The same fiery red hair, rosy cheeks and emerald green eyes. Ah, yes, emerald is a good omen. The sacred color of our beloved kingdom."

Reverting his full attention over to Daphne, the king asked her, "My dear, we are going to be family from now on. Come, do tell me more about yourself."

Taking a step forward, Daphne took a bow and said, "Thank you, Your Highness. My name is Lady Daphne Kassandra Galloway. I am the second daughter of the Earl and Countess of Galloway. As your son previously mentioned, I am the younger sister of Queen Violet of the West and the sister-in-law to King Maximus of the West, as well as the aunt to their two sons, Crown Prince Leopold and his brother, Prince Tristan. Also, I am the elder sister of Lord Adrian Galloway, the heir to the Earl of Galloway title, estates and fortune. And lastly, I am also the great-granddaughter of Ruby, the Elder."

"Splendid!" the king clapped, joyfully. "What a wonderful pedigree!"

A second later, the doors to the throne room flung wide open and about a dozen or so courtiers quickly flocked onto the premise.

"Is it true that the emerald prince has arrived back home? The rumor of his arrival are swarming throughout the palace," spoke his assistant.

"Yes, Atticus," the king spoke to his most trusted advisor. "As you can already see, Florian has returned. And now, we must act quickly."

Turning his attention to the rest of the palace courtiers in the room, King Titus happily announced, "Listen all, my son, Crown Prince Florian of the East, has found himself a new bride. This lovely and fair maiden is known as Lady Daphne Kassandra Galloway. She is the sister to the Queen of the West. And hence, from this day forward, she will be now known as Crown Princess Daphne of the East. Please, take a moment to honor your new crown princess, Princess Daphne."

Instantly, the crowd proceeded to bow down in front of Daphne and as a result, our heroine was at a loss for words. All of her life, she had dreamt of this magical moment, a hundred times over. And now, her dreams were finally coming true. Suddenly, everything that was happening in real-time, all felt so surreal.

"What should I do?" Daphne whispered over to Florian.

"Nothing," he replied. "Just smile on and enjoy the moment."

Following his advice, Daphne did just that. Afterwards, once the palace courtiers all rose up and stood back into place, they returned their attentions over to the king.

Meanwhile, King Titus looked straight at his staff and instructed them with the following, "Prepare the palace at once. The wedding shall take place first thing, tomorrow morning."

"Tomorrow morning?" Daphne promptly cried out, in surprise.

As much as she wanted to get married and become a princess, she didn't expect for it to happen so soon. A day wasn't enough time to plan for a proper royal wedding. Plus, she hadn't yet visited her sister, either.

"Trust me, my dear, you'll want this wedding to take place come tomorrow," spoke the king, sternly. "That is, if you still *want* a wedding to take place at all."

"What does he mean?" Daphne turned her attention over to her groom-to-be.

"Unfortunately, my father is right," Florian sighed, as he ran his hand through his thick golden crown of hair.

"How so?" she pressed on.

"Remember, when I mentioned that I had a fiancé?" he reminded her.

"Yes," Daphne recalled.

"Well, I should probably mention that she's also a wicked witch…"

"Which means," interrupted his father, "If you want to avoid any issues with Esmeralda, then we must act quickly and have you two wed, before any more havoc reaches our kingdom."

"Is your former fiancé dangerous?" Daphne asked, cautiously.

"Very," replied King Titus, in place of his son. "The damn witch is a nuisance. No offense to your great-grandmother, Ruby, the Elder, of course."

"Yes, Ruby is a well-respected sorceress and a good witch," Florian added.

"And we are forever grateful to her, as well as to your sister and brother-in-law for defeating Vera, the Evil Queen," King Titus chimed in.

Indeed, seven years ago, Daphne's sister, Violet, had traveled to the Great Kingdom, along with Maximus, to battle Vera, the Evil Queen, who had previously usurped the throne and unleashed a reign of terror out in the western kingdom. With the help of Ruby and Maximus, Violet was able to defeat their long-lost great aunt and reestablish peace throughout the land, once they ascended the throne.

"But," the king continued on, "I should never have allowed my late wife,

Ophelia, to have betrothed my only son to her best friend's daughter, while Florian and Esmeralda were mere babes in their cribs."

"To Mother's credit, Esmeralda wasn't yet a witch," Florian pointed out. "Plus, the Marquis and Marchioness of Clover are such dear and sweet friends of the palace."

"It doesn't matter how kind or sweet they were and still are," his father cried. "Either way, Esmeralda idolized and followed in the late evil queen's footsteps and delved into the occult. *Black magic.* She might be the daughter of the Marquis of Clover, but regardless, I won't have my son married to such a heartless wench, no matter how wealthy her family is. No, a sister to a western queen is a far favorable match. Besides, I've always admired your friend, Maximus, too."

"So, it's all settled, then?" asked Florian to his father.

"As far as I'm concerned, you found yourself a new bride. Therefore, your engagement to Lady Esmeralda of Clover is hereby annulled."

"Thank you, Father," spoke Florian, gratefully.

"But don't think that Esmeralda will quietly sit by and take this news so easily," his father forewarned. "No, if we want to avoid any further issues, then we must act quickly. Time is of the essence."

With Florian and King Titus now staring directly at Daphne, as well as the entire crew of palace courtiers all gathered around them, the king eagerly asked, "Shall tomorrow at ten o'clock in the morning be favorable for you?"

As much as Daphne preferred to have a longer engagement; however, given the dire circumstances now currently facing them, she ultimately caved in. And with a simple nod, Daphne found herself agreeing to their proposal. A second later, she was thrust into a busy crowd of palace courtiers, all eager to plan her upcoming wedding within the span of a single day.

# Chapter 3

## *A Royal Wedding*

"And with this ring, I, Prince Florian Apollo of the East, hereby take Lady Daphne Kassandra Galloway, as my lawful wife," the crown prince vowed, as he placed a shiny brass golden ring around his bride's finger.

A second later, the priest pronounced them as husband and wife, as well as the new eastern crown prince and crown princess, and the lawful heirs to the emerald thrones of spring. Additionally, for the first time since his curse was broken, Florian and Daphne locked lips as an ordinary mortal pair.

And just like that, come overnight, Daphne's entire life had drastically changed. No longer was she a young, unmarried and innocent fair maiden, wandering aimlessly through the fields of her father's grand estate.

Instead, after discovering a cursed prince and then, breaking his spell, Daphne was quickly whisked away to a foreign realm. And while *her kiss* might have transformed the little emerald green frog into a dashing and charming mortal prince; *his kiss*, in return, turned her into a real-life princess, as well. Thus far, they were *even*.

But the hours leading up to their grand wedding was certainly an adventure in the making. As soon as Daphne agreed to participate in the last-minute wedding ceremony, the palace courtiers quickly swept in and officially, they were off to business.

In no time, Daphne was met by an entire team of dedicated courtiers. There was Atticus, the king's right-hand man; as well as Marcia, April and May, her personal assistants and ladies-in-waiting.

Additionally, there was Lavinia, the wedding courtier and managing housekeeper, along with her assistant, Hyacinth. Meanwhile, introductions were in order with Caldwell, the palace chef; along with Fern, the butler; and Nike, the court messenger. Plus, Poppy and Chloe, the decorators; and Merrybelle and Honeybelle, the twin seamstresses.

Furthermore, there was also Pascal, the court jester and entertainer. Not to mention, Melody, Isabella and Isadora, the court musicians. And lastly, there was an entire army of royal imperial knights, including Atherton, her own newly appointed personal knight and bodyguard.

One by one, Daphne met with each member of the court. First, Atticus congratulated her with a warm hug and gifted her with a fresh bouquet of white dahlias. Afterwards, Lavinia and Hyacinth quickly introduced themselves to her as well and then, proceeded to present her with a glimpse of the wedding itinerary, which was already completed, all down to the very last of details.

Overwhelmed by the fast and high-paced environment that she was thrusted into, Daphne promptly agreed to all of Lavinia's and Hyacinth's suggestions, without a second thought. Therefore, upon her approval, Lavinia and Hyacinth immediately handed the wedding invitations over to Nike. Afterwards, the court messenger swiftly fled the scene in great haste, running straight through the palace's front gates, determined to deliver the last-minute royal wedding invitations to the invited guests.

A few minutes later, Daphne was met by Caldwell and Fern to review the banquet's menu. In honor of their eastern land, the crown princess and her entourage voted for the main dessert to be a lime green princess fondue cake, decorated with pale pink lilies and crimson red roses as its icings.

Furthermore, the kitchen committee also selected pink lemonade as the refreshment of choice, along with a generous feast consisting of baked pheasants, steamed vegetables and springtime fruit in honor of the royal occasion. And as soon as Daphne agreed to the menu's final selections, Caldwell and Fern were off to work.

Next, came Pascal, Melody, Isabella and Isadora. After previewing their musical talents on the spot— which consisted of serene and whimsical musical notes stemming from the harp, piano and flute— Daphne joyfully watched on as Pascal proceeded to dance, juggle and summersault to their pleasant tunes. Happily, the crown princess enthusiastically clapped on, as she eagerly watched the entertainment from the comfort of her seat.

By now, Florian and King Titus were long gone. At this point in the day, Daphne was alone in the throne room and left within the care of her ladies-in-waiting, along with her seamstresses and decorators.

Meanwhile, as Daphne quietly sat and watched the vivid performances held by her court jester and musicians, Merrybelle and Honeybelle quickly took advantage of this opportune time to take her measurements. Afterwards, they presented her with a collection of fine pearls and sparkling diamonds, as well as ribbons of gold and silver to select from.

In the end, Daphne decided to go with the pearls and silver ribbons to add onto her new wedding dress. And of course, as an eastern tradition, an emerald green ribbon was reserved to serve as her bridal belt, as well as the primary ribbon source to the hemmed lace found along the edges of her bridal gown. Meanwhile, her ladies-in-waiting all agreed to wear similar emerald green mermaid dresses in her honor.

Once the bridal gown and bridesmaids' dresses were all settled upon, Daphne met with her decorators, Poppy and Chloe, to coordinate the selection of floral arrangements for the wedding. In honor of the spring palace, it was mutually agreed upon to use pink lilies to serve as her official royal wedding bouquet.

Additionally, since the palace was also the home to about a hundred or so different types of native flowers— including white daisies, plum shaded dahlias, cherry red roses, baby pink tulips and canary yellow daffodils— Daphne agreed to also incorporate these spring flowers as the main décor used on the guests' tables.

Once everything was all finalized, Daphne exited the throne room with Atherton, by her side. Being the kind and sincere personal knight that he was, Atherton generously gave the crown princess a private tour of the palace, before eventually escorting her upstairs and into her bridal bedchamber. A room, where Daphne would ultimately come to spend her last night alone as a virginal maiden.

Flash forward to twenty-four hours later, Daphne was now seated at the head of the royal table located within the banquet hall. At long last, she was now a married woman with her new husband, the crown prince, by her side.

And even though she was surrounded by hundreds of foreign and unfamiliar faces, she still took great comfort in the fact that she wasn't entirely alone in this new transitional stage of her life. After all, her family were only a few feet away from her, seated at a separate table. Therefore, she took a deep sigh of relief.

Ever the adoring and trustworthy family, the Galloways— compromising of her parents, brother, great-grandmothers, sister, brother-in-law and nephews— all managed to attend her wedding in-person. Regardless of the short notice, her family still miraculously came to support her.

Luckily, for Daphne, her parents welcomed the happy but surprising news. Even though they were taken a bit aback by the sudden announcement; however, in the end, Lord Henry and Lady Kassandra were genuinely thrilled to bear witness to their youngest daughter's marriage to the crown prince.

Therefore, with her family's blessings, Daphne wed Florian. Even though their wedding was planned and executed all within the span of a single day, it still didn't prevent the mass crowd— by the hundreds— from attending their blissful union, including both royals and ordinary citizens, alike. Plus, judging by the luxurious setting and whimsical floral décor, this was truly a fairy tale style wedding come to life. Indeed, Daphne's wedding was really a spectacular and grand affair!

Not only was Daphne the ultimate belle of the ball, but with her long princess style ballroom gown that was decorated with hundreds of shiny white pearls all individually handsewn onto her bridal dress, along with bright silver and emerald green ribbons encircling her gown, she was also a living spring goddess brought to life.

Additionally, her long red hair was adorned with a floral wreath, which served as her royal crown. The floral wreath was comprised of pale pink lilies, accompanied by green ivy vines that were wrapped around to serve as its base. Lastly, Daphne wore a pair of opaque pearl earrings that her sister, Violet, had previously gifted to her before she left home to marry the western king.

Meanwhile, the party's festivities were in full action. Currently, the musicians were happily playing away, while Pascal, the court jester, was busy dancing to their merry tunes and juggling to entertain the plentiful guests in attendance.

Furthermore, hundreds more had already flocked over to the buffet table and were eagerly helping themselves to a generous serving of the scrumptiously cooked food. But if eating a delicious meal wasn't one's forte, then there was always dancing. And judging by the current mass sea of people, the dancefloor was as crowded as a school of fish.

"Shall I have the next dance?" Florian asked his new bride.

"I must admit," Daphne answered in shame, "I'm not too familiar with your style of dancing. Although I once tried to dance at my sister's wedding, held several years ago. But that was a western dance, not an eastern one."

"Then I shall make it my personal duty to teach you," Florian promised her. "But for now, just follow my lead. I'll go slowly, so that you can easily keep up with me."

And with that heartfelt vow, Daphne agreed to his request and followed her new groom over to the dancefloor.

As the music proceeded to play a slow tune, Daphne grabbed a hold of Florian's right-hand, as his left-hand wrapped tightly around her slender waist. Given that this was the very first time that Daphne had ever allowed him to physically touch her like this, she privately acknowledged to herself just how strange all of this now felt. Not only was she a wife in name; but soon enough, their bodies were destined to meet, as well.

Up until now, Daphne had never slept with a man before. Let alone, kissed one. In fact, Florian was the *first and only man* that she had ever kissed before. And now, with him standing so close to her, with his chest practically pressed up against her bosom, Daphne suddenly grew anxious.

"Don't worry, my princess," he reassured her, sensing her nervousness. "It will get easier with each move that we take, together. I promise to help guide you every step of the way."

With those comforting words, accompanied by his beaming smile that stretched from ear-to-ear, Daphne suddenly felt her heart skip a beat. Without any reason, her chest grew heavy and her heart continued to flutter with excitement. This was most certainly, an odd sensation. She had never, ever felt this strange way before!

Happily, the newlyweds continued to dance away on the dancefloor, hand-in-hand and as promised, Daphne followed in Florian's lead. As he moved, she moved. As he turned, she turned. And as he leaned over to his side, she also leaned over to her side. In perfect harmony, the couple glided across the dancefloor with such elegance and grace, that it was almost as if they were a perfect pair who were simply made for each other.

Although this was her first-time dancing alongside with Florian, Daphne soon found herself enchanted by his aura. No longer was he the same slimy green frog from when she first met him. Instead, he was transformed into the perfect prince. A man who not only guided her across the dancefloor with the utmost ease and suave debonair, but he also possessed the generous patience to wait on her, too.

Thus far, Florian genuinely seemed to check all the boxes. Indeed, he was charming, handsome, kind, respectful and admired by all who knew him. Honestly, Daphne couldn't have scored a better match than him. And now, dancing alongside with him in this magical palace, she was glad that she waited and saved herself for him.

Meanwhile, as they glided across the stage, Daphne suddenly caught sight of her sister, Violet, dancing away with her husband, Maximus. Much to Daphne's own surprise, not only was her sister dressed in a lovely sparkling violet silk empire gown, but she was also *very much pregnant*, once again.

Plus, judging by her overly large, extra round and protruding belly, Violet must have been well into the advance stages of her pregnancy. At least a good six months or so. But how could her sister have neglected to write to inform her about her third pregnancy?

Suddenly, the music ended and the dancing came to a halt. Determined to speak directly with her sister, she quickly excused herself from the crown prince's company. Meanwhile, as Daphne made her way over to her sister's side; Florian, in return, decided to pay Violet's husband, Maximus, a visit himself.

"Violet!" Daphne cried, as she rushed over to elder sister.

"Daphne!" Violet exclaimed, in return, as she quickly dashed off and then, threw her arms around her younger sister to give her a heartfelt hug.

"Many congratulation to you and Florian," Violet happily cheered, as she gently pulled herself away from their embrace. "I always knew that the two of you would make a wonderful pair!"

"Always? Whatever do you mean?" asked Daphne, in surprise.

"Don't you recall?" Violet asked her, in return. "At my wedding, I tried to introduce you to Prince Florian. I told you that he was a good friend of Maximus."

"You did? Unfortunately, I can't remember," Daphne admitted in earnest. "Back then, I think I was too lost in my world of books. Either way, our paths never previously crossed, until as of recently."

"Regardless, your paths *still* crossed, after all," Violet pointed out. "And in the end, that's all that truly matters."

Wanting to change the subject, Daphne was quick to retort, "Well, what about you? Pray tell me, dear sister, just when were you planning to tell me about my new niece or nephew?"

"Oh… well… I was planning to write to you," Violet gushed. "But then, Maximus thought it best that I surprise both you and our family in-person, instead."

"Hmm, so, when did you mean to inform us exactly?" Daphne interrogated her. "Once the child was born!"

"Of course *not*!" Violet laughed on. "We were planning to visit. But then, your wedding unexpectedly came about and so, what can I say, today is the big reveal!"

Proudly, her sister placed her hands above her round belly and happily smiled on. In the end, motherhood suited the queen so incredibly well.

"Either way, you're a fantastic mother," Daphne complemented her. "Leopold, Tristan and now, this little one, couldn't have been blessed with a better mother."

"Oh, thank you, Daphne," Violet blushed. "You know, being a mother is the greatest adventure that I've ever embarked upon. I might be a wife, a queen, a daughter and a sister, but motherhood trumps them all. I would sooner die a violent death, before allowing anything negative to befall upon my children. And one day soon, you'll also come to experience this same all-consuming and overwhelming feeling for yourself first-hand, too. Just you wait."

"I, a mother?" Daphne repeated, in surprise. "Please, Violet, I've only just gotten married. I cannot think of being a mother, just yet."

"Well, don't be too surprised," Violet warned her. "After all, Mother and I both had our first pregnancies, just a year shy into our marriages. Thus, assuming that you also follow in the same Galloway tradition, then I'm sure that your first-born child will arrive sometime by either the end of this year or by early next year, at the latest."

Unfortunately, little did Violet know that Daphne's marriage was actually a marriage of convenience. As of yesterday, she might have agreed to be Florian's wife; but now, come today, she wasn't entirely certain about the true status of their union. Especially, with regards to their relationship in the bedroom.

Therefore, as far as Daphne was concerned, a planned pregnancy was still a faraway fantasy that was miles away from her reaches. Either way, she didn't have the heart to admit all of this to Violet, right now. After all, her sister didn't need to know everything about her private life.

"Come now, Violet," Daphne spoke, "Enough about me. Tell me more about this new baby."

"Well, I'm expecting to give birth in a matter of a few short months…"

"A few months? Really?" asked Daphne, sarcastically. "Violet, you're practically ready to pop!"

"I know. But honestly, all of my pregnancies have been like this," Violet admitted. "I've always been exceptionally larger than most females, with my stomach being the size of a watermelon. But either way, Maximus and I are hoping for a girl."

"Aww, a baby girl. Finally, a niece. I'm sure Leopold and Tristan will simply adore her," Daphne gushed, happily.

Instantly, Daphne looked across the banquet hall and saw her nephews standing by her family's table. Leopold, age six, had a full head of bright blonde locks, silver eyes and sharply defined facial features, which he inherited directly from his father's side. Meanwhile, Tristan, age five, had midnight black hair, emerald green eyes and soft facial features, which he clearly took from his mother's side. A spitting reincarnation image of his maternal grandfather and their father, Lord Henry, Earl of Galloway.

Currently, both boys were playing sword fighting with their grandfather and uncle, Adrian Galloway, while their grandmother, Kassie, and great-great-grandmothers, Maureen and Ruby, watched on.

Although the boys were sweet and adorable children; however, at the same time, they were, just like their uncle in his youth, a wild pair to follow. As much as Daphne loved her nephews dearly to death, she was also secretly looking forward to having a niece.

"Yes, a niece will be ideal," Daphne spoke, with much conviction. "Any thoughts about a name?"

"Well, actually, yes," her sister answered. "If it's a girl, then we've been thinking about the name, Marigold. After all, marigold is another flower name, just like mine. Plus, the M initial will also honor her father, Maximus, too. And of course, it's the official flower of our western kingdom. Therefore, if it's a girl, then we plan on naming her Marigold."

"Princess Marigold," Daphne repeated, with a beaming smile. "You know, it's got a nice ring to it. I absolutely adore it."

"Thank you," Violet happily replied. "I knew that you would."

Suddenly, before Daphne could say another word, a loud banging noise instantly echoed across the entire room. Shortly, thereafter, it was promptly followed by an accompanying cloud of green smoke. Whatever ruckus this was, judging by the shocked expressions found within the crowd, this wild spectacle was entirely unexpected and most importantly, *unplanned.*

"Did no one else find *me* worthy enough to be bestowed with an exclusive invitation?" spoke the young woman, who now appeared behind the vanishing green cloud of smoke.

Like everyone else at this party, Daphne curiously directed her gaze over to this stranger. Whomever this woman was, she was an attractive young debutante. Most likely, a female in her early thirties.

Observing her from afar, Daphne noted that she had a pale face as white as snow, lips as red as a crimson apple, and silky hair that was long, straight and midnight black in color— almost identical to the shade of a raven. Meanwhile, her eyes were green, just like Daphne's, although it was a level darker than hers. While Daphne's eyes might have been emerald green, this lady's eyes were more jade-like in color and was covered with an extra thick set of dark lashes.

Apart from her attractive face, her figure was also just as lovely. A perfect hourglass shape, with a slender waist, a full plump bosom and a long pair of legs. But instead of wearing a conservative gown like the rest of the members of the court, this mysterious young woman was sporting a very revealing outfit that practical exposed all angels of her voluptuous body.

With an unforgiving plunging low neckline— stretching from the top of her neck and all the way down to the bottom of her stomach— this mysterious woman wore a thin sheer black chiffon and mermaid style gown, which showcased her perfectly curved figure.

Meanwhile, her breasts were barely hidden from public view on account of the thin straps of lace that hardly covered them in the first-place. Plus, the high slits found on each side of her dress worked to expose her long and bare legs. Furthermore, her slender back was completely left open from the behind, altogether.

Had she wanted to remove her dress, then it would literally take just one light push of her finger for the entire gown to fall down onto the ground, leaving her stark naked. But regardless of her choice of attire, she was still a stunning and ravenous beauty. A seductress muse, if ever there was one.

"After all," the mysterious woman continued on, "The crown prince is *my* *fiance*. Shouldn't *I* have been given the honor to sit at the front row and watch this public mockery take place? A laughable and illegitimate union? Besides, even my own parents are here, so why not me!"

"Darling, we thought it best that you stayed at home," replied the Marquis and Marchioness of Clover. "We didn't want your feelings to get hurt."

"Oh hush, Mother and Father!" their daughter scolded them, publicly. "This is between Florian and me… and now, that new whore of his!"

"Watch your filthy mouth, Esmeralda of Clover!" King Titus shouted angrily, as he banged his clenched fist against the head of the banquet table. "You shall address my new daughter-in-law by her rightful name, Crown Princess Daphne of the East, or simply, Princess Daphne."

"And as far as I am concerned," the king continued on, "Your previous engagement to my son was nonbinding. Therefore, his marriage to Princess Daphne is perfectly legal. Furthermore, if you prefer not spending tonight as a prisoner of my castle, kept inside within the darkest corners of my rat-infested dungeon, then I highly suggest that you leave this party… *at once!*"

"I shall go, when *I'm* ready to leave, my king," Esmeralda spoke up, in defiance. Fearlessly challenging the king.

Turning her attention over to Florian, she looked straight into his lapis blue eyes and said, "Enjoy your time with this fairy tale princess," as she pointed directly at Daphne, with her index finger in utter disgust.

"But once this honeymoon stage is over and done with, and you find yourself craving the touch of a *real woman* who can truly *please you*, then you know where to find me. Until then, I'll be waiting."

Afterwards, she blew Florian a kiss and then, she sent the crystal chandelier come crashing down towards the king's direction. A second later, Esmeralda vanished through another cloud of green smoke.

Luckily, Atticus was standing nearby and was able to push the king away towards safety. Meanwhile, the crowd was left utterly stunned and speechless. However, being the jolly man that he was, King Titus simply refused to allow Esmeralda to have the last laugh. After all, this was the grand wedding of his only son and heir.

"Come now, all," the king shouted to the crowd. "Your prince has found a new princess. Let the celebration continue!"

"Here, here," shouted the crowd in return, as they lifted their glasses high up into the air and cheered on as the music and festivities promptly reconvened.

Meanwhile, Florian rushed over to Daphne's side and swiftly pulled her away from her sister and back over to him.

"Sorry Violet," he apologized to his new sister-in-law. "But I really must speak with your sister."

"But of course," Violet agreed, without any protest.

Turning his attention over to Daphne, he said, "Come with me. You and I need to talk."

And just like that, Florian grabbed his new bride by the hand and dragged her out of the ongoing ceremony.

# Chapter 4

## *How the Emerald Prince Came to Be*

A few minutes later, the couple stood side-by-side outside on the balcony, which was located right behind the ongoing festivities and overlooking the imperial palace's royal gardens. From this view, everything down below appeared so pleasantly peaceful and beautiful.

However, even with the majestic scenery surrounding them, it still failed to undue the sadness currently reflected upon the crown prince's gloomy face.

"I'm sorry that you had to witness all of that," Florian apologized to her in great shame.

For all his worth, the crown prince was a true gentleman. Even though Daphne didn't yet know Florian all too well— after all, he was still, technically a foreigner to her— but even as a perfect stranger, she could already tell that he came from a kind, sincere and respectful lot.

"Florian, I don't blame you. Honestly, it's not your fault," Daphne was quick to help set him at ease. "Although, I wish I had known the truth about her true character much sooner, so that I could have better prepared myself mentally in advance. She might be a witch, but she's also a scorned woman more than anything else."

"To prepare in advance to face my psychotic former fiancé?" he skeptically asked, with a raised brow. "Come now, Daphne, you're a smart woman. Certainly, you must have already arrived to the inevitable conclusion that there was absolutely nothing in this world that you could have done to prevent Esmeralda from causing such havoc and destruction. Not to mention, her acting so utterly disrespectful towards you."

"Either way, I'd still like to know what I'm up against," she told him. "I'm not one to easily shy away. Besides, I might not be as powerful or as beautiful as her…"

"Beautiful?" he asked in surprise. "Daphne, there is no comparison."

"Oh," she replied.

If Florian found Esmeralda more attractive than her, then she was just going to have to accept this reality… *sadly*.

"Daphne, you're drop dead gorgeous," he told her, as he reached over to gently tilt her chin up with his hand. "Like I said before, there's no comparison. You are the new crown princess, *not her*. Absolutely beautiful, both inside *and* out."

Did Florian really just say that she was gorgeous? Beautiful? Prettier than the seductress, who had most recently crashed their wedding? This was certainly unexpected!

"I'm ashamed that she called you by that spiteful name," he confessed aloud.

By now, the crown prince moved his hand away from her face and was now, clenching it tightly in the form of a fist. "Especially, in front of your family. I only wish that I could have stopped her in time."

"Again, it's not your fault," she reassured him, as she gently brushed her hand against his face, forcing him to look at her directly. "You are not responsible for her actions. Besides, my family and I have dealt with worse villains in the past than Esmeralda. Trust me, I can deal with the likes of her."

"But still. I, at the very least, owe you the truth," he confessed, as he leaned his face against the palm of her hand.

"Yes, you do," she agreed, as she reached over and took a hold of his hand.

Surprised by her sudden act of affection, Florian happily smiled on and said, "Not how you imagined spending your wedding night? Standing outside on the balcony and discussing about my past love life, huh?"

"We cannot undue our pasts," Daphne told him. "However, we can at least try to control our futures. And as far as I'm concerned, you made me a princess. And for that, I am truly grateful."

"I suppose that there are far worse fates than being a royal princess," he deduced, with a beaming smile. A smile that stretched from ear-to-ear.

Surprisingly, for a second time in a row, Daphne felt her heart skip another beat. Really, these newfound emotions were all so confusing, even for her!

"Yes, that is true," Daphne agreed, as she blushed in the bright shade of red.

"Well," Florian sighed, "Since we're being honest, I want you to know the whole truth, straight from my own two lips."

"Go ahead, I'm listening," she encouraged him.

"As my father told you last night, Esmeralda and I were betrothed from our cribs. Our mothers were best friends. While she and I might have grown up alongside each other as childhood friends, but even as a young boy, I never felt anything romantic towards her."

"Do you mean that you've never been attracted to her?" asked Daphne, feeling almost a bit shy and nervous for prying into his personal life.

"No, I never was," he answered truthfully.

"So, what happened between the two of you?"

"Well, as we grew up, Esmeralda gradually picked up on my lack of affection," he explained. "She might have cared for me romantically; but as for myself, I could never see her being anything else beyond the role of a friend and nothing more. Certainly, not my future wife."

"Oh, so I see," Daphne secretly smiled to herself.

"But, unfortunately, my engagement to her wasn't something that I could easily escape from," Florian revealed. "To have gone against my mother's wishes would have been publicly viewed as a betrayal. And so, I kept up with the charade, with the high hopes that one day, maybe, just maybe, Esmeralda would opt to break our engagement, instead."

"And if she broke the engagement, then you'd be free from any potential scandal? With your family's honor still intact?"

"Precisely," he answered. "But unfortunately, that wish never came to be. However, five years ago, my mother passed away. And a few years later, my twin sister went on to marry the Duke of Starlight. By then, most folks had long forgotten about my betrothal."

"So, your mother's death inadvertently served as the justification to end your unwanted engagement?" Daphne curiously asked.

"Not exactly," Florian sighed again out of frustration, as he ran his hands through his thick and curly golden locks of hair.

"As much as I was saddened by my mother's passing," he emphasized, "But at the same time, I had secretly hoped that her death would also signal the end of my engagement. Except it didn't. It didn't because Esmeralda refused to end it. For you see, my fairest Daphne, in my kingdom, in order for an engagement to end, both parties must agree to the separation."

"I understand," Daphne acknowledged. "In other words, you needed Esmeralda's blessing to end the union?"

"Yes. Except, luckily, in my favor, I discovered a loop hole."

"A loop hole? Which kind?"

"Two words: *black magic*," he grinned.

"Black magic? As in, the occult?" asked Daphne, with a tremble.

In the past, the young princess never cared for black magic. Often times, such dark spells usually resulted in long held curses, devastation and destruction.

"Exactly," he replied. "After the academy, Esmeralda grew obsessed with the dark arts. In fact, she was a huge fan of your own estranged great-aunt, Vera, the late evil queen. And so, Esmeralda followed in her prime example. In many ways, reflecting back on it all, part of me thinks that she turned to dark magic in order to win me over. Or, at the very least, experimented with a few love potions or so, directed towards me."

"But true love can never be forced," Daphne interrupted him. "Anyone who reads enough fairy tales knows that magical potions or curses can never force true love. It must be organic and natural, in order for it to be true."

"Right again, my fairest Daphne," Florian agreed, with a glowing smile.

A smile that suddenly made her heart flutter, unexpectedly.

"So, how did Esmeralda's black magic affect your relationship with her?" the crown princess inquired, as she sought to conceal the excitement lingering within her chest.

"Well, once I came to learn about her new hobby, I then took it upon myself to review our law books here at the palace's library," he explained. "And upon my review, I discovered that even if both parties don't agree to the annulment, a crime against humanity can override it."

"Wait, so black magic counts as a crime against humanity?" she asked in confusion.

"Yes, it does, because that sort of magic can threaten both the stability of a kingdom, as well as the welfare of a nation and its people," he proclaimed. "Plus, after the evil queen's reign of terror in the western kingdom, the rest of the surrounding nations mutually agreed to recognize black magic as one of the key fundamental crimes against humanity. Furthermore, had it not been for your sister's defeat of the evil queen, then the rest of our kingdoms might have also perished in the last war, too."

"It all makes sense now," Daphne agreed. "So, Esmeralda's black magic freed you?"

"Almost," he said. "By then, I explained everything to my father. And of course, he was over the moon with joy. In truth, he, too, never cared for Esmeralda. He always found her to be a spoiled child. However, in order for my father, the king, to grant my request, it required one last essential thing."

"Which was?" she asked in anticipation.

"*You*," he pointed towards her.

"Me?" asked Daphne, in surprise. This revelation certainly caught her attention!

"According to our royal protocols, I needed a new bride to override the last one," Florian clarified. "Plus, with a new bride, Esmeralda would have no other choice but to back down. And so, I paid her a visit at her estate, Clover Castle, stole her grimoire, transformed myself into a frog and then, I finally ventured off into your world."

"Wait, *you* turned yourself into a frog? *Not Esmeralda?*" she repeated, in astonishment.

All this time, she naturally presumed that a witch must have cursed him to shapeshift into a frog. Plus, after discovering that his former fiancé was a witch… well… Daphne logically presumed that Esmeralda *must* have been the culprit. *She had to be, right?* After all, who would ever willingly turn themselves into a slimy emerald green frog to begin with? Out of their own fee will?

"Yes, it was me. I'll happily admit that it was *I*, who turned myself into a frog," he shrugged, nonchalant.

"All this time, I foolishly believed that it was Esmeralda who cursed you and not the other way around!"

"What can I say, Daphne? I was desperate," he confessed. "Plus, I always wanted to visit the lands of Earth. And so, I did."

"So, that's how the emerald prince came to be. Or, at least, the frog version," Daphne concluded.

"But then again," she pressed on, "Why do they call you the emerald prince? It's not just because of your past status as a frog, is it?"

"For you, perhaps, it might seem that way. After all, you technically, met me in my previous frog state," he replied, as he reached out to grab a loose strand of her red hair and gently tucked it behind her ear.

"But in truth, the emerald prince is also an honorary title bestowed upon to the heir apparent to the spring throne," the crown prince revealed. "Throughout history, all of the previous eastern crown princes have always been referred to by that special esteemed title, as well. After all, we are said to be the bringers of eternal spring. The hope for tomorrow. The source of seeds, in which to plant our lineages into the wombs of our maiden brides to bear our future heirs. And so, because of these reasons, this is why my eastern kingdom will sometimes refer to me as the emerald prince, in addition to the title of the crown prince."

"So, if you're the emerald prince, then does that also make me the emerald princess now, too?" Daphne inquired.

"Yes, I suppose it does," Florian happily laughed on. "Now, aren't you glad that you kissed that slimy frog prince, after all?"

"Yes," Daphne blushed out of shame, now feeling embarrassed by her previous poor and prejudicial attitude towards his former green form. "But why go through all that trouble? Why didn't you just run away to my land in your regular humanly form?"

"As I told you before, I always wanted to visit Earth. Plus, it's easier to travel in a smaller form. A perfect disguise," he winked.

"But how did you escape from Esmeralda's residence, Clover Castle?"

"Like me, her family also owns a magic mirror. Most of the royal houses do."

"But why didn't you use your father's belonging, instead?" she pressed on.

"Because, as I'm sure you'll soon come to learn first-hand, there are several eyes that are constantly affixed upon us at the palace, at all times," Florian explained. "Daphne, what can I say, there are plenty of courtiers, hidden everywhere. And if they knew what I intended to do, then they would have stopped me."

"So, let me get this straight," Daphne pondered aloud, "You invited yourself into Clover Castle, tricked Esmeralda, reviewed her grimoire, transformed yourself into a frog and lastly, snuck through her magic mirror to arrive into my world?"

"Exactly," he grinned.

"Does this mean that your mission was always set on finding a new bride? As in, an earthly bride?" she decided to ask him the million-dollar question.

"It was always my hope," he admitted in earnest. "And luckily, for me, I found you."

"Yes, you most certainly did," Daphne agreed, as she reflected upon their first encounter back at her father's garden.

"But," she went on, "How did we end up arriving to the eastern kingdom through your father's magic mirror, if you originally used Esmeralda's magic mirror to depart?"

"Ah, well, magic mirrors are quite unique," he remarked. "For you see, a magic mirror or an enchanted cave will take a traveler to the place where they desire the most. And in our case, it was the imperial palace."

"Oh, that does make a lot of sense, now," she concluded.

"But as happy as we ought to be right now," he forewarned, "I'm also afraid that after tonight, Esmeralda will continue to try to make our lives utterly miserable, from here on out."

"Then, we don't let her," Daphne held on to his hand tightly.

"Listen, Florian," she began, "As of now, we might not know each other too intimately. Plus, this could very well be a marriage of convenience for the both of us—"

"I needed a bride to free myself from the clutches of an obsessive witch, while you needed a husband to leave home and become a princess?" Florian interrupted her, with a sly smirk resting upon his handsome face.

"Exactly," she smiled back at him.

What else could she say? After all, he did have a valid point!

"But either way," Daphne continued on, "We can still build a happy home for ourselves. We shouldn't be afraid to stand up to a witch."

"Truer words have never been spoken," he agreed, with a warm smile. "Which is why at first sight, I always knew that you were the one."

"What do you mean?" she asked in surprise.

"Ah, nothing," he shyly glanced down at his feet.

Suddenly, it finally dawned upon Daphne that their night of celebration was soon coming to an end. In a matter of hours… no… minutes… Florian and her were expected to retire for the evening into their new bedchamber and complete the final ceremonial act, cementing their sacred wedding vows. To *consummate* the marriage.

At this moment, Daphne was still a virginal bride. Unfortunately, for her, she had never previously bothered to formally ask her elder sister or mother about the private affairs of the bedroom. Although she had listened to the girlish chatter involving various sexual scandals and wild sex tales as told by her sister and friends at past parties; however, she was still ignorant about the specific details surrounding the act of intercourse, altogether.

Somehow, in the back of Daphne's mind, she always assumed that the art of sex would simply come natural to her. That, when confronting a lover, then she'd know exactly what to do. But lo and behold, when faced directly with the matter concerning sex, Daphne was a true coward.

"About tonight…," she nervously gulped.

"Yes, what about tonight?" Florian took a step forward, moving towards her direction.

Instantly, Daphne could feel the warmth of his body, standing right next to hers. Florian might have been fully dressed in a fine suit, but she could still feel his muscular body hidden from underneath.

As fearful as she was, she was also equally curious as to how he looked, once all of those layers of clothing were peeled off. Leaving her emerald prince *stark naked.*

"Are you in want of something, *Daphne?*" he seductively spoke her name, using a deep and sultry voice.

A sound, that she had never heard him use before… *until now.*

"I…," she nervously stuttered.

"Do you want me to make you scream my name?" he leaned in and whispered into her ear. "Or better yet, have *me* scream your name? Would you like that? Do you have any specific desires that you wish for me to fulfill?"

"I… don't know…," Daphne admitted nervously in shame. "I've never been with a man before… I don't think… I just thought…"

A second later, Florian pushed himself away from Daphne. Afterwards, he gave her the biggest surprise of their entire evening

"You're right, Daphne," he spoke, quietly. "Our marriage might be a convenience. One stone for two birds. But they don't know that."

"Yes, I suppose that's true," she had no other choice but to agree.

"And because they don't know," he took another step back away from her. "We should probably keep up with the charade."

"Charade?" she asked in confusion.

"I promise not to touch you," Florian vowed, as his body leaned against the railings of the balcony.

Meanwhile, the moonlight shined against his face, making his lapis blue eyes sparkle against the backdrop of the night sky.

"But with that promise," he continued on, "You must also promise to share my bed, in return."

"Your bed?" she blinked twice.

"We're husband and wife now," he pointed out. "Naturally, they'll expect us to share the same bedchamber."

"However," he further added on, "While we might share the same bedchamber, I will also keep to myself. The world might see us as a married couple, but you and I shall be the best of friends."

And with that faithful promise, he graciously offered her his hand. Reluctantly, Daphne took it and a second later, Florian escorted her upstairs and into their new bedchamber.

# Chapter 5

## *Royal Wedding Night*

While the rest of the wedding guests partook on the joyful celebrations taking place downstairs— many of whom, were currently busy enjoying the bright burst of active fireworks illuminating the night sky as the skillful musicians continued to play their sweet melodies that could be heard all throughout the palace's grounds— Daphne, in contrast, found herself whisked away from all of these happy festivities.

Much to her disappointment, she was isolated and tucked away in a quiet room, within the privacy of her new husband's bedchamber.

Meanwhile, as the kingdom continued to dance and celebrate downstairs, Daphne curiously observed her new surroundings. Much to her surprise, Florian's room was rather simple. For a crown prince, it wasn't at all luxurious or as fancy as she had previously imagined for a royal's private quarters to be.

Instead, Florian's bedchamber was humble and modest. Overall, it housed a minimal amount of furniture. It included the following: a pair of velvet green reading chairs by the stone fireplace; an oak wood armoire that included carvings of lily pads on all four corners; and finally, a single large king-sized bed that leaned against the back of the wall, located towards the center of the room.

Apart from these essential items, there was little else left in this perfectly sparkling white marbled royal bedchamber— with the exception of an oversized glass window and a balcony that provided an exclusive view of the imperial palace's royal gardens.

Although Daphne had expected more luxurious decorations, shiny collectables and priceless artifacts to be displayed within her husband's private space; however, she assumed that the lack of décor must have stemmed from her husband's past as having lived as a long-term bachelor.

"Your new vanity and armoire should arrive sometime this week," Florian announced, as he casually strolled into the room.

Judging by Daphne's curious face, he must have read her mind about his humble abode. Already, he could sense her displeasure.

"Do you have any special preferences about our bedchamber?" he further inquired. "Lavinia and Hyacinth can help you to redecorate it. Furthermore, if you dislike your new furniture, then you can always have it changed, too."

"Any type should suffice," Daphne was quick to reply, hoping not to offend his kind generosity.

"Really?" Florian asked, as he pulled off his shirt and thereby, exposed his perfectly muscular chest.

A chest, that no doubt, hundreds of other women in their kingdom would have adored to touch, first-hand. No wonder Esmeralda acted so difficult. Who wouldn't want to keep Florian all to themselves? He was sexy and gorgeous!

Instantly, Daphne gulped. Indeed, she was nervous.

"My fairest Daphne, you need not be shy," Florian grinned. "You are free to be yourself at my court. My courtiers are now *your* courtiers, too."

"Thank you," is all that she could say.

Even though Florian promised not to touch her, Daphne still

couldn't help but feel butterflies form within the pit of her stomach. Apart from her family, she had never been left alone in the company of a man before. Let alone, a husband. *Her husband.*

"It's weird that we're married now," she confessed.

"Weird, how?" he curiously asked her, as he proceeded to peel off the rest of his clothing, leaving nothing behind but his breeches.

"It's just that I've never…"

"Never what?" Florian asked her; now, standing practically naked right in front of her face.

"I've…," she gulped.

"You've…," he pressed on.

Goodness, Daphne was so incredibly nervous! But like Florian said before, they were friends. *The best of friends.* Besides, if they were going to be best friends for the remainder of their lives spent together, then she needed to start acting more confident around him.

"It's just that I've *never* seen a naked man before," Daphne sighed, as she tugged at her wedding gown with her hands.

"Naked? Who's naked?" Florian asked in surprise.

"Well, *you* of course!" she snapped.

Instantly, Daphne covered her eyes with her hands. Goodness, wasn't it obvious that *he* was the one who was practically naked in this room and certainly not her, Daphne thought to herself.

"Ah, but technically, I'm not naked, my fairest Daphne," Florian was quick to point out.

"Daphne, if you can open your eyes, then you'll see that I've still got my breeches on," he explained with a wicked smirk.

"Besides," he added on teasingly, "You've seen *less* clothing on me, back when I was a frog."

"What???" cried Daphne in surprise, as she promptly removed her hands away from her face.

"You *weren't* naked, when you were a frog!" she shouted in defiance.

"Oh, but that's not entirely accurate," Florian explained, with a careless wave of his hand. "When I was a frog, was I or was I not wearing a blouse?"

"No, you were not wearing a blouse," she answered.

"And was I wearing a pair of trousers? A cape or even a pair of boots to go along with it?"

"No, neither."

"And did I have my breeches on, as well?" he asked this time, with a raised brow.

"No, you didn't," she replied.

"Exactly," he grinned. "I was *completely naked*, when you first met me."

"And furthermore," Florian continued on, "When you kissed me, you kissed me, while I was entirely in a naked state, too. Therefore, Daphne, there's no need to be shy. You've already seen me in my birthday suit."

"But that doesn't count!" she exclaimed. "You were *a frog… not a man*!"

"Man or frog, it was still *me*," he retorted.

Suddenly, Daphne was at a loss for words. Technically, he was *right*. Indeed, Florian had a valid point. She did, in fact, witnessed him *naked*. Therefore, her past stance on never seeing a man naked before, wasn't… well… entirely accurate anymore.

Witnessing Daphne's dumbfounded reaction, Florian instantly burst into laughter.

"Come now, Daphne, don't be so rigid," he laughed on. "Like I said before, I won't touch you."

"*However,*" he emphasized, "If we're going to be living together, then you might as well get used to seeing me naked in the flesh. Because, my darling, that's how I prefer to sleep."

"What???" she cried in horror. "You actually sleep naked???"

"Nature's best rest," he mischievously grinned from ear-to-ear, showcasing that perfectly charming smile of his.

A second later, Florian abruptly pulled down his breeches to reveal his very long and thick cock.

Instantly, Daphne was mesmerized. Not only had she not seen a naked *human* man before, but this was also the first time that she had ever seen a man's cock with her very own two pair of eyes. And lo and behold, it was out on display, right in front of her!

Had it not been for her pride, then Daphne was almost compelled to abandon their friendly charade and to give in to this new wicked desire that she felt brewing in between her thighs. And for the first time ever, she actually felt a wet sensation developing from down below. But more than anything, she also wanted to kneel down in front of him and suck his…

But before Daphne could fully indulge in this naughty fantasy of hers, Florian was quick to change into a pair of shorts. No longer was his cock fully out, flaunting itself for her private viewing.

"I believe that's enough of a preview for one night, don't you agree?" he teased her

"Yes, I agree," she turned her head to the side, with her face blushing in the bright shade of red.

"While I much rather sleep in the nude, but for you, my fairest Daphne, I will make the exception," he smiled on, all the while, perfectly knowing how much his wild behavior had vexed her, too.

Who knew just how much fun marriage could be, after all!

A second later, Florian hopped right onto bed, landing on the left-side of the mattress.

"Looks like the right-side is your lucky spot, my love," he winked at her.

"Wait, are we going to be *sharing* the *same bed, too*?" she asked, nervously.

"But of course," he replied, nonchalant. "I thought that I was rather clear downstairs about my expectations?"

"Yes, but when you said sharing a bedchamber…"

"No, Daphne," he interrupted her. "I did specifically say the word *bed*."

Recalling their last conversation downstairs on the balcony, Daphne replayed the entire scene over again in her head. Sure enough, Florian was right. He did propose to her about sharing a *bed*. *His bed*, to be precise.

But somehow, in the midst of their past conversation, she foolishly presumed that he meant a single bedchamber with two beds, not one.

"I suppose you're right," she sighed in defeat. "You did say that, didn't you? Plus, there doesn't look to be any other beds in here, either."

"Don't worry, Daphne," Florian comforted her, while he padded the right-side of the bed and invited her over to join him. "We can share the same bed and still not touch each other."

"Here," he suggested, as he reached over to grab a spare pillow. "We can use this as a divider. As long as we have this pillow placed between us, then you've got nothing to fear."

As silly as all of this was, seeing that thick and fluffy pillow brought a great sense of comfort to Daphne's dwindling nerves. At least with a solid barrier, even in the form of a feathery pillow to serve as a protective wall, she felt more at ease.

One way or another, Florian successfully managed to relieve her from the newfound pressures associated with her expected wifely duties.

"For now, it shall do," she told him.

A moment later, Florian yawned out of exhaustion. Afterwards, he stretched his arms and pulled the bedcovers over his body.

"Well," he said to her with his eyes closed. "Aren't you coming to bed, now?"

"Me?" she repeated.

"Yes, *you*," Florian replied, as he reopened his eyes wide again.

"It is getting late, after all," Daphne agreed. "I should change… but…"

"But what?" Florian asked her.

"Technically, I have no clothes in your bedchamber," she hesitated to reveal to him. "In fact, I don't really have much clothes at all. Except for a few spare dresses kept in the last room that I was previously occupied in the night before our wedding."

"Well, then, first thing tomorrow, I'll arrange for Merrybelle and Honeybelle to take your measurements and prepare you a whole new wardrobe," he boldly promised her, as a simple matter-of-fact.

"Why, thank you, Florian," she graciously replied. "I'd like that very much."

"Good," he smiled.

And then, taking a second glance at his new bride, Florian instantly observed the stressful expression still lingering upon Daphne's face.

"What's wrong? Why do you still look so anxious?" he inquired.

"It's just that I have nothing to wear, *right now*!"

Once again, Florian happily smiled to himself. It was true. Technically, Daphne had nothing to wear. Apart from her bridal gown, she had nothing else. Therefore, she was left with two alternatives: *his clothes or her nakedness*.

"Well, I have two options for you," he told her, as he wickedly grinned.

"And they are?" she asked, with a raised brow.

"You can either borrow one of my blouses or…"

"Or…," she repeated

"You can sleep naked," he proposed with a smug expression.

"Me naked? Are you serious?" she asked, dumbfounded by such a prospect.

"That's your options. Take it or leave it," he replied with his arms folded around his bare chest.

"Dear God! This is insane!" she shouted, out of frustration.

"Come now, Daphne," he reassured her. "I'm your husband now. While I promise for us to remain celibate; but surely, you being naked in my company isn't the end of the world. After all, walking around in the nude within the privacy of our own bedchamber is perfectly normal. Especially, amongst newlyweds."

Sadly, Florian had *yet* another point. They were alone in their own bedchamber. And most importantly, like he said, they were married. Plus, he had already promised not to touch her. Therefore, being naked around him shouldn't be so incredibly bad, right?

"Given that your blouses are far too big for my petite body, I suppose that I'll opt for the nude," she proclaimed, with her chin held up high.

"However, you are to close your eyes, as I strip down," she ordered him. "I might be naked, but I still don't want you to see me."

"But I already *see you, right now.*"

"That doesn't count!" Daphne exclaimed. "I'm wearing clothes. Therefore, you see me *in my clothes*. No, I don't want you to see me… well…"

"Naked?" he asked, with a raised brow.

"Exactly," she sighed.

"Very well, for now, I'll close my eyes," he said. "Go ahead and change. I promise not to take a peek."

With that faithful promise, Daphne quickly tore off her bridal gown and undergarments, and tossed them aside to the opposite end of the room. Afterwards, she quickly hopped onto her side of the bed and threw the bedcovers over her chest, leaving nothing else exposed but her face, neck and long red hair.

"Okay, you can open your eyes now," she told him.

"Comfortable?" he asked.

"Very," she yawned.

"Alright my fairest Daphne, in that case, I'll bid you a goodnight."

A second later, Florian blew out the flickering flame to their candle and fell fast asleep. And as her new husband slept beside her, Daphne fantasized on how it would feel like to have him touch her. To have him explore her plump breasts, curved buttock and slender waist— all the while, feeling the warmth of his sturdy hands pressed in between her legs.

Meanwhile, as she daydreamed about these wicked fantasies, Daphne closed her eyes shut and within the darkness, she began to touch herself. Secretly, she dreamt about how much fun it would feel like to have Florian play with her folds. Even though she still lacked the courage to ask him directly in real life; at least for now, Daphne decided to pleasure herself.

# Chapter 6

*Life as a Princess*

*(aka Being a Princess Takes Hard Work!)*

The next morning, Daphne awoke to find herself alone in Florian's bed and surrounded by a host of palace courtiers by her bedside. From her ladies-in-waiting, Marcia, April and May; to her seamstresses, Merrybelle and Honeybelle; and even the housekeeper, Lavinia, and her assistant, Hyacinth. In the end, Daphne was practically ambushed by her new entourage.

"Rise and shine, Your Highness," Lavinia announced loudly, as Hyacinth promptly pulled opened the velvet green curtains to their sides to bring forth the bright sunlight coming from the outside garden and peeking through the oversized windows.

"What time is it?" asked Daphne, as she rubbed her eyes and adjusted her vision to the newfound lighting.

After last night's whirlwind of events, come the next morning, the crown princess felt utterly exhausted.

"It's almost noon," Lavinia explained.

"Noon! I slept in that late!" Daphne exclaimed in surprise.

Suddenly, the night before flashed across Daphne's memories. There was the wedding. The unexpected news concerning her sister's surprise pregnancy. Followed by an angered Esmeralda— aka her husband's former scorned fiancé— who managed to crash their party unannounced. Soon afterwards, she found herself upstairs and alone with Florian… and *naked*. And then… well… after playing with herself into the late hours of the night, she awoke to now find herself surrounded by a team of courtiers, all eager to attend to her every need.

"After your fitting, we shall discuss about redecorating your new bedchamber," Lavinia instructed. "And then, once that matter is all settled, we'll begin with your lessons."

"Lessons? What lessons?" Daphne asked, out of curiosity.

Previously, she was not privy to any such thing.

"Why, lessons on *how* to conduct yourself as the new crown princess of course," Lavinia stated, as a simple matter-of-fact.

"Come now, Your Highness, you cannot assume that one can simply become a princess overnight, just by marriage alone," Lavinia added with caution.

"You can't?" Daphne asked her directly.

"Certainly not," Lavinia huffed in annoyance. "No, Your Grace, being a princess takes *hard work*."

With that honest admission, Daphne was given a silk baby pink and white lace robe and promptly escorted out of bed, while Merrybelle and Honeybelle got straight to work by collecting her measurements. Afterwards, Marcia, April and May prepared a warm bubble bath. A luxurious bath filled with scented fresh water, which was decorated with crimson red rose petals, along with a generous splash of lavender oil, all prepared in honor of their new crown princess.

Over the course of the next several proceeding weeks, the newly crowned emerald princess was trained in almost all areas concerning the official imperial palace's royal protocols.

Even though Daphne was the youngest daughter of an earl; however, her formal etiquettes still reflected *English* protocols and not necessarily, the laws, traditions and customs pertaining to the Kingdom of the East. Another foreign realm that she was still growing accustomed to.

And so, Daphne, without complaint, graciously immersed herself with her new lessons and dedicated her precious time to learn about the eastern table etiquettes, as instructed by Chef Caldwell. In addition, the palace chef also taught her about their local food customs found within the region, as well.

According to Caldwell, fresh fruits, berry tarts and herbal teas were considered to be the staple food sources of their kingdom. Furthermore, green pea and onion soup, roasted lamb, baked freshwater fish and lemon asparaguses were amongst the most popular food dishes that were beloved by all within their nation.

Apart from dining, Daphne was also tutored by Lavinia and Hyacinth, regarding the histories of both the Great Kingdom as a whole continent and their own land, the Kingdom of the East. From their legendary mystical queens of the past to their most recent monarch, King Titus, the newly crowned princess was taught about all of the previous kings, queens and other respected nobles who were famously revered throughout their land. And according to Lavinia, her husband's family directly descended from an ancient bloodline, who were the original founders of their emerald dynasty.

As for the kingdom's local culture, Daphne learned about the latest and upcoming fashion trends by Merrybelle and Honeybelle. According to her seamstresses, most eastern ladies wore long and sheer chiffon empire style gowns in springtime hues, and made from extra-soft and breathable materials. From emerald green to cool lilac, to soft baby pink to magenta, and lemon yellow to silvery opal, ethereal and fairy-like shades were the most popular and frequently worn gowns found throughout their kingdom.

Furthermore, eastern ladies traditionally wore less jewelry than the rest of the other ladies residing within the neighboring kingdoms. Often times, eastern ladies wore either a single pair of earrings, a necklace, a bracelet or a ring— but rarely as a complete set. Additionally, pearls and opals were the most popular gems worn during commonly held balls; whereas, emeralds were reserved for more highly-esteemed or official royal balls and other important social events.

For their hairs, most ladies sported long and flowing manes, which normally grew below their shoulders. Occasionally, they wore floral and straw bonnets or wide round hats. For accessories, they often decorated their manes with freshly picked flowers, typically adorning their hairs with a single poppy, lily, daisy or a rose, to name a few.

However, a full floral wreath was specifically reserved for royalty. Therefore, only the eastern royal family were permitted to use these floral wreaths during state affairs and other important public events.

As for the men, they wore a combination of black or brown top hats or feathered bures. With regards to their attires, most of them sported loose cream blouses or tunics, with some designed in ruffles and others using a plain pattern.

Meanwhile, their slick and straight cotton trousers generally came in the colors of jet black or chocolate brown, and were accompanied by a pair of leather black boots, loafers or wingtip oxford shoes. Often times, most men wore capes, suits or petticoats, primarily in the shades of honey yellow, pure white, jet black, navy blue or rustic brown. However, emerald green capes, suits and petticoats were specifically reserved for the eastern royal family to wear exclusively.

In terms of the arts and entertainment sector, Daphne was schooled by her ladies-in-waiting and court jester. With regards to art history— including the kingdom's most famous portraits and highly esteemed sculptures— her ladies-in-waiting lectured her about them, along with their respective artists; many of whom, had artworks that were featured at their local museum.

But if art history wasn't enough, then it was her court jester, Pascal, who personally taught the crown princess on how to play the most popular games played at the palace's court, including various card games, boardgames and even, how to juggle a trio of recently harvested red apples, too! Imagine that!

Additionally, in honor of the sacred songs performed about their region, musical lessons were also provided to the princess by her palace's musicians, Melody, Isabella and Isadora. Through this trio, Daphne learned how to play the harp. Although the crown princess was already classically trained by her own mother, Kassie, to play the piano forte; however, adding another instrument to her long-list of accomplishments was welcomed wholeheartedly by the princess.

As for dancing, this is where Daphne's dear husband, the crown prince, stepped in. Each day, at precisely four o'clock in the afternoon, Florian arrived to the palace's ballroom to demonstrate a new dance number with his wife.

Much to Daphne's own surprise, she was indeed, a quick learner. Thus far, most of the eastern dances weren't too incredibly difficult to learn and master. Plus, they weren't relatively too different from the dance styles practiced back in her homeland of England. With a fast step here and a twirl there, Daphne quickly grew accustomed to her new role as Florian's leading lady and dance partner.

But if that wasn't enough, Daphne was also trained in the fine art of combat by her own personal knight, Atherton. Taking a detailed note from his brother-in-law's handbook, apparently, Florian also firmly believed that the crown princess needed to be properly trained and fully prepared to defend herself at any spur of the moment, should the unfortunate opportunity to fight ever present itself to her.

Even though the crown princess was highly protected by her palace guards around the clock, the crown prince still desired for his new bride to possess the utmost confidence and skilled ability to protect herself with the use of a sword, when faced with an unsuspecting adversary.

And so, Daphne trained with Atherton on a daily basis. Additionally, if she wasn't practicing sparring or wrestling, then she also participated in kick boxing, knife throwing and horseback riding lessons, too. Even though Daphne was already a classically trained equestrian, like her elder sister before her; in the end, she, too, also needed to sharpen her skills, when riding a war horse, as well.

Overall, learning to become a royal princess took lots of work. *Hard work*. Apparently, as Daphne came to learn first-hand, simply kissing a frog wasn't enough to make her princess. Neither was her marrying an emerald prince, either.

Instead, to be a *respected* royal, an emerald princess, who was beloved and greatly admired by all of her people, Daphne needed to adapt into their world. A world, in which her own sister also had to previously learn to adjust in, too. And thus, following in her elder sister's footsteps.

Meanwhile, as Daphne memorized all of the key names to her fellow peers and surrounding court members, she decided to also welcome them into her inner circle, too. Therefore, Daphne took great lengths to draft each of them heartfelt letters, personally inviting them over to visit her palace for an afternoon session of high tea.

As far as the crown princess was concerned, the more diplomatic relations that she established early on with her neighbors, then the better off her kingdom would be in the future, in terms of both lasting peace and prosperity.

"And now, Your Highness," Lavinia proudly declared, "I believe that the time has come for you to host your first ball."

"Do you really think that I'm ready, Lavinia?" asked Daphne, as she placed a pad of paper down above her writing desk in her study.

"More than ready, I do declare," Lavinia proudly complemented her. "You've been a splendid student, thus far. In fact, King Titus, Prince

Florian and myself, all feel that it's about time that you finally make your formal debut out in public."

"Thank you, Lavinia," Daphne replied, graciously. "I couldn't have done this all, without the entire palace's support."

"You are most welcomed, Your Highness," she said with a bow.

"And now," Lavinia continued on, "Once you've selected your color template and font, then the invitations shall go out immediately. Hopefully, by the end of this week."

"In that case," Daphne said with a bright smile, as she lifted up her pad of paper from off her desk. "I believe that I shall go with the emerald green cards, using the all-cursive font. After all, it's to be an Emerald Ball, is it not?"

"Indeed, an Emerald Ball it shall be."

# Chapter 7

## *An Emerald Ball*

Once upon a time, Daphne Galloway used to read about magical and princess-like royal balls from the pages of her favorite storybook called, *An Encyclopedia of Fairy Tales*. Furthermore, within that book contained epic and romantic tales about princes, princesses, knights, villains, battles, curses and most importantly, stories about *true love*.

And just like the enchanting balls held within the pages of her beloved storybook, tonight, the palace was everything that Daphne had ever imagined for a royal ball to be. Whimsical. Ethereal. Breathtaking. But most importantly, *real*. A literal dream *come true*.

Indeed, the Emerald Ball was a spectacular and thrilling event. In celebration of Daphne's marriage to the crown prince, the famous ball was thrown in their joint honors.

Dressed in an oversized, puffy and luxurious cream colored ballroom style princess gown, which was made from a combination of silk and chiffon materials, Daphne's debut outfit was intricately designed and personally handsewn by her two highly-talented seamstresses, Merrybelle and Honeybelle.

In addition to her stunning cream ballroom gown, Daphne's dress was also adorned with a generous collection of miniature satin heritage green hued ribbons that were carefully sewn on, starting from her decolletage and all the way down to her stomach, resembling a traditional corset.

Additionally, her sleeves were designed midway in length, resting alongside her elbows. Furthermore, they were covered with an extra layer of sparkling fern green lace, along with a hint of sparkling gold and silver glitter scattered within them.

Meanwhile, her hips had an additional layer of sheer gold fabric on both sides to produce an overskirt, creating an extra weight to her already heavy dress. Furthermore, there were several hundreds of sparkling silver beads in the form of lilies that were individually stitched onto her gown.

And on the center of her ballroom dress, resting alongside her chest, was an embroidered laurel tree. Its leaves stretched across the upper layers of her gown, and was located right below her cleavage and ended towards the bottom of her breasts.

But apart from her enchanting gown, Daphne's fiery red hair was also swept away into a half bun. While her top mane was carefully pulled away from her face, the bottom half of her hair was curled into bright red locks of curls that gracefully dangled against her back. And above her head rested a wreath of pink lilies, which served as her official royal crown.

As for accessories, Daphne wore a diamond studded and emerald teardrop-shaped stone necklace with matching earrings, along with a sparkling golden lace and feathered fan. Lastly, her shoes were satin slip-on kitten heels, which were gold and adorned with lime green pearls decorated along its topline.

Finally, as the crown princess glided across the floors of the grand party, she took in a moment to admire its magical scenery.

All throughout the banquet hall and ballroom, the palace was decorated with spring flowers that blossomed all throughout. From pink lilies to bright yellow poppies, to bluebells and crimson red roses, flowers were strategically placed around all of the numerous tall columns and high ceilings, encircling each open space with a generous collection of floral décors.

Meanwhile, the entire venue was dominated by the color of emerald. From the carpets to the curtains, and the tablecloths to the vases, the bright shade of emerald was found *everywhere*. If ever there was an emerald palace that housed the emerald prince and emerald princess, then this castle was *it*.

Additionally, the antique chandeliers were all shined and polished to absolute perfection, without a single trace of dust spotted anywhere. Furthermore, the sparkling silverware, crystal glasses and fine porcelain plates— which included a bright pink waterlily emblem in the middle, encircled by a golden crown— were all proudly out on display.

Indeed, the waterlily was a sacred symbol that was also used on their kingdom's flag. An emerald green flag, with an identical floral crest found in the center. The official flag of the Kingdom of the East, the Land of Eternal Spring.

Overall, the Emerald Ball was like a magical wonderland, in which hundreds of guests arrived, all elegantly dressed in their finest gowns and tailored suits. A real fairy tale-like ball come to life, if ever there was one.

Furthermore, tonight's event appeared to be a full house. It seemed that everyone residing within the Great Kingdom came to this cherished ball. People, whom even our very own emerald princess had not yet had the pleasure to meet before— at least, not until now. And so, using her trusted cue cards, Daphne managed to recognize a few faces from amongst the busy crowd.

Stemming from her own eastern kingdom, there was the Duke and Duchess of Snowdrop. A young royal couple aged in their mid-to-late twenties, who resided in Castle Snowdrop, famously located within the western reaches, bordering the neighboring Kingdom of the West. And their castle, in particular, was the home to a majestic garden known throughout the region for its magical splendor and its rare collection of rich soft purple and pink sugarplum dianthus flowers.

According to Lavinia and Hyacinth, in addition to their famed sugarplum flowers, the Snowdrops' red tulips, orange poppies and crimson red roses were all famously cultivated to brew some of the loveliest and most enchanting perfumes found within the Great Kingdom.

In fact, it was often rumored that any young or single fair maiden residing within the land who purchased one of these refreshing perfumes, then it was believed that this blessed maiden was guaranteed to land a husband before the end of the current courting season.

Next, there was the Baron and Baroness of Azalea. They were an elderly pair, who lived on the eastern shores of their kingdom. Like the Snowdrops, they too, resided in a famous and prestigious abode, known as Castle Azalea.

Similar to their counterparts, the Azaleas' maintained a luscious garden, which produced the most exquisite azalea flowers found throughout their land. In fact, their azaleas were so incredibly beautiful and beneficial to the local economy due to the fact, that most of their flowers were exported to the other neighboring kingdoms. In reality, the azaleas accounted for at least ten percent of the Kingdom of the East's total GDP.

And then, there was Lord and Lady Bleeding Heart, as well as Lord and Lady Cherry Blossom. Like their namesakes, they resided in Bleeding Heart Manor and Cherry Blossom Hall. In addition, they also came from very old, established and wealthy families. Ancient linages to be precise.

In fact, Florian's own mother, the late Queen Ophelia, was a descendent from both houses. Bleeding Heart from her father's side, and Cherry Blossom from her mother's. And it was during one of these past Emerald Balls, where a young Ophelia of Bleeding Heart eventually came to capture the heart of the former Crown Prince Titus. And the rest, is well… history.

But apart from Daphne's kingdom, there were also other elite members of the aristocracy attending this ball, traveling from the nearby neighboring kingdoms, as well. According to the portraits that she had previously studied at the palace's library, ahead of her stood King Cyrus and Queen Leyla of the South. A royal couple who appeared no older than

Florian and herself.

With their sunlit bronzed skin and caramel eyes, the southern royals were a handsome pair, who recently welcomed a new bundle of joy of their own, Crown Prince Atilla.

Meanwhile, next to them stood the Earl and Countess of Citrine. According to the circulating rumors, the Citrines owned a monopoly of mines in the south, which produced hundreds of sparkling gemstones— including diamonds, rubies and emeralds— that were used to export across the entire continent.

However, even with a monopoly, the Citrines were no match to the Baron and Baroness of Onyx. In reality, the Baron and Baroness of Onyx were the *true* wealthy socialites from the southern kingdom.

According to Hyacinth, while the Citrines' possessed most of the southern gemstones, the Onyx family mined all of the gold. So much gold, that they even successfully arranged for their only daughter, Leyla, to marry the southern king. As it stood, Leyla, was *the* new Queen of the South, as well as the mother to the heir to the southern throne.

Traveling further along the ballroom and standing right in the heart of the room, was the Grand Duke and Grand Duchess of Svane from the north. As it currently appeared, they seemed to be the only representatives from the northern kingdom.

Unfortunately, due to a recent severe snowstorm, the northern royals were unable to attend tonight's festivities. Luckily, the Svanes, who were previously vacationing out in the west, were able to travel to the east to attend the Emerald Ball in their Highnesses' honors.

Even though they weren't the official northern king or queen, the Svanes' still arrived to the party, both elegantly dressed in a matching suit and gown made of silver. In fact, they alone, easily outshined the other nobles who surrounded them.

Had Daphne failed to have known ahead of time that they weren't the true northern reigning royals, then she could have easily mistaken them for the northern king and queen. As it currently stood, the young pair were simply enchanting to gaze upon and exhumed glamour and royalty at the highest of degrees.

Observing the Svanes from afar, Daphne noticed that the Grand Duke possessed the darkest shade of black hair that she had ever witnessed before on another person. It was so incredibly dark and jet black, just like a raven. Additionally, his face was as pale as snow, and his lips were as red as an apple.

Meanwhile, his wife, the Grand Duchess, was just as equally lovely. With her hair as fair as ice, and her eyes as crystal blue as a frozen river, the Grand Duchess of Svane was as beautiful and as elegant as a gentle swan found in winter.

Of course, there was also Daphne's elder sister and brother-in-law, Violet and Maximus, minus their two young sons. Currently, Violet was tightly holding on to the arms of her beloved husband, while she was busy conversing with the Viscount and Viscountess of Tourmaline and the Marquis and Marchioness of Clover, with the exception of Esmeralda. Meanwhile, Maximus was eagerly chatting and laughing away with Florian. From the looks of it, their husbands appeared to be very old and dear friends.

Although Daphne was aware that Florian was acquainted with her sister and brother-in-law; but at the same time, she also hadn't realized as to just how incredibly close they all were in each other's companies. And for some reason, their relationships made Daphne feel a tinge of jealousy on her part.

From afar, it was like watching an exclusive inner circle of friends happily mingling together, minus her. A prestigious old social club that she was not yet made a part of. Even though it was rather silly for Daphne to feel negative in this particular way; however, she couldn't help herself. After all, her own sister and brother-in-law, all *knew* her husband far better than she did. Heck, she hardly knew him at all, to begin with!

Suddenly, Daphne felt incredibly sad. Even though their union was based on a marriage of convenience; but still, she secretly longed for more. In reality, she wished that in due time, that perhaps, their arranged marriage could blossom into something more meaningful and *real*. Just like the waterlilies that grew within their enchanted garden.

Maybe… just maybe… their relationship had the potential to grow and for them to develop into becoming true friends… the *best of friends*, as Florian so eloquently previously described them to be. And with friendship, then perhaps, their relationship could even graduate to love? True love? One could only *hope*.

Meanwhile, as Daphne stood in the center of the ballroom, she was soon approached by Florian's twin sister, Diana, and her husband, Orion, Duke of Starlight. Much to Daphne's surprise, Diana was the spitting image of her twin brother. With the same curly and golden blonde locks of hair, piercing lapis blue eyes and soft pale skin, she was the female equivalent of her younger brother.

Princess Diana Luna of the East, Duchess of Starlight, was truly just as beautiful, elegant and enchanting in-person, as previously described in all of the circulating rumors. Indeed, all of the tall tales and musical lyrics describing the beloved princess were true.

Within a moment's glance, Daphne was simply taken away by her ethereal beauty. In fact, Diana was far lovelier than all of the famous ballads and sonnets written about her. Truly, those works of art did her no justice.

Just by staring at her, Daphne secretly hoped that if she and Florian were ever to have a daughter one day in the near future, then the crown princess wished that her child would be just as elegant, lovely and equally beautiful, like her paternal aunt.

"We finally meet at long last," Diana happily gushed.

Before Daphne knew it, the duchess promptly wrapped her arms around her new sister-in-law.

Pulling away, Diana said, "You are far lovelier and charming in-person. Truly, my brother's letters concerning you, simply do you no justice."

"Florian wrote to you about me?" asked Daphne, in astonishment.

Never did she ever imagine that her husband actually took the time of day to write about her whereabouts to another person. Especially, to his beloved twin sister.

"Of course, he did," the duchess confessed. "My brother is a born poet and a talented musician. And you, Daphne of the East, is the muse that he's long searched for!"

Florian, a poet and a musician? And she, a muse? Each day really was the unraveling of another mystery for our heroine!

"Truly, you are far too kind, Princess Diana Luna," Daphne blushed, out of embarrassment.

She might have been the new crown princess, but Daphne was still growing accustomed to this newfound spotlight. Especially, after recently learning that Florian spoke so highly of her to others. Apparently, he knew more about *her* than she did of *him*!

"Please, do call me Diana," her sister-in-law insisted. "After all, we are sisters now. And I've always wanted a sister, too."

"Very well, *Diana*," Daphne addressed her, with a warm smile.

"And please, call me Orion, as well," spoke her new brother-in-law.

Standing beside his wife, the Duke of Starlight was a giant. At first glance, he over towered his bride by several feet. In fact, the duke, most likely, stood around six feet and seven inches tall.

But apart from his height, he was also a dashing young nobleman. With his hair a lighter shade of blonde than his wife's, it resembled more like the color of pale corn. Meanwhile, his eyes were deep grey, like steel.

Overall, the duke was a handsome gentleman. Plus, judging by his close proximately to his wife, one could easily detect his overwhelming love and protection of her.

"Indeed, Diana and Orion, it's truly a pleasure to finally meet with the pair of you," Daphne spoke in earnest.

After all, it was a good development to meet with Florian's extended family. Hopefully, the more she learned about them, then the better insight she'd gain about his personality and private life, too.

"And once you and Florian are more settled down, then you must pay us a visit at Starlight Castle," Diana pleaded. "The north might be a lengthy trip by carriage; however, the scenic view there is like no other."

But before Daphne could respond, she felt a new presence arrive beside her. Quickly, she turned to her side and sure enough, it was Florian.

Dressed in a white satin suit with gold and silver sparkles, it was an outfit custom designed to match Daphne's gown. Furthermore, he wore an emerald green velvet cape, which was adorned with several bright and golden pins. Medallions. Meanwhile, above his head, he wore a wreath made of pale pink waterlilies. A royal crown that also matched the same wreath worn around Daphne's head, too.

Overall, the emerald prince was as handsome as could be. Meanwhile, his golden locks shined brightly against the candlelight and his lapis blue eyes sparkled, just like a pair of sapphires. Remarkably, to her own surprise, Daphne suddenly felt her heart nervously skip a beat.

"I'm sorry to interrupt this happy introduction," Florian intervened, as he sandwiched himself in between his sister and new bride.

"But, being that we're still newlyweds," he continued on, "I'd like to share the first dance with *my wife.*"

Without bothering to wait for Diana's response, Florian quickly took a hold of Daphne's hand and within the blink of an eye, the pair were off to the dancefloor.

"My fairest, Daphne, not only do you look like a goddess in this gown, but you also smell absolutely divine," Florian remarked, as he got a whiff of her intoxicating scent.

Cedar, with warm notes of laurel leaves. A concoction that was truly a scent brewed straight out of heaven.

"Thank you," Daphne blushed by his sincere complement.

A second later, they quickly got into their positions. With their hands locked in an embrace, Florian proceeded to rest his left-hand alongside her waist. At this point, the couple were practically pressed up against one another, just noses apart.

"Recently, I've received word that you've exceeded beyond everyone's expectations with regards to your lessons," he proudly complemented her.

"Yes, Lavinia did express to me that she thought that I was doing rather well with my studies," Daphne modestly replied. "Although, it did take a good amount of hard work to study and see it all through."

"Indeed," he agreed, with a beaming smile. "Plus, you've also mastered the art of dancing. The hardest lesson above all else, if I might add, too."

A second later, Florian gave Daphne a light twirl around. Afterwards, once she returned back to face him again, he said, "And given that you've already mastered our eastern dances, I believe that we'll need to step up your upcoming lessons and have you practice the dance steps from our neighboring kingdoms, as well."

"Will you be teaching me these new steps or another?" Daphne curiously asked.

In truth, Daphne was hoping that Florian would say the word: *yes*. Secretly, she enjoyed their dances. The time they spent together in each other's company.

Given their busy schedules, Daphne seldom saw Florian except for their nightly dinners and bedside. Therefore, dance lessons with him was an excuse to be around in his company. Plus, she *liked* the *feel* of his touch against her skin. Even if it was only limited to just her hands and waist.

"Yes, it shall be me," he replied, quietly. "Besides, I can't imagine anyone *else* touching you but *me*."

In that instant, Daphne couldn't help but detect an ounce of jealousy on his part. Was it possible that he disliked her dancing with another man? Another male royal or courtier who would ultimately, be forced to touch her? Even within the simple constraints of a dancefloor?

"Either way, I promise to educate you on all matters concerning dancing," he vowed. "Anyways, who else could possibly be a better partner for you than myself, my fairest Daphne?"

"I suppose you're right, Florian," Daphne agreed. "Plus, I've grown rather accustomed to your style of teaching, too."

"Oh, and how so?" he curiously inquired. Now, eagerly seeking to press her for more information.

"Well, for starters," Daphne began to explain, "Whenever I execute a move correctly, the left-side of your lips curls upwards.  Plus, when I master a particular given dance, then there's a gleaming violet sparkle that shines within your lapis blue eyes."

"And in the short amount of time that we've spent together, you've managed to catch all of this?" he blinked, in surprise.

Already, the prince was taken aback and highly impressed that his new bride even cared to take notice about these intricate details surrounding himself.

"Yes, I do catch on quickly," she shyly admitted. "Especially, when it comes to… *you*."

Without realizing it, Daphne blushed in a bright shade of pink. Meanwhile, Florian instantly happily smiled from ear-to-ear.

Discovering that his wife paid such close attention to him, brought a surprise joy into his blooming heart. Her confession to him alone was so incredibly sweet and heartwarming.

"Oh, and by the way, come tomorrow, the jeweler will be visiting the palace," he announced, quickly changing the subject. "After all, you're due for a formal tiara fitting. That, along with a few other things."

"A tiara? As in a *real* princess tiara?" asked Daphne in excitement.

All of her life, Daphne had always dreamt of this very moment. A chance to be crowned as a real princess. And while her mother might have adorned her with their family's collection of tiaras; in the end, none of them were actual royal tiaras. *A princess tiara.* At long last, her childhood fantasy was finally coming true!

"But of course," Florian stated, as a matter-of-fact, "Did I or did I not promise to bequeath you with an endless supply of tiaras and jewels, when we first met? As I recall, I vowed to adorn you with strings of sparkling pearls and glimmering rubies, along with precious emerald tiaras to go along with it. After all, an emerald princess can't travel across the kingdom and participate in official royal business, without a proper emerald tiara of her own to showcase. Otherwise, it'd simply be improper."

"Yes, you really did promise to do all of that back at Galloway Manor," Daphne agreed. "But in truth, I wasn't entirely sure if this childhood dream of mine was really going to happen in the first-place. After all, at the time, you were a cursed frog, when you made that initial vow to me."

"And?" he challenged her presumptions.

"Well, naturally…" she struggled with her words, "I just presumed that you promised me all of those things, just so that I could… *kiss you.*"

"Why, my fairest Daphne," he sighed in great disappointment. "I'm saddened to hear this. Especially, given your lack of faith in me."

"Oh, no I didn't mean…"

"At this rate, you might as well have left me to face that cruel cursed fate alone. Because, right now, my dear, I do believe that you've successfully managed to wound my pride, after all," he shamefully admitted, with a pale and cringed face.

Regrettably, Daphne was disappointed by her own harsh choice of words. Ever since they arrived to the imperial palace, Florian had been nothing short but wonderful. Indeed, thus far, he did keep true to all of his promises to her. And for a whole second, Daphne was fearful that her thoughtless words might have inadvertently crushed his prideful spirts due to her own personal and meritless doubts.

"My dear, I never back down from a promise. *Never*," Florian swore. "I promised you, Daphne, my love, to serve all of your dreams on a silver platter. Come hell or high water, I will gift you the entire world and everything in it. Every desire, hope and wish, traveling upon a shooting star. All of these, I shall personally deliver them to you, until your heart is fully content."

A second later, the music came to an abrupt end. And as Florian took a final bow to his princess, he gave her a light kiss alongside her hand and said, "Until tonight, my fairest Daphne. For now, duty calls."

Afterwards, Florian excused himself to meet with the neighboring royals to discuss various trade deals. Upon his departure, she decided to return back to her seat at the royal table.

However, unfortunately, for Daphne, her trip was short lived. For at that precise moment, she managed to run into her nemesis, Lady Esmeralda of Clover. Apparently, she, like her parents, still came to the ball, after all.

Dressed in an overflowing and velvet midnight black colored ballroom style gown with silver sequins, Esmeralda's attire was far more conservative than her last appearance at Daphne's wedding.

This time around, Esmeralda's chest was completely covered in fabric, with her neck and decolletage fully concealed... as well as everywhere else for that matter. Although the lady was dressed in a gloomy dark shade of midnight black, the only pop of color that she wore was a pair of emerald green earrings and a matching bracelet to go along with it.

"Do you honestly think that *you*, could ever please him?" Esmeralda hissed, with her hands placed against the sides of her hips.

Immediately, she decided to cut straight to the chase, without a moment's delay. Already, she managed to corner the crown princess in the middle of the ballroom.

"You know *nothing* of him," she sneered in disgust.

"Meanwhile, I, on the other hand," Esmeralda continued on, "Have known him, since he was a toddler. I know his likes and dislikes… *everything*. And trust me, *Princess Daphne*, you're not Florian's type!"

At this point, Daphne was curious about Florian's ideal woman. Kind? Charming? Independent? Witty? Ambitious? Blonde? Brunette? *Redhead?* Alas, the princess couldn't help but wonder as to which sort of female was the emerald prince's *type* to begin with?

"Type or not, he's still married to *me*," Daphne quickly pointed out. "So, you might as well accept it. Because I'm *not* going anywhere. Florian is *my husband* and *I am his wife.*"

Instantly, Esmeralda cringed and closed her eyes in despair. For all of her talk, she was truly in the losing corner. Either way, Daphne was his wife and most certainty, *not her.*

"Perhaps, you're his wife, for *now*," Esmeralda retorted, "But that might not always be the case. In time, he'll come to miss me. After all, we grew up, alongside each other. Best friends and partners for everything. Eventually, he'll come to miss me. It's an inevitable fact. Whether you love or hate something, *familiarity is everything.* And no matter how much you try, *Princess Daphne*, you can never undue the past that he and I, alone, share together."

"In time," she continued on, "He'll grow tired of you. Like a shiny new toy. He's like that, you know. Right now, you might be the golden apple of his eyes, but soon enough, you'll eventually fade away from his admiration. In the end, he'll come back to *me*. After he's had his fun with you, Florian will restore his obligations to honor his late mother's dying wish and thereby, take me as his new bride. Just wait and see. After all, I was born to be Esmeralda, the Emerald Princess. It's why I was *named* Esmeralda to begin with. It's because our mothers always believed that I was destined to become the crown princess of this land."

"Listen, Esmeralda," Daphne spoke fiercely, with her index finger pointed towards her foe this time around.  "Thus far, instead of *enjoying* my first Emerald Ball, I've been forced to endure and listen to your endless whining."

"Whining? *Me?*" asked Esmeralda in astonishment.

Already, she was offended by the accusation.

"Yes, *whining*," Daphne huffed, in annoyance. "And as far as whining goes, you're worse than my younger brother, Adrian. And trust me, he's the ultimate *king* of whininess and destruction!"

Alas, Esmeralda was left utterly speechless. A first, for the daughter of the Marquis of Clover.

"*You* might be *his past*," she continued on forcefully, spoken just like a true queen-in-waiting, "But *I* am *his future*."

With much strength, Daphne, proceeded to walk past her foe, brushing herself forcefully against Esmeralda and slamming her shoulder, almost tripping her along the way. And as the lady struggled to catch her balance, the princess quickly fled the scene.

As Daphne swiftly glided across the floor and traveling towards the opposite side of the ballroom, she was mere inches away from the refreshment table, when she suddenly heard a loud cheer, followed by a round of clapping.

"Bravo, sister!" Violet happily clapped on.

Apparently, the western queen had witnessed the entire ordeal from afar.

"You certainly handled that confrontation rather well, too, might I add," her sister beamed proudly, as she quickly grabbed a hold of Daphne's arm and interlocked it within hers.

"Come, let's take a turn around the ballroom together," Violet suggested.

And as the Galloway sisters took a stroll together on the floor and smiled at the other guests attending the ball, Daphne whispered over to her elder sister and said, "Violet, I'm sorry that you witnessed my heated argument with Esmeralda. Personally, I wish that unfortunate scene wasn't broadcasted so publicly out in the open, like it did."

"But it wasn't your fault," Violet was quick to defend her younger sister. "Daphne, sometimes in life, we are faced with unforeseeable challenges.

Obstacles that we have no other choice, but to stand up and tackle. And tonight, I'm very proud of *you*."

"You proud of *me*?" Daphne asked, in surprise.

Her sister, Violet, might have been a hero in the last war, but Daphne was just an ordinary debutante. She'd never been forced to confront an enemy of war; let alone, a regular bully before. Especially, at a royal court. But one way or another, Daphne was forced to deal with newfound challenges, head-on.

"Of course, I'm proud of you, Daphne," Violet beamed on with a proud smile. "You stood up for yourself *and* for your honor, too. Plus, you didn't resort to any violence, either. Instead, you opted to use your wits and tongue to defend yourself. Just like a *true princess*."

"Thank you, Violet. I really appreciate it," Daphne replied, sincerely touched by her sister's kind spoken words.

"Listen, Daphne," her sister began, "I think that some time away from this court, will do you and Florian a lot of good."

"Violet, what do you mean?" she curiously inquired.

"Come and stay at my palace," Violet advised. "If I stand correct, you and Florian haven't yet celebrated with a proper honeymoon, right? Plus, it's been ages since you last visited our castle. Also, I know that my boys, Leopold and Tristan, will be thrilled to have their aunt and uncle over for a visit. They certainly do miss their aunt."

"Violet, are you sure? Especially, with you being so close to delivering?" Daphne sought to ask, not wanting to impose upon her sister's generosity.

"More reasons for you to come. Honestly, I could use your company to help me to prepare for the new baby," Violet insisted. "Besides, Maximus will have plenty of fun spending time with Florian, too."

"But what shall I tell the palace? They're still awfully insistent on managing my daily affairs to no avail," Daphne sighed.

"Then, we'll say that it's a trip to further promote diplomatic relations between our two neighboring kingdoms," Violet explained. "It will be a win-win decision for us all."

"It does sound rather tempting," Daphne admitted.

"Also," Violet wickedly smiled on, "It will give you a chance to be away from any prying eyes. Our autumn woods are very secluded. Plus, Granny Ruby still owns that cottage. Perhaps, you and Florian can enjoy a romantic evening alone there, together? With no palace courtiers around to interfere?"

Little did her sister know about her true romantic relationship with Florian. But either way, a trip traveling away from the eastern palace was welcomed wholeheartedly. Plus, an excuse to avoid any potential future run-ins with Esmeralda wasn't a bad thing, either.

"Alright, I'm convinced," Daphne happily agreed. "Before I retire for the evening, I'll speak to Florian about this matter. But most likely, I'm sure that he'll agree. He always does."

"Splendid!" Violet gushed on. "A magical trip to the Kingdom of the West, the Land of Eternal Autumn it shall be!"

# Chapter 8

## *A Bumpy Carriage Ride*

An eight-hour carriage ride brought the royal couple over to the neighboring autumn region, better known as the Kingdom of the West. As it turned out, it didn't take much effort on Daphne's part to convince Florian to join her on this trip, either.

In truth, the crown prince was looking forward to an extended trip with his new bride. Plus, there were also several business arrangements to discuss with King Maximus, including their ongoing trade deals, strategic warfare preparations and joint military operations rehearsals.

As trusted allies, their two kingdoms were constantly in contact with one another. Generally, taking place over an exchange of numerous letter correspondences. Therefore, a trip in-person to discuss their professional and personal matters, were warmly welcomed by both parties.

Meanwhile, along their journey, Daphne peeked through their carriage's window to stare outside. Comfortably, the crown princess sat in an elegant and exquisite horse drawn carriage, which resembled the famous pumpkin carriage found within the classical tale: *Cinderella*.

However, rather than traveling in an orange hued vehicle, the carriage in question was of course, painted in the royal shade of emerald green and was adorned with hundreds of crimson red roses and pale pink waterlilies along its sides. Looking forward to her new travels, Daphne anxiously gazed out of the window to admire the lovely scenery surrounding them.

Upon departing their eastern kingdom, the crown princess observed the thick blankets of lush greenery, which were decorated with hundreds upon thousands of soft, elegant and pastel-inspired spring flowers. Traveling further down the road and eventually, crossing the border into the neighboring kingdom, Daphne was in awe by the majestic scene before her.

In contrast to her country, the western kingdom was the stark opposite of her blooming nation. Instead, the autumn land was covered in deep layers of warm and jewel toned foliage, which were all generously scattered across the open dirt roads.

Alas, no longer were they surrounded by fresh greenery. Instead, the scenery was replaced by rows of dark, tall and ancient looking oak trees. Trees, which were currently, sporting dried leaves on the ends of their branches.

Meanwhile, the sky reflected a cold, cloudy and autumn-inspired feel to it, too. As opposed to the brightly green, sun-drenched and floral land that Daphne had recently grown accustomed to; her sister's land was like venturing into an overcast and bronzed colored world. A world, centered around a copper-based sun; which in return, was also surrounded by a hunter green, burgundy and tangerine hued forest.

Although the western kingdom lacked flowers in their land; however, there was at least one particular golden flower that bloomed in the heart of this withering season: *marigolds*.

Suddenly, an unexpected smile formed across Daphne's face. In a few short weeks, her sister was going to deliver a child. Hopefully, a baby girl. In fact, she could simply sense the baby's gender as an intuition, predicting that a new princess was going to be born.

Soon enough, Daphne was going to become an aunt for a third time around, and her newest niece was going to be the name bearer of such a lovely and exquisite flower. Truly, her name couldn't have been more perfect for an autumn princess.

"What are you thinking?" Florian curiously asked his wife, as he admired her expression from across his seat.

"Oh, nothing in particular," she answered, reverting her attention over to her husband. "I was just thinking about how everything that thrives within this continent is so incredibly lovely. Both the spring and autumn lands."

"The Great Kingdom is beautiful," he agreed. "But Earth is just as equally lovely, too."

"Perhaps, but if I'm being honest…," she hesitated to say.

"Yes, do go on," he encouraged her.

"England never really felt like home to me," the princess admitted in earnest.

"Why?" the prince inquired.

"It's just that I never really felt like I belonged," Daphne revealed. "And even though I was born and raised in England; in truth, I never wanted to actually stay there, forever."

"Is it because you felt like you belonged elsewhere?" he asked, now intrigued by her statement.

"Yes, actually, I did," Daphne replied. "Especially, after my sister got married and moved away to the Great Kingdom. When she left, a part of me felt like I, too, belonged here, as well. Two sisters destined for the same continent."

"Then, why did you stay back there? In England? Why didn't you come any sooner into our realm?" Florian implored, curiously.

"Obligation," she sighed, as she fidgeted with her hands.

"To your family?" he inquired, with a raised brow.

"Yes," she admitted. "Plus, as a middle-child, I felt well… stuck."

"Stuck in which way?" he pressed on.

"Well, after my sister got married, my brother, Adrian, departed home to attend a strict military academy in London. Meanwhile, I was left behind and alone in the company of my parents," she began to explain, "And looking back at it all, I think my mother was especially grateful to still have at least one of her children close by her at home. But truth be told, I didn't mind it so much at the time. Especially, at first."

"At first?" he repeated.

"Yes," she continued on, "But as the years went by, and I grew up and found no one of interest to marry… well… I was afraid that staying behind in my small village as an aging maiden was going to be my ultimate fate. Unfortunately, sometimes, that really is the fate of a middle-child. And I was *almost* ready to accept it, too. That is, until *you* came along."

"Do you feel more at home, here?" he asked, eagerly.

"Yes, actually, I do," Daphne happily replied. "More than I initially thought so at first, too."

"And you do *belong* here," he added on, with much conviction. "Just so you know, my fairest Daphne, you are the *perfect* emerald princess. I honestly couldn't have kissed a better maiden than you."

Afterwards, Florian gently placed his hands above hers. Although it was a friendly gesture; however, as Daphne carefully gazed at his handsome face, she could swear that she also saw the look of longing, just lingering within those sparkling pair of lapis blue eyes.

In that moment, he wore an expression, which reflected admiration, passion and hidden desire. If she hadn't known any better, Daphne was almost inclined to think that perhaps, Florian harbored genuine feelings for her. Feelings that went just beyond friendship and maybe even possibly… *romantic love?*

But this was impossible, right? After all, their marriage was based on a matter of convenience and not related to true love. He needed a wife, and she needed a husband. A bride to break his miserable lifelong engagement to a witch; and she, an excuse to flee from her family's home to marry a real-life prince. Thus, their marriage was based solely on friendship. That was all. Nothing less and nothing more.

However, as his hands lingered above hers, Daphne felt her heart begin to flutter. It was racing so incredibly fast, that her face couldn't help but blush in the bright shade of red.

"I say, Daphne, are you alright?" Florian inquired, out of concern.

Embarrassed by her flushed reaction, Daphne quickly replied, "It's just the carriage ride. I think I might be suffering from motion sickness."

"Here, let me help you," he offered.

A moment later, Florian was no longer seated across from her in the carriage. Instead, he was now resting right beside her. Within seconds, the crown prince quickly reached over her flushed body to open a window nearby to allow some fresh air to circulate inside of their stuffy and overheated carriage.

"The cold air should help," he told her.

However, before Daphne could enjoy a breath of fresh air, the carriage suddenly jolted, as it hit an unexpected bump on the road. Thus, sending the crown princess flying high up towards the ceiling and almost tumbling out of the cracked open window. A second later, she slammed back down onto her seat and struggled to regain her balance. Meanwhile, her hair was tangled into a knotted mess.

"Oh dear," Daphne declared, as she attempted to tame her unkept hair.

"No, this shall not due," Florian spoke sternly, as he clicked his tongue in disapproval.

Without a further notice, the crown prince swiftly grabbed a hold of wife and placed her above his lap, wrapping his arms tightly around her waist.

"Ah, Florian…," she gulped, out of nervousness.

"Shush," he told her. "Just sit and relax. Enjoy the fresh breeze, it will calm your nerves. I promise to look after you, until we arrive to the castle."

Quietly, she shook her head and gave in to his request. One way or another, Florian was trying to help console her. *To protect her.* And in truth, it was awfully sweet of him to care so much about her welfare.

But as Daphne sat above on Florian's lap, she could also feel his body pressed against hers. He was warm, muscular and firm. In truth, he was certainly far more comfortable than just sitting above on the rigid seats found within this darn carriage!

Suddenly, Daphne got a whiff of his scent. It was bold and refreshing. A combination of lilies and honey. A sweet and floral scent that sent her nose on fire. Oh, how much she adored it! How much she wanted nothing more than to join her naked body with his and bathe in that intoxicating scent!

And then, to Daphne's surprise, her bottom managed to accidentally glide against his length. It was *hard*. He was so aroused!

"Umm… are you alright?" she asked him.

"I'm fine," he gulped, trying his best to ignore his obvious struggle.

"Florian, I think I'm alright now. I can sit back down on my own seat again," Daphne suggested, out of pure mercy for her obviously struggling spouse.

"Are you sure?" Florian hesitated to ask. "If not, I can manage."

Manage my ass, she thought to herself! Really, this entire situation was all laughable, too! Even though Daphne *liked* the feel of him from underneath her, she also wasn't a cruel wife, either. No, it wasn't fair for Florian's body to react in this way, if nothing romantic was expected to happen between them, right now.

Therefore, Daphne took in a deep breath and said, "Florian, it's alright. Thanks to you, I feel much better. Plus, we still have quite a way to go on our journey. In the meantime, I think it's best if I try to sleep."

"Are you certain?" he asked her, once more.

Again, Daphne could feel his hardened cock rising another inch by the second. And to be fair, she was also growing wet down below, herself.

If she wasn't careful, then whether or not they were ready, at this going rate, by the end of this carriage ride, they were ultimately going to have sex. With her body resting comfortably above his lap, and his cock ready to slide right into her wet opening.

Because, at this point, all roads led to this inevitable path. Unless, however, Daphne took swift control of this tempting situation and diverted this bumpy encounter, altogether.

"Yes, I'm certain," Daphne answered and this time around, she took the liberty to hop off from his lap and sat herself back down on the opposite side of the carriage.

A second later, she was lying down and had her head popped up and resting against one of the spare decorative pillows.

"Well, as long as you're alright," he finally conceded.

"Let's sleep," Daphne suggested, as she threw him a second spare pillow.

"Very well," Florian agreed.

Meanwhile, as they rested across from each other, Daphne secretly smiled. From this angle, his hot length was practically ready to pop straight out of his trousers, just like a jack-in-the-box. Furthermore, instead of using his pillow to rest his head, Florian kept it down below to cover his arousal.

As much as Daphne wanted to giggle at this funny scene, she ultimately decided to hold it in. Finally, with great satisfaction, she realized that although she might not be Esmeralda, she could still ignite a burning desire within her husband, either way.

# Chapter 9

## *The Kingdom of the West, the Land of Eternal Autumn*

Several hours later, Florian and Daphne arrived to the western imperial palace. By now, it was nightfall and the moonlight was shining down below and across the royal grounds. Upon entrance through the front gates, they were instantly greeted by a delighted Violet and Maximus, along with their two excited young sons.

Even though it had been a few seasons since Daphne last visited the western palace; but still, upon their arrival, she was instantly transfixed by the palace's spectacular beauty. It was almost as if, it had been her very first time traveling to this enchanting castle.

Like her own eastern palace, Violet's abode was built using pure white marble. Marble that shined and sparkled, just like a translucent and opaque pearl. Meanwhile, the palace was filled with large glass windows, stretching from its ceilings and down to its floors, on all sides and ends.

In fact, during the daytime, the gleaming sun would often shine through these openings to cast a rainbow of light against the castle's floors. However, it was only during the night, when the twinkling stars from the night sky managed to peek through these glass windows to project a golden starlight glow; which in return, was dispersed throughout the open space.

"We feared that your carriage wouldn't arrive until morning," Violet addressed them.

"Not so much *us*, for say," Maximus admitted. "It's the boys who've been anxiously waiting for your arrival. Haven't you boys?"

Almost immediately, Leopold and Tristan ran straight towards their aunt's direction and quickly threw their arms around her. A second later, Leopold pulled himself away from Daphne's clutch and practically tackled Florian down onto the floor. Before she knew it, the young crown prince was crawling up her husband's arms and was now, seated on top of his shoulders.

"Calm down you two!" Violet shouted at her young sons in frustration, embarrassed by their naughty outbursts and ungentlemanly behaviors.

"It's quite alright," Florian reassured his sister-in-law. "After all, it's been some time, since I last saw the boys. Isn't that right, Lee?"

"Uncle Florian, can we venture out into the forest again, together? Tristan and I want to learn to play the lyre! And only you can teach us!" shouted a determined Leopold, with his hands resting alongside his uncle's shoulders.

"The lyre? Since when did you boys take an interest in the lyre?" their father asked, most curiously.

Learning to play the lyre, well, that was certainly news to him. Up until to today, his sons had never previously shown any interests on any particular musical instrument. At least, as far as he was aware of.

"Since the last time Uncle Florian played it back in the forest, while Lee and I danced along," Tristan responded this time.

"Very well, come tomorrow, we'll do just that," Florian proclaimed, wanting to appease his young nephews.

"The four of us will have a grand adventure out in the woods. What do you say, Daphne?" he winked.

"Oh, please, Aunt Daphne, you must agree," Tristan cried. "Uncle Florian won't go, if you don't."

"Yes, especially, now that you're married to him," Leopold added on.

"He always talks about you, you know," Tristan blabbed aloud.

Her nephews' choice of words, certainly caught Daphne by surprise. Their admissions were truly interesting. Not only had Florian written letters about her to his twin sister, Diana, but according to Leopold and Tristan, he also spoke about her to their own nephews, too.

This revelation was most curious, considering the mere fact that they had only been married for just a matter of weeks. But apparently, Florian still found the time to converse about her with their young nephews.

"Of course, I shall come," Daphne promised her nephews, as she playfully tousled her youngest nephew's head of dark locks.

"But," she said, "Does Uncle Florian even have a lyre on hand with him?"

"Oh, I'm sure that we can arrange to find one, if he doesn't," Violet chimed in.

"No worries," Florian reassured them. "I always carry a spare lyre in my luggage."

"So, it's settled," Violet happily beamed. "Come tomorrow, you two can enjoy a nice trip into the woods with Leopold and Tristan by your sides."

"Yes, it looks like we'll be one big and happy family," Florian smiled on.

In that moment, Daphne couldn't help but suspect that Violet was somehow secretly thrilled about the prospect of them spending a day out together in the woods. To spend quality time away from the prying eyes of the castle. Was it possible that her elder sister knew the truth about their platonic relationship?

"In the meantime," Maximus interjected, "It's time to get these two into bed. Come on boys, it's getting late."

And as the king carried his young sons upstairs and into their beds, Violet escorted Daphne and Florian into their guest bedchamber.

"Supper will be served in exactly one hour," Violet announced. "It will just be us four adults, so feel free to dress comfortably for the occasion."

Afterwards, Violet closed the door shut and both Florian and Daphne collapsed onto their bed and took a brief nap.

An hour later, Florian and Daphne joined Violet and Maximus at the dinner table, located inside of the grand banquet room. Her sister was dressed in an oversized velvet scarlet red empire style gown, which complemented her bright red hair that was elegantly swept aside from her face and secured into a neat bun. As a symbol of the west, Violet wore a diamond encrusted and pumpkin-shaped hairpin, which she used to clip her hair up.

Meanwhile, her brother-in-law, Maximus, wore an outfit that was similar to Florian's. Both men wore an identical cream ruffled blouse, black trousers and brown leather boots. The only exception were their capes, in which Maximus wore a red satin one and Florian wore a green velvet version.

And just like his pair of silver eyes, Maximus sported a silver crown, which was adorned with an amethyst heart-shaped jewel in the center that rested above his chestnut brown head of hair. A matching crown, which Violet also wore tonight for the occasion.

As Daphne and Florian took theirs seats at the table, the princess gently adjusted her tiara. Since getting married, tonight marked the first time that the crown princess had worn her tiara out in public. Up until now, she primarily used a floral wreath as a mark of her royal status.

However, while visiting her sister's kingdom, it was highly recommended by her palace courtiers to showcase a more traditional tiara, during her diplomatic trip to the western kingdom. A golden tiara adorned with an amber oval-shaped gem, which just-so-happened to match her golden silk mermaid style gown that she wore for tonight's dinner engagement.

"Daphne, you look absolutely lovely," Violet complemented her younger sister. "You're as bright and as beautiful as the sun."

"Thank you, Violet," Daphne blushed on.

In truth, she wanted to wear a similar golden color to match Florian's bright locks of blonde hair. Hair that was almost identical to the radiant sun.

"So, what's for supper?" Florian eagerly asked.

Indeed, after nearly spending an entire day traveling by carriage and sporadically snacking on some fruits and dried nuts along the way, the emerald prince was practically famished.

"We have a feast prepared for the occasion," Maximus replied, proudly.

A second later, the king promptly snapped his fingers and instantly, a host of palace servants suddenly appeared with full plates on hand. Peeking through the crowd, Daphne saw plates of several meats, including baked chicken, quail, rabbit and fish. There were also plates consisting of roasted potatoes, carrots, squash and raw cranberries. Additionally, traditional western delicacies were also served, including pumpkin stew, caramel apples, mint tea and pumpkin pie.

"Dig in folks," the king happily proclaimed.

"Thank you, Maximus and Violet, for the lovely meal," Daphne complemented them. "I can't tell you how happy Florian and I are to be served with such a grand meal. Especially, after traveling so long out on the road today."

"But of course, my dear sister," Violet replied, warmly. "I must admit, I've always wanted the opportunity to host the two of you and now, I finally have my long-awaited chance."

That statement certainly caught Daphne's attention. Previously, had Violet secretly desired to serve as their matchmaker? Based on her choice of words, it certainly seemed that way.

"I say," Florian began, "Shall I send that order of flower seeds to your palace to compensate for the lost village, destroyed by that dreadful fire? Previously, Lord and Lady Bleeding Heart wrote to me to confirm that they have plenty of spare berries and vegetable seeds in their possession. According to my calculations, we can send them over in time for the upcoming harvest season."

"Yes, thank you, Florian," Maximus replied, as he wiped his mouth clean with a napkin. "That's most kind of Lord and Lady Bleeding Heart. Please give them my sincerest regards to their kind generosity. Furthermore, I'll request for my courtiers to get in touch with your palace to complete the transfer."

Curious as to which village they were referring to, Daphne inquired, "And where might this land be located at?"

"One of the former villages on the western front," Maximus replied. "Sadly, it's one of the lost villages that Vera, the Evil Queen, burned down during her reign of terror."

Seven years ago, before her sister had married the current king, Vera, a wicked witch, had previously invaded the western territory and stole Maximus' kingdom. Upon unleashing a brutal rebellion, Vera murdered Maximus' father and brother, the late kings, Elryk and Leopold. Afterwards, she went on to usurp the throne for herself and thus, crowned herself as the ruthless evil queen.

Unfortunately, as it was later revealed, Vera was also the same witch who previously cursed Violet's and Daphne's own father, Lord Henry Galloway, into becoming the infamous Dark Horseman. It wasn't until their mother, Kassie, came along into the picture a century later, that his curse was ultimately broken by their enduring belief in everlasting true love.

Years later, Violet traveled into the Great Kingdom as the savior and eventually, defeated Vera, once and for all. Afterwards, she and Maximus married and were crowned as the new King and Queen of the West. But the most shocking of all revelations, was that Vera was also the estranged sister of their late grandmother, Sarah. In the end, the late evil queen was also the paternal great-aunt to both Queen Violet of the West and Crown Princess Daphne of the East.

"Unfortunately, our late aunt and her dark army destroyed several small villages and hamlets during her brief reign," Violet chimed in. "And even though Maximus and I have been on the throne these past seven years or so, there are many lost and destroyed territories that still needs our attention for cultivation and rehabilitation."

"And so, with these seeds from your nation," Maximus spoke on, "We can continue to slowly rebuild these ruined lands, one seed at a time."

"So, I see," Daphne spoke, as she took a sip of her wine. "In that case, I think that this trade deal between our nations is absolutely brilliant."

"I couldn't further agree," Maximus nodded in approval. "Which is why, I, too, plan on sending some pumpkin seeds your way in time for this year's harvest, as well."

"By the way," Florian joined in, "We should also discuss about our knights' training. Shall I host this year's practice at my court or yours?"

Meanwhile, as the two men plotted away, Daphne turned her attention over towards her sister.

"Oh, by the way, Daphne," Violet gushed on, "The new crib and linens have recently arrived. Perhaps, you can help me to decorate Marigold's new nursery, during your stay? I'd be most grateful for your input."

"Wait," her husband interrupted. "When did the baby's new things come in? Why wasn't I informed about the delivery?"

Being the possessive husband and father that he was, Maximus wanted to know absolutely everything and anything that pertained to his growing family. Especially, anything connected to his youngest child.

"Oh, it recently came in this late afternoon," Violet replied to her husband. "A few hours before Daphne's and Florian's arrival."

"So, is it really going to be a girl?" asked Florian, this time. "How can you be so sure? After all, you already have two boys. Isn't it more likely that you're carrying another son?"

"Well actually, apart from the fact that Maximus and I are secretly hoping that it's a girl, Daphne recently wrote to tell me that she also had a dream confirming much of the same," Violet confessed.

"A dream?" asked Florian, curiously. "And pray tell, what does Daphne's dream have to do with any of this?"

"I'm surprise that you don't know," Violet stared at him in disbelief. "Daphne, have you not already explained to your husband about your unique talent?"

"What talent?" Florian inquired, while turning his full attention over to his wife.

"Nothing, it's just that sometimes, my dreams come true," Daphne confessed.

"More than sometimes," her sister interjected. "Daphne, is a born seer. Her dreams serve more like prophecies. What she sees in her dreams, often comes true in real life."

"Except, most of the time, hardly anyone believes her," Maximus added on.

"Why don't others believe in your dreams?" Florian asked her directly.

"I can't really say for sure," Daphne shrugged. "Perhaps, it's the curse of being a middle-child. I may speak the truth, but rarely does anyone listen to my prophecies."

"Well, Maximus and I certainly take your dreams seriously," Violet sternly spoke.

"May I ask what this dream concerning the baby was about?" Florian further inquired.

"According to Daphne's last letter," Violet answered in her sister's place, "She saw Maximus and I standing in a nursery made of gold and rocking a baby girl in our arms. The newborn child smelled just like a marigold flower and there was a bright and flaming fire burning inside of the fireplace."

"So, based on that dream, you interrupt it to mean that you shall give birth to a daughter?" asked Florian.

"Yes," Violet replied. "Plus, in my heart, I already know that it's a girl, too."

"What about you, Maximus? What are your thoughts?" the emerald prince posed his question over to his brother-in-law.

"I agree with my wife," the king spoke. "I, too, feel like it's a girl. But either way, son or daughter, I'm just grateful to have another child with my beloved."

And then, Maximus reached over, grabbed a hold of his wife's hand and happily smiled from ear-to-ear.

Meanwhile, as Daphne watched them embrace, she felt a strange pain in her heart. For some reason, seeing her sister and brother-in-law so happy in their marriage, made her *almost* wish for the same sort of love in her own.

Suddenly, as if reading her mind, Daphne felt Florian grab a hold of her hand from underneath the table. His touch was soft and warm. Surprisingly, it brought her much joy and happiness. And as he held on to her hand, her heart bloomed with mirth.

However, a minute later, Daphne recalled that their embrace was hidden underneath the table. As far as their hosts were concerned, no one other than themselves were aware of such affection. Was it possible that Florian truly wanted to hold her hand, even when no one else was looking?

Furthermore, if no one else was looking, then what was the point of it all? It's not like he was forced to hold her hand, for the sake of their charade. Therefore, was it possible that her husband wanted to hold her hand, out of his own free will? After spending all this time together, Daphne was starting to develop a strong attraction and attachment to her husband.

"May I ask what the gold and fire represents in this dream, then?" Florian asked, as he continued to hold on to Daphne's hand.

"You know, I'm not entirely sure," Violet replied, as if she, too, had only recently acknowledged this part of the dream, as well.

"The gold and fire are significant," Daphne answered, this time. "However, that's as far as I know. Only time will tell the truth."

"Either way, as long as the child is born healthy, then that's all I care," Maximus declared.

And then, for the remainder of their evening, the family feasted on the rest of their supper, before eventually, retiring off to bed.

Later on, that evening, Daphne was resting inside of her bed, while suffering from a bad case of abdominal cramps. Apparently, tonight's epic feast had been a bit rough on her already sensitive stomach. Just as she had previously declared during their ride in the carriage earlier in the day, it seemed that she *really did* suffer from motion sickness, after all.

"I've brought you some warm chamomile tea with a dash of lemon and honey to help sooth your aching stomach," Florian announced as he stepped into their bedchamber, while carrying a cup of herbal tea in his hand.

"You're too kind," Daphne spoke, as she tried to sit back up on their bed to lean against the headboard.

"Here, let me assist you," her husband cried, as he practically ran over to her side to help aid her.

The next thing Daphne knew, Florian had abruptly pulled her back up towards him into a standing position. And without any warning, he began to undress her.

"What are you doing?" she nervously asked.

"Shush," he told her. "Don't worry. I'm just going to help you get changed into something more comfortable for bed, that's all."

A second later, her sparkling golden gown fell straight down and landed on the bottom of the floor, leaving her completely exposed and wearing nothing else but her corset and undergarments.

"Shall I remove the rest, or will you?" he asked her, with a sly grin.

"I… I…," she gulped.

This was the first time that Florian had held her body so close to him, with little else than her undergarments. At this point, there was only a thin layer of lace separating them, between his hands and her naked body.

"Relax," he whispered into her ear. "Here, allow me."

Silently, Daphne nodded and slowly, Florian began to peel off the rest of her clothes. First, he gently undid the laces to her corset, letting it fall across her abdomen, until it reached her hips and then, down onto the floor.

"Much better," he remarked with approval.

By now, Daphne's breasts were fully exposed, while he stood right behind her. Meanwhile, as his thick length rubbed against the curves of her buttock, she closed her eyes and took in a deep breath.

At this point, whether or not she was suffering from a stomach ache, she no longer felt it. Instead, she felt numb.

"Allow me to undue your hair, too," he begged.

"Yes," Daphne sighed, keeping her eyes closed.

A moment later, Florian released her hair from the clip that had previously held it together. In one sweep, her fiery red hair tumbled down and floated across her bare back and chest.

By now, Daphne was completely lost in the moment. So, this is what it felt like to stand fully exposed and practically naked in front of a man, she thought to herself. It was both terrifying and liberating at the same time.

Afterwards, Florian sat down on their bed and brought Daphne down along with him. As she sat above his lap, she opened her eyes and saw his reflection in the mirror. From her vanity dresser, she saw him grab a hairbrush. A second later, Florian proceeded to use that same brush to comb through the ends of her red hair, one stroke at a time.

Right now, Daphne couldn't have felt more comfortable. No longer was she nervous about sitting above Florian's lap, like she did back in the carriage. Instead, she was at total ease. And although she could feel his length hardening right from underneath her, this time around, she didn't mind it all so much.

And so, as Daphne closed her eyes, Florian carefully brushed her hair, working her back layers and eventually, moving to the front locks covering her chest. Meanwhile, as he gently brushed through the knots resting alongside her bosom, his other hand managed to accidentally glide across one of her breasts.

Nervously, Daphne sucked in another breath. However, instead of a brief touch, Florian's hand seemed to linger there, resting above her right breast and hovering over her nipple.

"Ah," Daphne couldn't help but release a sigh.

"Do you like this?" Florian mischievously asked her, having previously caught sight of her pleased reaction to his touch.

"Yes, I do," she shyly admitted.

"Then, shall I touch you, again?" he asked her cautiously.

Amazingly enough, this was the first time that he had sought her permission to touch her. Technically, there was no need for him to ask. This wasn't a part of their arrangement.

And yet, regardless of their prior agreement, Daphne still wanted him to do so. Yes, she very much desired for him to touch her. And badly, too.

"Please," she begged.

Much to her delight, he did just that. Slowly, he placed the hairbrush down onto the bed and using both free hands, he began to gently massage and caress her breasts, while taking extra care of her nipples.

"Do you like this, Daphne?" he seductively whispered into her ear, using a low and deep sultry voice, as he flicked away at her pink and hardened nipples.

"Yes," she sighed, again.

Pleased by her response, he moved to squeeze both of her nipples hard with his fingers; which in return, forced Daphne to release a desperate cry.

"There's my girl," Florian happily laughed on, as he leaned in and placed a gentle kiss alongside her head.

Meanwhile, as his left-hand continued to play and fondle with her breasts, his right-hand wandered down below her abdomen and stopped right in front of her lace undergarments.

"Shall I help you to forget about your pain?" he dared her.

By now, Daphne was rocking against his lap, instinctively rolling her hips alongside his body. Whether or not her mind warned her to stop, her body simply craved for his touch.

"Yes, please," she pleaded.

Instantly, Florian slipped his hand inside of her undergarment and traveled all the way down to her lady parts. Slowly, he began to massage her folds, gently stretching them with his fingers. Carefully, using his thumb to caress her opening.

Even as an inexperienced virgin, his touch was like the awakening of a hidden beast that resided deep within her. A side of herself that up until now, she never knew existed. And as he fondled with her most private of parts, Daphne began to rock and roll her hips against his fist.

Sensing her sexual frustration, Florian decided to help relieve some of her inner tensions. And so, as she rocked against him, he took swift action and removed the rest of her clothing. Afterwards, his fingers poked at her core and to his delight, she was completing soaking wet.

Again, Daphne had never been with a man before, so this entire experience was brand new to her. Honestly, she wasn't entirely sure if she was doing all of this… or *whatever* this was… correctly.

Even though she was supposed to be a wife; however, up until this point, their marriage hadn't yet forced them to explore any real intimate physical relations with each other. At least, not until tonight.

By now, Daphne didn't know what to expect next. Either way, she was thoroughly enjoying this newfound experience with her husband.

"Relax," he told her, already sensing what she was secretly thinking.

"Tonight, it's not about me," he vowed. "It's about *your pleasure*. My personal desire to please you."

His words instantly sent a shiver down her back. *Pleasing her. Pleasuring her.* It was all about *her. Not, him.*

No longer did she need to feel afraid or nervous. All she needed to do was to trust in Florian and surrender herself over to his care. An arrangement that she was happily ready to do, too.

"Alright, I trust you, Florian," Daphne whispered into his ear. "Please, make me feel good."

Based on her high level of trust and confidence in him, Florian's heart happily soared. Determined to please his wife, he gently pulled her from off his lap and carefully placed her down onto their bed, with her back lying against the bedspread. Afterwards, he kneeled down in front of her on the floor and slowly, he began to spread her legs wide open before him.

Being stretched before her husband, Daphne took a deep breath in. This was the first time that she had ever been so exposed to anyone in this position before. Let alone, a man.

But now, with her permission, Florian was kneeling in front of her, like a real-life knight in shining armor. And as she gazed upon him, Daphne noticed the intense desire reflected within his piercing blue eyes. Whatever he was about to do next, he desperately wanted to do it. And *badly*, too.

"Daphne, can I taste you?" he begged her, with such longing in his voice.

"Taste me?" she blinked in surprise. What did he mean by that, exactly?

"Yes, taste you," he repeated.

"I guess—"

Not a second later after agreeing, Florian's lips instantly glided against her inner thighs, with his tongue making its way up into her opening. At this point, Daphne was dripping wet and Florian was licking and sucking her dry. Cleaning her sinful desires, all by the power of his glorious tongue.

"Aaaahhhh...," Daphne sighed deeply, as her toes curled and her hands griped the satin bedsheet.

Meanwhile, Florian held her legs above his shoulders and buried his head in between her thighs. And as he continued to feast upon her soaking flesh, Daphne closed her eyes, rolled her head backwards and then, released a blissful moan.

So, *this* was *pleasure*. *This* was *pleasing one's wife*. If this was a preview to sexual relations with her husband, then Daphne was truly at a loss for words.

Meanwhile, as Florian's tongue glided across her body and licked her womb up and down, his hands were busy caressing her inner thighs; all the while, wickedly introducing himself to her awakening body. Similar to a spring flower that was blooming right before him.

Slowly, Daphne reopened her eyes, lifted her head up and watched him work his magic. Instinctively, she grabbed a hold of his head and ran her fingers across his golden locks of hair. And as she played with his golden strands like a field of wheat, she noticed that his length was hardening by each growing second. He might have been pleasuring her, but who was pleasuring him?

"What about you?" she innocently asked him.

"Don't worry about me," he paused in between his sucks.

As a result, Daphne almost regretted asking him this very question in the first place. Honestly, it was pure torture to have him stop feasting upon her. Even for a mere second!

"There will be other times," Florian promised her. "But for now, it's about *you*."

Passionately, he continued to suck her, sticking his tongue into regions of her body that she didn't even know existed before, until now. Soon after, she closed her eyes and surrendered herself over to her new lover.

With each new lick, Daphne found herself rolling her hips along the way, thrusting her body over his head. It was so wrong, but oh, how it felt so right, too!

Without even thinking, her body was moving in a cosmic rhythm that had her riding Florian's face. Even though her wild movements were entirely indecent and unladylike; but regardless, it was also incredibly pleasurable on her part, too.

And so, as she rode him, she stared across in the mirror and saw a wicked grin form along her husband's cheerful face. And in that moment, she realized that he was also enjoying this sexual encounter, just as much as she was, too.

A few minutes later, they both reached their versions of heaven, equally exhausted and satisfied in their union. Afterwards, Florian cleaned Daphne up and placed a nightgown over her body.

Once she was ready for bed, he tucked her inside of their blankets, before blowing out the flame to their candle and joining her bedside. Lastly, even after all that they had experienced tonight, the infamous pillow barrier remained in between them.

"Do you feel better, now?" he asked her.

"Yes. After everything, I most certainly do," Daphne instantly blushed.

Yes, of course, she felt better, she thought to herself. How could any wife not feel better? Especially, after experiencing the pleasurable services as performed by one's husband!

"In that case, I do believe that's enough for one night," Florian smiled, before he finally dozed off to sleep.

And now, alone in the darkness, Daphne deeply reflected about what had just recently transpired between them. After tonight, she was forced to acknowledge as to just how truly wonderful Florian looked after her. Both emotionally and physically, too.

After growing up as the forgotten middle-child, for the first time in Daphne's life, she had someone who was solely dedicated to her. *Just her.* Never before, had she experienced such caring attention.

Back at her childhood home, her elder sister, Violet, used to get most of their mother's attention as the first-born child, while her younger brother, Adrian, was their father's shadow, carefully groomed by the earl, himself. After all, Adrian was the heir to the Galloway title, estates and fortune, regardless of how much of a nuisance he was.

Therefore, due to these reasons, this often-left Daphne by herself. Alone with her books. Perhaps, that's why she loved reading fairy tales so much. It was an escape from her lonesome world.

However, after marrying Florian, everything changed. No longer was she the forgotten middle-child, but a princess who was personally looked after by the palace courtiers. And while Daphne was grateful for her staff, she still missed having the attention of a loved one, too.

Perhaps, this is why she was previously hesitant about the prospect of consummating her marriage bed. It wasn't just about physical intimacy alone. Instead, it was also the *emotional* intimacy associated with the act of love. To give one's heart freely to another. And after holding onto her heart for many years; in the end, Daphne was just afraid of getting hurt. Of being abandoned.

However, with that being said, remaining within Florian's constant company was starting to change her opinion about love. Seeing how thoughtful and kind he was towards her consistently around the clock, only further warmed her heart.

As a crown prince, he didn't have to bring her tea. After all, there were servants for that. Plus, he didn't have to dress her or brush her hair, either. There were maids for those tasks, as well. Furthermore, he also didn't need to touch her to make her feel better tonight, too.

Instead, it seemed like Florian truly wanted to do all of these things, just for her. It was almost as if everything that he did, really was for her sole benefit. But was it because he was a kind and generous prince who helped everyone around him, or did he truly harbor genuine feelings that were reserved only for her?

In the end, Daphne realized that only time would tell.

Turning to his side, she whispered, "Thank you, Florian, for taking such good care of me. I'm glad that I waited and married *you*, after all."

Even though Florian was sound asleep, Daphne secretly blew him a kiss and then, she closed her eyes and went to sleep.

105

# Chapter 10

## *A Journey Through the Woods*

The next day, Florian, Daphne and their nephews, Crown Prince Leopold and Prince Tristan of the West, traveled together through the woods, conveniently located just a walking mile or so away from the palace's grounds. Carrying their picnic basket in hand, they packed a light and delicious lunch, consisting of pheasant sandwiches, mint lemonade, pumpkin pie and cinnamon spiced apple tarts.

Once breakfast concluded, the happy family departed from the imperial palace by horseback, with Leopold riding alongside with his uncle, Florian, and Tristan partnered with his aunt, Daphne. Together, the foursome traveled through the rustic woods, passing by several ancient oak trees along the way.

Eventually, their journey brought them to a saltwater lake, which was located right in the heart of the forest. A whimsical spot that was a short distance away from their family's private cottage, which was owned by Daphne's great-grandmother, Ruby, the Elder.

After tying their horses to a nearby tree, the family proceeded to walk over to the lake's shores to set up camp. Meanwhile, as Daphne threw a red and white gingham picnic blanket over their special spot overlooking the scenic view of the lake and its surrounding oak trees, Florian and the boys helped to prepare some cold refreshments.

"It's still too early for lunch," their aunt forewarned them.

"Can we at least drink some mint lemonade?" asked Leopold.

"Of course, you can, Lee," Daphne nodded in approval.

A second later, Leopold and Tristan rushed to gulp down their lemonades. Apparently, after a short trip traveling by horseback, the young princes were absolutely parched.

"Don't drink too much," their uncle spoke, this time. "Come on, boys, let's use this opportunity to get some fresh air and exercise."

Before Daphne knew it, Florian and the boys were off frolicking through the forest. Together, they ran like a pack of hyper wolves, jumping and tumbling across the dirt ground. However, if that wasn't enough, the boys even began climbing up trees, while Florian eagerly chased right behind them.

Meanwhile, as Daphne watched her family happily play together in harmony, a part of her wondered on how her sister possessed the stamina to manage these extra hyper and wild boys, including her own adult husband. Growing up, Daphne hardly had the patience to deal with her naughty younger brother, Adrian. And yet, Violet had two of them. Honestly, her sister must have been a saint to maintain the patience and strength to keep up with her active boys on a daily basis.

However, at the same time, watching Florian and the boys playfully rough house with each other, brought an unexpected smile across her face. Witnessing just how well her nephews got along with their uncle also gave her a new sense of pride and joy. Indeed, it was heartwarming to see them all getting along so incredibly well. Bonding like a true family.

Meanwhile, as Florian and the boys moved on to play a round of sparring, Daphne couldn't help but giggle and remember about her own youth. Years ago, when her siblings and herself were still children, they, too, used to wander inside of the enchanted forest back in their homeland of

England. Playfully, she and her sister used to pose as princesses in distress, while their younger brother was tasked to save them from the fictional wicked villain.

Back then, Daphne wished to marry a prince and become a princess. And even though, she eventually grew up to become one, she never imagined for her real-life prince to be so well… *perfect…*

"That's enough of that," Florian declared, as he dropped his sword down onto the ground.

"But we're only just getting started," Tristan pouted, with his sword still in hand.

"Ah, but if we spend all day practicing sparring, then how shall you and your brother ever learn to play the lyre?"

"That's right," Leopold beamingly smiled with excitement, while agreeing with his uncle's suggestion.

"Come on, Tristan," the crown prince told his brother. "Let's take a break with our sparring match and concentrate on the lyre, instead."

A few minutes later, Florian and the boys joined Daphne's side. Together, they sat above the picnic blanket and stared across at the majestic scenery. With the fresh air, clear lake view and the hundreds of tall trees surrounding them, Daphne felt like she was back at home in the enchanted forest.

"Isn't the view lovely from here, boys?" she asked her nephews.

"Yeah, it is," Tristan answered. "But next time, we should go fishing!"

"Always looking for the next grand adventure, huh, Tristan?" Leopold asked his younger brother, sarcastically.

"Of course, that's what heroes do," replied the younger prince.

"Well, apart from a grand quest," their uncle interrupted, "Heroes must also learn to play the lyre, as well."

"Really, why?" asked Tristan, as curious as ever.

"Because, a hero might find himself in the company of a fair maiden one day. And so, naturally, he might want to charm his lovely lady with some serene music."

"Charm a fair maiden? Why, who cares about girls!" the younger prince huffed.

And then, both Leopold and Tristan had a good giggle.

"Come now, boys," their aunt scolded them. "That isn't very funny!"

"Besides," she continued on, with a wicked grin, "You might not like girls *now*, but that might change in the future."

"Aunt, I would sooner be a villain than to ever glance at a silly girl," Leopold proudly declared.

"Me, too," Tristan chimed in. "I, too, would rather be a villain, as well. Or, at the very least, I'd rather marry a rose full of thorns than to woo a damsel in distress!"

"Boys!" exclaimed their aunt, in disappointment.

"Don't you know that girls aren't just damsels in distress?" she clicked her tongue in disapproval. "Why, take your mother, for instance. She was never a damsel in distress. Instead, your mother was a former knight, who defeated an evil queen. Meanwhile, your grandmother broke a hundred-year-old curse. Plus, your great-great-grandmother is a famous sorceress, too. And I, your aunt, am certainly not one to be trifled with, either!"

"Apologize to your aunt, boys," Florian advised his nephews.

"Very well," Leopold sighed. "Aunt Daphne, I'm sorry."

"Yes, Aunt Daphne, I'm sorry, too," Tristan agreed.

Witnessing the adorable and apologetic expressions upon her nephews' faces, Daphne couldn't help but smile. One way or another, she held a soft spot in her heart for those rambunctious boys.

"Very well, let's enjoy the rest of our afternoon," she told them. "But first, we must eat our lunch, before we start on your lessons."

"Now the trick to playing the lyre," Florian began to explain to the young royals after lunch, "Is that music alone, is not enough to entertain."

"It isn't?" asked Tristan, as he sat cross-legged near his uncle's side.

"No, it certainly is not," the emerald prince answered, as he pulled out his white ivory lyre from out of his traveling backpack.

"Then, what is it?" Leopold inquired.

"My dear, Lee, the answer is simple. It's poetry."

"Poetry?" the boys cried out.

"Music, song and dance," Florian told them. "These three elements are essential, when playing the lyre."

"So, where does poetry come in?" asked Leopold, with a curious expression resting on his youthful face.

"Poetry are the lyrics to the songs that we sing," their uncle explained. "When we read or speak them, then they're considered as a form of poetry. However, when we sing them aloud, along with the use of our harmonious instruments, then together, they transform into music. A magical world of song, that's celebrated by all who are blessed to hear them."

"So, that's the magic of music?" Leopold inquired. "Using words and melodies to express our feelings?"

"Sometimes," Florian continued to lecture them, as his long and slender fingers grazed against the strings of his lyre to produce its first set of musical notes.

"Music and poetry are a special way to express one's true inner feelings," he furthered added. "Emotions that many folks, otherwise, cannot publicly admit aloud in real life."

"Ah, so that's where love sonnets come in," Leopold deduced.

"Exactly," the emerald prince agreed.

"But why music?" asked Tristan, in confusion. "Why not just speak from the heart?"

"Because my boys," their uncle sighed, "When it comes to the matters of the heart, we are all lost fools."

Meanwhile, as Florian spoke these words out loud, he stared straight at Daphne's direction and smiled at her. Instantly, her heart fluttered, while she blushed in the bright shade of red.

"And this song," Florian happily announced, "Is a song that I wrote for your aunt."

And as the boys began to cheer and dance, Florian gazed at Daphne once more and gave her a wink.

Taking in a deep breath, the emerald prince played his lyre and sang the following song:

*"My fairest Daphne,*
*Treasure of my eyes,*
*Pearl of my heart,*
*Whose beauty is as lovely,*
*As a blooming laurel tree in spring,*
*With eyes as green as sparkling emeralds,*
*And hair as bright as a burning fire,*
*At first sight, this fair maiden captured my heart,*
*As she silently sat there,*
*Reading underneath a laurel tree,*
*While patiently waiting for her prince to come,*
*One glimpse at her and I knew,*
*That I was lost to her forever,*
*Even in my curious green state,*
*With nothing else to hold,*
*But my lily pad floating above the pond,*
*Alas, I understood,*
*That she was the one,*
*The owner of my beating heart,*
*If only she but knew."*

Afterwards, the boys each took their turns to test out the strings of their uncle's lyre, before they eventually, decided to switch gears and practice on a round of archery, instead. Unfortunately, Leopold and Tristan were highly active boys, with extremely *low* attention spans.

Meanwhile, as Daphne stayed behind at the picnic station, she was left pondering about Florian's song that was solely dedicated to her. Was his performance this afternoon all for show, or did he really mean all of those heartfelt words that he sang?

After all, Florian, himself, previously admitted that songs reflected the hidden desires of one's heart. Words that could not be freely spoke out in public; unless, otherwise used within the contexts to the lyrics of a poem or a song. Therefore, did Florian truly care for her? More than just as a friend?

With much admiration, Daphne silently watched on as her husband played with her beloved nephews. And in that happy moment, she realized that he'd make an excellent father.

Because the truth was that not only was he a wonderful spouse to her, but he was also a kind, thoughtful and generous person to all those around him, as well. And after spending all of this time within his company, Daphne soon recognized that she wanted more out of life, other than simply being limited to the status of a royal princess.

Now, instead, she also wanted a loving family of her own. A family, just like her sister had. A life with Florian by her side, along with children of their own to cherish and love.

*If only it could be…*

# Chapter 11

## *If Only it Could Be...*

Seven years ago, Florian sat at the back row of an overcrowded cathedral to witness the royal wedding held between his best friend, Maximus, and his new bride, Lady Violet. It was proclaimed to be the wedding of the century, which united a foreign savior with the newly crowned western king.

As such, everyone throughout the Great Kingdom traveled far and wide to attend this momentous occasion. From the neighboring royals to ordinary everyday citizens; young or old; rich or poor; female or male; locals or foreigners, practically everyone who resided within their realm attended this historical wedding. Most notably, the bride's own family, a foreign clan who traveled great distances from a land called Earth.

Meanwhile, as Florian silently sat there in his seat, his eyes wandered across the busy crowd occupying the room. As predictable, the royals stemming from the northern and southern kingdoms all came, as well as a few other notable dukes and earls from his own eastern kingdom, as well. Faces, that Florian had seen a hundred times over and none of whom, he was at the very least, interested in conversing with.

Unfortunately, for the emerald prince, apart from Maximus and Violet, there wasn't anyone else in his vicinity, whom he was inclined to mingle with. Naturally, out of duty, he *should* have sat with his parents and twin sister, of course; however, Florian wanted to use this wedding as an opportunity to mingle with different people. A chance to have an adventure. An excuse to meet someone *new*.

Luckily, for him, his fiancé, Esmeralda, and her parents, the Marquess and Marchioness of Clover, were nowhere in sight. Hopefully, they failed to attend this wedding. For God only knows just how much he desperately needed some distance away from his unrequited love.

Sadly, as a result of their mothers' mutual wishes, starting from an early age, the emerald prince was betrothed to the Marquess of Clover's daughter. Although he considered Esmeralda to be nothing more than a friend; she, on the other hand, *did* harbor romantic feelings for him. Much to his own dismay.

And now, sitting near a crowd of strangers, Florian couldn't help but notice and admire the blissful smile currently bursting across his best friend's face. For all his worth, Maximus genuinely appeared to be besotted with his new bride, the queen.

The King of the West might have long held the reputation of a brutish prince and a notorious heartbreaker; but now, after meeting Lady Violet, everything had drastically transformed for his lifelong friend.

Indeed, overnight, this reformed rebel blossomed into a devoted husband. Just one glimpse at the newlywed pair and instantly, it was beyond obvious to all who witnessed that Maximus was madly in love with his new wife and she, equally in love with him, in return.

If only, he too, could experience much of the same, Florian thought to himself. Unfortunately, as it currently stood, he could never love his fiancé in that same way. He could never bring himself to love her, as much as she loved him.

Any future union shared between them would only serve as a marriage of convenience and nothing more. If forced to, then he could easily give her his name, but never his heart. That alone, belonged to him. And as far as Florian was concerned, he wasn't someone who could willingly give his heart away so easily.

Meanwhile, as he scanned across the room, his eyes suddenly landed upon the bride's family. Together, the Galloway clan peacefully sat at the front, several rows away from him.

According to the groom, Violet's parents, siblings and great-grandmothers were all in attendance. For the past week or so, the close-knit family resided at the imperial royal palace as esteemed guests of honor.

At first glance, Florian noted that Violet's father presented himself as the ideal and proper gentleman, finely dressed in a sleek black suit, accompanied by an oversized dark tanned petticoat— elegant clothes which showcased his tall and strong built physique. Apart from his attire, his daughter, the bride, also seemed to closely resemble her father's facial features a great deal, too. Especially, with regards to their shared emerald green eyes.

Meanwhile, her mother appeared to be a refined and sophisticated aristocratic lady. Dressed in a cornflower blue silk gown, which highlighted her petite waistline, along with a string of shiny pearls adorned around her neck, the Countess of Galloway was as flawless as ever. Like her daughter, the countess also shared the same wild and fiery red hair as the new queen.

Then, there was the queen's young brother, who sat close by to his two aging great-grandmothers. Already, the young teenager looked dreadfully bored by the ongoing ceremony. As a result, Florian, himself, couldn't help but laugh at the mere sight of it. After all, weddings weren't exactly the ideal place for active teenage boys to attend— regardless, if the new royal was his own sister.

And then, suddenly, a second later, he saw *her*. Violet's sister. Similar to a cupid's shooting arrow, at that fateful moment, Florian heart felt like a spear had pierced straight through his beating heart. For right before his eyes, it was as if an angel had been sent down to earth, traveling straight from heaven above.

At first sight, she had already managed to light up the entire cathedral by her ethereal beauty. With her fiery red hair, pale skin and sparkling emerald green eyes, Florian was instantly smitten. She might have shared a similar face to her elder sister, but there was also something refreshingly unique and precious in appearance with regards to the younger Galloway daughter.

His dream girl was dressed in an emerald green silk empire style gown with traces of gold sparkles, which shined against the rose hued light, as reflected through the cathedral's mosaic glass windows. Wearing a pair of translucent pearl earrings and a pair of white satin gloves, she resembled a lovely, prim and proper young debutante.

Meanwhile, her Rapunzel-like long red hair was left undone and elegantly floated across her back, well beyond her behind. Just one glimpse at this fair maiden and already, Florian wanted nothing more than to run his hands through her wild and flaming red locks of loose hair.

Instantly, the emerald prince was bewitched. It was almost as if a spell had been cast upon him. Because at that precise moment, Prince Florian Apollo of the East, fell madly and hopelessly in love with his best friend's sister-in-law.

However, it took him some time to find her. Unfortunately, for the young prince, fate had other plans in store for him.

Determined to introduce himself to the Galloways' youngest daughter, Florian abruptly stood up from his seat. Hoping to place a proper name to this nameless beauty, the crown prince eagerly pushed his way through the busy crowd to reach her family's side. However, by the time the prince finally arrived to the front row, the Galloways had already departed the cathedral.

Later on, that evening, Florian eventually tracked down her family at the banquet hall. By the time he finally introduced himself to her parents, brother and great-grandmothers, the young lady was no longer by their side.

With his mystery woman still missing, Florian kindly excused himself from her family's company, while he continued to search high and low for his fair maiden.

Impatiently, the prince wandered throughout the entire ballroom, desperately seeking to locate her. Meanwhile, as he declined all of the dance requests from the other available debutantes, he anxiously encircled the entire premise by foot and still, he could not find her.

Out of frustration, Florian was almost ready to give up on his search. And so, as he ventured off into the garden, he grabbed a pebble stone from off the ground and threw it directly into the pond. As his stone bounced past a floating waterlily, before eventually, landing into the water, Florian held his breath in and made a wish.

"If only I could meet her...," he wished aloud.

And as he released his breath out into the open air, Florian stared across at the lush garden and hoped for the best.

Suddenly, much to his sheer surprise, he saw a young lady seated right across from him. There, underneath a laurel tree, was his fair maiden. Quietly, she sat there, with her legs tucked underneath her dress, while she held a book within her hands.

Alas, she was reading. Apparently, she must have wandered away from the wedding ceremony to find a quiet place to read her book in solitude.

Silently, Florian watched her from afar. Even then, she was so incredibly beautiful. But apart from her outer physical beauty, Florian also admired her relentless spirit. Regardless of the venue, this maiden still found a way to read her book. To him, that took dedication. Clearly, this young lady was both determined and clever. Beauty and brains, equally woven together to form the ideal woman.

Judging by her attitude, Florian concluded that she was not a follower, but a leader. After all, this girl danced at her own rhythm, royal wedding or not. Plus, it was rather unusual for young and single maidens not to be dancing with a male partner at the ball. After all, that's what balls often served as: a means to meet and mingle with other young and available bachelors. Obviously, this girl didn't care for any of that. Instead, she was a true rebel.

For most of his life, Florian was always told on how to act by his courtiers or scolded on what to say by his parents. Not to mention, constantly advised on how to dress or what to eat. Which instruments to play or which sorts of books to read.

As the crown prince to the spring throne, his life had been meticulously planned to absolute perfection, with little to any say on the matter from his part. Even his own marriage was decided for him. The bride hand-selected by his mother. A marriage destined to a girl, whom he could never love. Never care for. Let alone, envision himself ruling his kingdom by her side.

Overall, it was extremely rare for Florian to form his own opinions about anything. But tonight, within the blink of an eye, everything changed. For the first time ever, Florian had formed an opinion, all on his own. For once, he selected on whom to bestow his heart to. At long last, *he decided* based upon his own free will, as to whom he wanted to love.

For years, Florian read countless heartfelt sonnets and romantic poems; particularly, in the subject concerning love at first sight. Before tonight, he used to laugh at them all. After all, what sane man could ever possibly fall in love with another person at first glance?

This fact alone, seemed entirely impossible. Especially, in the case of Esmeralda. Because for the past several years, Florian had stared at his fiancé a million times over and never, ever, did he experience anything remotely resembling a form of true love. Love at first sight simply didn't exist within the same vocabulary as Esmeralda.

But tonight, Florian realized that love at first sight was actually, *real.* For indeed, that's what he secretly felt for this maiden. Already, without knowing her name, he instantly knew that he loved her.

Even though he still hadn't yet gotten the proper chance to formally meet with her; but in his heart, he swiftly acknowledged the inevitable truth. The premonition was already there, lingering within his chest. One way or another, this young and fair maiden, hidden underneath the laurel tree, was his soul mate.

With much determination, Florian was convinced that he simply had to meet with her. The sooner, the better. One way or another, he needed to introduce himself to her. Otherwise, he'd simply die out of anticipation. And so, mustering up much courage, Florian made his way across the field, traveling in the direction of the laurel tree.

Unfortunately, for Florian, by the time he reached the laurel tree, she was long gone. And instead of finding his maiden, he found a single laurel leaf that was left behind. It was the same leaf that the young maiden had previously used as a bookmark. Somehow, this cherished leaf must have fallen out of her book, when she abruptly departed the scene.

In memory of her, Florian kept that laurel leaf inside of his pocket. Guarding it safe and near to his heart; treating it as if it was the most precious gift in the entire world.

Days later, after much persistent inquires, the prince eventually came to discover the identity of his fair maiden: Lady Daphne Galloway. Indeed, as he suspected, she was the sister to Queen Violet of the West. And like the rest of her family, Daphne resided in the land called Earth.

By then, Florian had practically begged on his hands and knees for Maximus and Violet to introduce him to her. And as much as the queen was thrilled to play the role of a matchmaker, the timing of their planned meetings never went according to plan.

For every time that Daphne came over to visit the western palace, Florian was often preoccupied with other courtly affairs and diplomatic tours that prevented him from traveling abroad. And in return, each time that Florian visited Maximus and Violet at their imperial western palace, Daphne always managed to return back home to Earth, right before his arrival. Needless to say, fate played a rather cruel trick on the young and love-stricken prince.

And so, as result of these misfortunes, Florian had no other choice, but to patiently wait for the opportune time to finally cross paths with his true love. Plus, there was still the matter concerning his estranged fiancé, Esmeralda, too.

Two years after that fateful day when he first saw Daphne, his mother, Queen Ophelia, had tragically passed on. As much as Florian was saddened by the loss of his late mother; but at the same time, he also secretly hoped that her death would inadvertently signal the end of his engagement.

However, much to his disappointment, Esmeralda refused to budge. Even though Florian knew that she cared from him; however, a part of him also believed that she only *loved him* as so far enough to become the emerald princess. To her, love had its limitations. *The crown.*

And by then, Esmeralda was growing more powerful with each passing day, by the use of her forbidden black magic. If the prince ever dared to challenge her, then he knew that he'd find himself in hot water. Therefore, Florian kept up with the public charade; however, he also secretly plotted his escape to pursue his beloved, Daphne.

Miraculously, after spending countless hours in the royal library, he eventually discovered a loop hole in the law, concerning the dissolution of an engagement of marriage resulting from a clause concerning black magic. With a copy to this legal clause safely secured within his hand, Florian eagerly informed his father about his intention to seek an annulment from his unwanted engagement.

In the end, Florian always loved Daphne. He loved her at first sight. Furthermore, after waiting seven long years for her, he was finally determined to meet with her. A miracle made straight from heaven. The ultimate wish come true. But finding Daphne took a great effort on his part.

Soon afterwards, Florian snuck into Esmeralda's home at Castle Clover, using the excuse of visiting his so-called fiancé. Thrilled by his unexpected visit, Esmeralda welcomed him into her home, without a second thought.

Meanwhile, as the young witch was busy playing hostess, Florian wandered off into her laboratory, stole her grimoire and turned himself into a frog. Afterwards, he hopped through her magic mirror and traveled across the realms to arrive to Earth, with the sole mission of finding his beloved, Daphne.

For several days, Florian waited for the young maiden at the pond, which was located inside of her family's private estate. All the while, secretly hoping to catch a glimpse of her. And after years of waiting, he finally did.

Much to his heartfelt joy, Daphne was just as beautiful as he last remembered. In fact, she was even far lovelier than ever before, having blossomed just like a flower in spring. With her flaming red hair shining against the bright sunlight, and her emerald green eyes sparkling just like a precious set of gems, the emerald prince was absolutely enchanted by the sight of her.

In the years that passed by, Florian befriended her elder sister. Through Violet, he learned almost everything there was to know about Daphne. From her likes to dislikes, to her dreams and ambitions, and everything else in between.

And so, while in disguise in his greenly form, Florian patiently waited for her at the pond. Quietly, he sat above the floating pink lily pad, hoping to catch another glimpse of her. A chance to finally properly introduce himself.

And then, one day, she finally came. Once again, she quietly sat underneath a laurel tree. However, much to his disappointment, she failed to notice him. Instead, Daphne was too deep in concentration and was actively reading her book. Ever-so gracefully, too.

But either way, Florian watched and admired her from afar, nonetheless. Some days, Daphne read, while on other days, she sat in silence and daydreamed. But each time, she was ever-so quiet and graceful. With the look of constant longing. She wanted a life outside of here, he realized. And then, after much inner reflection, he came up with a brilliant proposition.

At first, Florian traveled all the way to England to serve as an excuse to finally meet with his dream girl. In truth, he knew that if he bribed Daphne, then she'd be kind enough to kiss him. After all, he knew the true history about her family's curses; therefore, naturally, she'd be inclined to help rescue him from his own curse.

However, what Florian failed to realize at the time, was that he'd come to fall even more madly in love with her, with each passing day. That not only was he willing to trade rubies and pearls for her kiss; but that he truly wanted to marry her, too. That he'd make her his bride at all costs.

And then, suddenly, out of the blue, he heard her wish... spoken out loud.

As Daphne threw that pebble into the pond, he noticed her say the word *princess*. That was her wish. Daphne Galloway wanted to be a princess. And he was a prince. He could make her one, if she'd agree to marry him.

Like lightning, the wheels were in motion. The plan was as clear as day. Without a further delay, Florian decided to make his formal move.

And so, on that fateful day, he chased her down in that garden and cornered her underneath that laurel tree. Being the clever prince that he was, Florian knew that Daphne would never agree to marry him as he was. Therefore, he decided to make her a bold proposition. An enchanting offer that she couldn't refuse.

To her, it might have appeared as a marriage of convenience; but to him, it was so much more. Regardless of his prior claims pertaining to his royal duty to marry a foreign bride; the real truth was, that he simply *wanted her*. To him, their marriage was *real*. It was real, because by now, he had already loved her so dearly, even if she remained ignorant about the truth.

No, a marriage to Esmeralda would have been a marriage of convenience; but a marriage to Daphne would be nothing else short but a marriage based on true love.

Alas, now, Florian was indeed, married to his beloved, Daphne. His wife and crown princess. The honorable emerald princess.

However, as he sat across from her in the forest, with their young nephews by his side, Florian realized that he wanted more out of their marriage. Instead of being a husband by name, he also desired to be with her physically too, as a real husband. To ultimately, become the father of her unborn children.

*If only it could be…*

Hoping to clear his mind, Florian decided to take the boys over to the lake. Meanwhile, as three of them threw pebbles into the water, once again, the emerald prince held his breath in and made another wish.

Afterwards, he smiled over at Daphne and gave her a playful wink, leaving her standing with a raised brow and a confused look upon her sweet and lovely face.

# Chapter 12

## *Emerald with Envy*

Aweek into their stay, Violet and Maximus threw a ball at the western palace in honor of their esteemed guests. Better known as the Autumn Ball, the party hosted about a thousand or so attendees. Folks who traveled far and wide to attend tonight's festivities, along with other locals who resided within the western kingdom.

All throughout the grand imperial estate, the palace was decorated with rustic autumn décor. From tangerine orange hued silk ribbons that wrapped around all of the shiny white columns to golden marigold garlands that encircled each ceiling of every room, to bright pumpkin and red juicy apples that were graciously placed out on display and found on all of the guests' tables, and dark evergreen carpets that were placed above the sparkling marbled floors. Overall, the entire scenery displayed at the castle represented the various harvest season's colors that were naturally reflected within this enchanting autumn land.

In honor of her kingdom, Daphne arrived to the ball wearing a velvet emerald green traditional princess style ballroom gown, which was embroidered with golden lace stitches found along its ruffled edges. Meanwhile, her red hair was swept away, with half of her hair clipped up using a crystal encrusted lotus flower hair ornament, while the rest of her hair was left down and arranged in fine curls that flowed across her back.

Although Daphne did not bring a purse with her to the ball; she instead, wore a pair of white satin gloves and carried a forest evergreen feathered fan to serve as her primary accessory, which she held tightly within the grasp of her hands.

Upon their arrival to the ball, Florian quickly joined Maximus' side, while Daphne was met by her sister, the queen. Like she, Violet was also dressed in a similar traditional princess style ballroom gown, except her attire was in the shade of lilac and included golden stitches of marigold flowers that were embroidered onto the edges of her dress.

Additionally, she carried an amethyst feathered fan alongside with her, as well. It seemed that the ladies of the western court frequently attended these balls, with their respective fans and white satin gloves as their primary accessories.

"Come now, sister," Violet began, "It's time to acquaint you with the other royal houses residing within these lands."

Observing Violet's lead, Daphne watched on as her sister began to use her amethyst fan to causally point at their invited guests. To their immediate right, stood Lord and Lady Pumpkinbeater, an elderly couple, who owned a large pumpkin patch located within the heart of the western kingdom.

According to Violet, their pumpkins were notorious for winning the annual pumpkin patch competitions. Furthermore, some of their kingdom's best pumpkin pies came straight out of the ovens from their prestigious bakeries.

Continuing on, to their far left was the Duke and Duchess of Appleby. They were a middle-aged couple, who managed and cultivated several acres of apple orchards. Their estate hosted the annual apple fairs, in which caramel green apples were served as a staple western treat, accompanied by their famous cinnamon spiced apple cyder. According to the queen, their fairs were so popular amongst the locals that most townsfolks often participated in their infamous apple bopping contests.

Furthermore, across on the opposite side of the room, was the Earl and Countess of Sunflower. Standing in the far corner, the royals were currently conversing and mingling with the Baron and Baroness of Chrysanthemum.

Representing the northern kingdom, there was the Grand Duke and Grand Duchess of Svane. And besides them, was Lord and Lady Bleeding Heart, as well as Lord and Lady Cherry Blossom. The Grand Duke and the two lords were currently smoking a round of cigars, while their wives were busy chatting and drinking a serving of cherry infused wine.

"Don't look now, but approaching us is Lady Aster," Violet gently whispered, while using her amethyst feathered fan to hide the lower half of her face.

"Who is Lady Aster?" Daphne curiously asked, as she too used her own green fan to conceal her lips.

"Lady Aster is from my kingdom," Violet replied, while continuously waving her fan against the bottom half of her face. "She's a very sweet girl. In fact, I think that the two of you will get along rather well. Lady Aster, formerly known as Petunia Blackberry, recently married Lord Ivan Aster, the heir to the Aster fortune."

"What's their fortune related to?" the crown princess inquired.

"Her husband deals with matters concerning steel," replied the queen. "In my opinion, you should consider inviting her over to your palace for tea, sometime soon. Perhaps, you can convince her to persuade her husband to invest on a project to build a future bridge to link our two kingdoms together. It would certainly benefit us by cutting the traveling time in half."

"That does sound agreeable," Daphne concurred.

A moment later, Lady Petunia Aster was standing before them. Without any hesitation, she swiftly hugged the queen. Afterwards, she turned her attention over to the crown princess.

"And you must be Princess Daphne of the East," Petunia happily beamed.

"Your wedding was absolutely magical! Furthermore, I must commend you for doing such a fabulous job on throwing this year's Emerald Ball, too. But of course, I shouldn't be so incredibly surprised. After all, you are Violet's younger sister."

"Petunia, you are too kind!" Violet gushed, as both she and her sister snapped their fans closed shut in unison.

At first impression, Daphne liked Petunia. Overall, she had a sweet and wholesome face, with her long honey blonde hair brushed aside and secured into a neat ponytail.

Wearing a chiffon and tangerine hued mermaid gown, along with a matching satin orange ribbon, which was used to tie her thick hair that dangled across her slender back, Petunia was a cheerful breath of fresh air. Possessing both a lovely and positive demeanor.

"Now, as you know, my sister is new to the Great Kingdom," Violet carried on. "She's still acquainting herself with our high society."

"Indeed," Petunia agreed with the queen. "And might I add, you're doing a fine job on settling in. As for myself, I can only imagine the sorts of challenging adjustments that you must be currently undergoing as the new crown princess, let alone as the new wife of the crown prince. In fact, when I first married my husband, I thought that I'd never settle in."

"Really?" asked Daphne in surprise. "And why was that?"

"Because marriage, as you'll soon come to learn, is full of many surprises," Petunia laughed on.

"I couldn't agree anymore," Violet chimed in. "The things one learns about their husband post-marriage is truly a wonder. In fact, it wasn't until after we got married, that I discovered that Maximus suffers from insomnia. An ongoing and lasting side effect, caused by his past sleeping curse."

"Same here," Petunia concurred. "It wasn't until after my marriage to Lord Aster, that I eventually came to learn about my husband's peculiar hunting habits. In truth, Ivan loves to depart in the early mornings to hunt. However, the problem is that he never has the heart to shoot anything.

Therefore, whenever he returns home in the evenings, he always comes back empty-handed. So really, it's not a hunting expedition for say; but instead, it's more like a general walk through the woods."

"It's true. Especially, when it comes to my boys, too," Violet also added. "Maximus, Leopold and Tristan are always searching for the next grand and wild adventure. But the problem is that the three of them can never agree on just *one single* activity to engage in. So, in the end, they either resort to wrestling or aimlessly wandering off through the woods. Sadly, they can never seem to finish anything."

And then, both women released a deep sigh.

Meanwhile, Daphne admired on how affectionately Violet and Petunia spoke about their respective husbands and families. In truth, she was still learning about hers. By now, she knew little about her prince. However, from what she had recently gathered thus far from passing conversations, she was aware that he was a poet and a musician.

In fact, he loved all of the great arts. Plus, the crown prince had a warm and charming personality. Additionally, he was also very kind and thoughtful, too. Come to think of it, perhaps, Daphne *really* did come to learn more about her husband, after all. Heck, she certainly knew him better *now*, than when she first met him back at the pond.

"Lady Aster, you must visit me for an afternoon session of high tea," Daphne eagerly announced. "I'd simply love to have you and Lord Aster over as esteemed guests at my castle. Please tell me, that you'll come."

"Oh, but of course I shall, my princess," Petunia beamed with pride over the royal invitation. "It will be my sincerest honor. Besides, I'm certain that Lord Aster and Prince Florian will have much business to discuss, as well."

Afterwards, Lady Aster insisted that the crown princess address her by her given name, Petunia; to which Daphne graciously accepted. Thereupon, the emerald princess promised to send Petunia a formal letter addressed to her by the imperial palace via mail in the days to come. Happily, Lady Aster told her that she was anxiously looking forward on receiving the upcoming invitation.

Once Lady Aster left the royals to join her husband's side, Violet and Daphne decided to take a turn around the room. After walking about ten steps, the sisters managed to encounter another member of their extended family.

Standing by the table of refreshments, was their very own great-grandmother, Ruby, the Elder. Dressed in a long and overflowing scarlet red column style gown, which was made from thick velvet and adorned with black lace found alongside its edges, their granny's bold attire graciously glided across the marbled floor, with each step taken by her red satin heels.

Meanwhile, her grey hair was swept aside into a tight bun and the only piece of jewelry that she wore was her signature ruby heart-shaped necklace, which hung around her neck.

Covered in deep wrinkles, their great-grandmother was as old as time; although no one really knew her true age. Ruby was the mother to their paternal late grandmother, Lady Sarah Galloway. Sarah, the youngest of their granny's two daughters, was also the wife of their late grandfather, Lord Henrick Galloway, and the mother of their father, Lord Henry Galloway. Tragically, Lady Galloway had died several years prior, during childbirth.

"I'm glad that you've finally decided to take some time off to visit us, Daphne," her great-grandmother confessed, as she joined her great-granddaughters' sides.

"Granny," Violet spoke up first, "Can Daphne and Florian stay at your cottage? I was thinking that a secluded trip to the outdoors might be beneficial for my sister and brother-in-law. After all, it will finally give them an excuse to spend some quality time alone together."

"Alone? Do they not already have enough alone time spent at the palace?" their granny asked, with a raised brow.

"They do," replied Violet. "But, as you know, there's always courtiers hovering around them. Perhaps, a chance to enjoy the fresh air in the outdoors, shall do them some good."

"And what do you think about this prospect, Daphne? Do you really want to stay at our family's cottage?"

In truth, Daphne was not entirely sure as to how she felt about partaking on this unexpected trip. Unlike Violet, the crown princess had never previously stayed at granny's cottage before.

After all, it was rumored that Violet and Maximus first became lovers, while staying at this very exclusive cottage. Furthermore, it was also the former site where her late Aunt Vera came to fall for the late monarch and Maximus' father, King Elryk, as well. Thus far, the cottage was notorious for bringing couples together, *romantically.*

"If it's available, then I have no objections," Daphne replied, at long last.

"Very well, then I shall leave the key with your courtiers," their granny replied. "I'll be traveling soon on business anyways, so come whenever you'd like. Preferably, within the next week or so. Otherwise, I would hate to catch the two of you in the *act.*"

Instantly, Daphne almost choked at the very thought of such an unghastly scene. *Never, ever* would she allow for herself to be caught in a sexual act and witnessed by any passing bystanders. Especially, in front of her own granny!

"Oh, come now, Daphne, don't be such a prude," Ruby scolded her. "I'm not so ancient that I can't remember young love. After all, I was married to your great-grandfather from long ago."

"You know," Violet reflected aloud, "You've never actually spoken about our great-grandfather to us before. Who was he exactly?"

Instantly, Ruby broke into hysterical laughter.

"You'd never believe me, even if I told you," she sneered.

"Oh, come on. Granny, do humor us," Violet pressed on.

"Yes, Granny, do go on," Daphne joined in.

"What can I say, back then, I was known as Ruby, the Fair and he was another sorcerer, like me," Ruby revealed. "But more than anything, he was a real wolf in the bedroom. And by day, he also worked as a huntsman, too. In fact, that's why we lived out in the remote parts of this kingdom, hidden away in that small cottage. One day, he cornered me in the woods and tricked me into marriage. By the time I bore my second child, he died shortly, thereafter."

"Granny, what was his name?" Daphne inquired, most curiously.

"Alfred, the Wolf," Ruby answered. "He was my late husband and your great-grandfather."

"Actually," their great-grandmother continued on, with a deep smile lingering on her face in remembrance of her late husband, "Your grandmother's and aunt's maiden names were Fille de Loop, also known as the daughters of the wolf. However, neither Sarah nor Vera decided to use it. They both disliked the surname greatly."

A moment later, Daphne proceeded to scan the room, all the while looking for Florian. A few minutes ago, he was standing by Maximus' side. But now, that no longer seemed to be the case.

"Do either of you know, where Florian might be?" she asked her sister and great-grandmother.

"Wasn't he with Maximus?" Violet inquired, in return.

"No, it appears that he's left the king's side some time ago."

Suddenly, the lights dimmed low and the orchestra began to play a tune. As the guests quickly flocked over to the dancefloor, Daphne glanced across the room once more. To her surprise, at long last, she finally spotted her husband.

Alas, Florian arrived onto the dancefloor with a female partner in hand. A woman with long raven black hair, who was dressed in an extra revealing black mermaid sequin gown, with a plunging neckline and a high slit, which showcased her plump breasts, tiny waistline and slender long legs. Ultimately, leaving very little to a man's imagination. *A seductress.* A woman who was none other than her rival: Esmeralda of Clover.

"What is *she* doing *here*?" Violet hissed, as she frantically began fanning herself. Already, her pregnant sister was vividly angry.

"Was she invited?" Daphne asked her elder sister.

"Certainly, not," the queen furiously replied, instantly offended by her sister's question.

"I would *never* invite *her* to any of my balls. I'd never have the audacity to go against your honor," the queen insisted. "No, it appears that Esmeralda of Clover has invited *herself* to my Autumn Ball. Imagine, the nerve of that girl! Apparently, my guards failed us here tonight, too."

But as Daphne quietly stared away and observed her husband dancing within the arms of his former fiancé, she suddenly began to feel the first pangs of jealousy. So, *this* is how it felt like to experience the pains of one's heart.

Perhaps, their so-called union really wasn't such a marriage of convenience anymore, after all. One way or another, Daphne had developed strong feelings of attachment to her prince. Indeed, she secretly adored him. Cared for him. *Loved him.*

Furthermore, although he had been nothing shy of presenting himself as a true gentleman to her, Daphne was also fully aware that he, too, was a man. And men, no matter how honorable they were, also had their own biological and physical desires.

In the end, she was no fool. The truth was simply staring at her, right in her face. Sooner or later, if she failed to freely give herself to her husband, then eventually, he'd find another mate. Esmeralda or not.

Sensing her great-granddaughter's frustration, Ruby rested her right-hand above Daphne's shoulder and said, "Don't fret, my dear. Remember, *you are his wife*, not her. As a word of advice, don't let him forget about this important fact, either."

Afterwards, her sister added, "Perhaps, a weekend away at the cottage won't be such a bad idea, after all?"

"Indeed," Daphne answered, with much determination. "It's time for this marriage to graduate onto the next level."

# Chapter 13

## *Convenience No More*

Later on that evening, Daphne and Florian quietly exited the ball and returned to their bedchamber. After a long night of celebration, rather than immediately retiring off to bed, Daphne was instead, consumed by the awful memories of her husband dancing with her nemesis at the ball. Every time that she closed her eyes shut, she envisioned him holding his former fiancé, gliding with her across the dancefloor and touching her hips…

This vision was simply too much to bear! To be fair, Florian wasn't at fault. To deny Esmeralda a single dance at the ball, it would simply have been plain rude. After all, he was the crown prince. The emerald prince of spring. Naturally, he was expected to dance with all of his many subjects… including, his former fiancé.

Although Florian appeared unmoved by that past dance; Daphne, on the other hand, predicted that this particular encounter was only just the beginning. One way or another, Esmeralda had made it publicly known to all in their land that she was determined to win over Florian's affection—regardless, if he already had a wife.

Sooner or later, she'd corner him again. Perhaps, by then, his past feelings concerning the unrequited love aimed at his lost fiancé would eventually change for Esmeralda's benefit. After all, Daphne wasn't really a *true wife* to him. Their marriage was based more on friendship than anything else. And maybe this fact alone, was the *true dilemma* to her inner woes.

However, being jealous of Esmeralda wasn't the entire root of the problem. Rather, Daphne genuinely cared for her husband. Through his consistent acts of kindness, generosity for her overall welfare and placing her needs above his own, his good will and selfless deeds ultimately, won her heart over.

Apart from his dashing good looks, charming personality and generous heart, Daphne adored Florian for the man that he was. Furthermore, even if Esmeralda wasn't a part of the equation, then she'd still long for a lasting romantic relationship with him.

In the end, it wasn't enough to live each night posing as brother and sister. Therefore, Daphne decided that if she intended to keep Florian as her mate for the long-term, then she was finally ready to give all parts of herself to him, both body and soul. Plus, she secretly desired to do so, too. *Oh, so desperately!*

After living with Florian these past few months, the princess regarded him to be her own dearest and sweetest friend and husband. But apart from their genuine friendship, Daphne was also curious about the other side to marital relations. By now, she was overwhelmed with this new yearning desire to experience the physical aspect of love for herself, too.

At long last, tonight, she was finally ready to explore this growing curiosity of hers. After all this time shared together, it was now or never to push forward.

"Ah, Florian," Daphne broke her prolonged silence as she stood in front of a tall mirror, which hung above the wall located within their bedchamber. "Do you mind helping me out of my gown?"

Upon her request, Florian instantly appeared by her side. Standing behind her, he gently placed his large hands above the back of her gown. Slowly, he began to caress behind her neck, making his way down to her golden beaded buttons, which were located near her midsection, resting right above her buttock.

"May I?" he asked, as he prepared to unhook the first button.

"Please," she sucked in the surrounding air, anticipating his touch.

One by one, Florian unbuttoned her gown, until her dress finally gave way and fell mid-length towards her hips. Afterwards, the prince was about ready to leave her side, when Daphne suddenly caught a hold of his arm, instead.

"Can you please help me to remove the rest?" she turned around to meet him, face-to-face.

Immediately, his eyes widened with excitement by her unexpected request.

"Really? Are you sure?" he gulped, as his Adam's apple bulged against his throat.

"I am," Daphne confirmed, with much confidence. "Florian, I want *you* to undress me. Fully. And *now*."

"As you wish, my princess," he immediately replied, with a graceful bow.

A moment later, Florian proceeded to remove the rest of her gown. Peeling layer after layer, until all of her clothes were left unattended on the floor. Thus, leaving nothing else remaining on her body, except for her lace corset and undergarments.

"Ah, aren't you forgetting something?" she asked him, with a raised brow.

"Forgetting…"

Without allowing him the opportunity to back away from her request, Daphne swiftly grabbed a hold of his hands and delicately placed them above her slender hips and told him, "These, too. I want you to remove *everything*."

"*Everything?*" he repeated nervously, with his heart pounding rapidly against his chest.

"Yes, *everything*," she happily confirmed.

"But that will leave you completely *naked*," he was quick to point out.

"I know," she clarified, with a proud smile. "That's why I want *you* to do the deed and no one else."

"Daphne," he sighed, as he shook his head. "If I do this, then I can't make any promises not to touch you. Even I'm *not* a saint. As a man, I do have my limits."

"Yes, I'm fully aware," she told him, as she gazed deep into his piercing lapis blue eyes, which were surrounded by a thick layer of blonde eyelashes that were also the exact color as a grain of wheat.

Eyes, that were currently, filled with excitement and splendor.

"Which is why afterwards," she continued on, "I want you to make love to me."

"Make love to you?"

By now, his heart had practically stopped beating, altogether.

"Yes, Florian," she confirmed. "After all this time that we've spent together, I must confess that I care deeply for you."

"And I, you," he told her.

"Which is why I think it's now the right time for us to do this," she explained. "Besides, I'm not afraid anymore. Plus, not to mention, I'm also curious, too."

"Curious?" he asked, now, highly intrigued by her admission.

"Yes, curious," Daphne answered, with much determination. "I know that you might want us to remain just as friends but—"

"No, Daphne," Florian interrupted her, as he softly placed his hand against her flushed cheek. "That's not entirely true."

"It isn't?" she asked in surprise.

"Being just your friend was a lie," he confessed, as he stared down at the floor in shame. "The truth is that *I always* wanted so much more from you."

"Always?" she repeated, in amazement. "If so, then why didn't you tell me about your true feelings, any sooner?"

"I… I… just didn't want to pressure you," he revealed, as he locked eyes with her. "You married me so quickly. I just… didn't want… to scare you away."

Eagerly, he tilted her head up and with her chin resting within the palms of his hands, he told her, "Daphne, I've *always wanted you*. From the first moment that I laid eyes upon you, seven years ago. It was always love at first sight. Then *and* now."

"Seven years ago? What do you mean Florian? We've only met just a few months ago," Daphne reminded him.

"A few months *formally*," he emphasized. "But in all honesty, I've loved you since the moment that I first saw you at your sister's wedding. Back then, you were silently sitting underneath a laurel tree and reading a book. That day, I tried to approach you, but you left so quickly. And ever since that fateful day, I've been chasing after you ever since."

"You have?" Daphne's emerald green eyes widened out of pure shock.

"Yes," he breathed in heavily. "And it's why I've kept this with me after all these years."

Reaching deep within his pocket, Florian proceeded to pull out a single dried laurel leaf. Gently, he placed the laurel leaf into Daphne's palm.

"What's this?" she asked him, as her green eyes took in a moment to observe this curious ornament.

"That's the leaf that you previously used as a bookmark on the day of your sister's wedding," he replied, recalling that memorable afternoon with a warm smile. "You left it behind in the garden, and I've kept with me ever since as a cherished keepsake. It was the only item of yours that I had to cling on to. At least, until now."

"My God, Florian, that's so incredibly sweet," Daphne acknowledged, with tears streaming down her cheeks.

"This is the real reason as to why I could *never* go through with my engagement to Esmeralda. Or anyone else, for that matter," he confessed, with teary eyes of his own. "Honestly, I can't ever imagine myself married to anyone else other than *you*."

"So… does this mean that Esmeralda was never your type?" Daphne hesitated to ask him, as she attempted to wipe her tears with her hands.

However, midway, Florian stopped her.

Instead, he slowly leaned in, until they came face-to-face. Once they locked eyes, the prince bent down and proceeded to lick away all of her tears. Leaving her eyes and cheeks completely dry.

"Of course not," Florian was quick to clarify, after cleaning her face. "I've only liked a certain redhead of mine."

"Oh, Florian!" she happily exclaimed, as another round of tears began to form within her sparkling emerald green eyes.

"In truth, I stole Esmeralda's grimoire and transformed myself into a frog, just to meet with you," he revealed with a heavy heart. "I traveled to your land in order to find *you*. As much as I tried for us to be formally introduced to each other in my land; somehow, our paths just never crossed. And so, in the end, I decided to take matters into my own hands."

"Wait," cried Daphne, "Do you mean to tell me that you turned yourself in a frog, just to meet with *me*?"

"Precisely," he admitted, with a sly grin.

And then, placing her hands within his, Florian told her, "I was willing to do anything to meet with you. To find you. To simply be with you."

"Florian, I don't know what to say," Daphne began to cry, once more.

"Why, didn't you tell me any sooner?"

"Well," he began, "Even though my heart was ready to embrace you whole; in return, I wasn't entirely sure as to how you felt about me. That's why I did what I did. Given your family's past history of curses, I knew that you'd kiss me to break my curse. Although, truth be told, promising marriage to you was a bit of a gamble. However, when it comes to you, my fairest Daphne, I'm willing to bet on the impossible."

"Florian, I love you," she finally confessed the hidden words that she had desperately longed to share.

"Daphne, I love you, too," he also acknowledged, as tears began to stream down from his own lapis blue eyes, as well.

"Then, let's consummate our marriage," Daphne proclaimed. "Let's rejoice in our union."

"Yes, we will," he told her. "But not tonight."

"Why not?" she asked in surprise.

After all, didn't Florian just confess that he loved her equally, too?

"Because when I finally claim your innocence," he slowly whispered into her ear using a deep and seductive voice that sent a chill down her back. "I want it to be somewhere special. Far away from any prying eyes. A place, where we can be alone together, as man and wife."

One way or another, Florian was a true gentleman at heart. Even now, he still wanted their first time spent together to take place at a special and memorable site. Luckily, for the them, Daphne had the perfect idea.

"If that's the case, then I know the ideal spot," she revealed to him. "My granny suggested that while we're visiting here, then we should spend some time alone at my family's cottage. It's quiet and secluded over there by the lake. No one will ever find us. Perhaps, we can spend our first time together at the cottage?"

"That sounds like heaven," Florian happily agreed to her suggestion, with an approving smile.

"But what about tonight?" Daphne asked him. "I wanted us to be together. Aren't you at least a bit disappointed by this outcome? After all, you did strip me down bare?"

"For now, an embrace will be enough," Florian answered, as he wrapped his arms around his wife.

And for the remainder of the night, the happy couple slept naked together in their bed, embraced in each other's loving arms.

# Chapter 14

## *Confessions of an Emerald Prince*

After confessing their love for one another, Florian felt like he was in heaven. Alas, after all these agonizing years spent yearning over Daphne, at long last, he finally conquered his beloved's heart. Not only did he wed her, but she also miraculously surrendered her heart over to him, too.

In the end, *she loved him*. And now, she was ready to become his true wife, not only in name but in action, as well. Ultimately, Daphne's declaration of love was a wonderous dream come true.

In truth, Florian, the infamous emerald prince, was about ready to jump into the air and shout for joy so that the entire world could hear his wonderous mirth. To openly acknowledge that his beloved emerald princess loved him in return. To publicly declare to all that their royal marriage was not a marriage of convenience nor a political union, but rather, a marriage based on real love.

Most importantly, in their world, a loving marriage was something that no spell in the entire universe could create. Instead, their love was free. It was effortless. It was special. It was true.

And so, the following day after the ball, the happy couple bid their family adieu. Afterwards, they traveled deep into the western woods to spend their weekend getaway tucked inside of Ruby's cozy and private property.

The cottage was a small hovel located in the far edges of the forest, situated close by to the saltwater lake that the crown prince and crown princess had previously visited with their nephews. Near the front entrance, was an abundantly sized herb garden, along with several tall oak trees that encircled the estate. And apart from a thatched roof, the rest of the structure was built out of sturdy grey stone blocks.

Upon entrance, the cottage appeared to be even smaller in-person from the inside. Consisting of a one level darkened flat, the property included two miniature sized windows, a main living quarters located within the center of the estate, which included a red brick fireplace and accompanied by a large black cauldron, along with a rectangular wooden table and a set of chairs. At the back of the home, there was a single bedroom that housed one large and spacious bed, along with two smaller beds that appeared to have been specifically crafted for children.

"It's not exactly as glamorous as the castle," Daphne admitted in guilt, feeling half embarrassed by the shabby décor's appearance, as well as her own original suggestion on having them stay at this dreary site for the duration of their weekend in the first place.

"Nonsense," Florian huffed, nonchalant. "It's a charming place. It will do."

Granted, the cottage was *less* than ideal for a permanent residence. However, traveling anywhere with Daphne was well worth the effort.

"Shall we give it a go?" she asked nervously.

Taking a step forward and moving towards her, Florian looked deep into her emerald green eyes and said, "Right now, we don't have to do anything. If you want, I can start a fire, and we can just peacefully sit and relax together in perfect silence. Simply being in your company is enough for me, no matter what we promised to do earlier. My fairest Daphne, I just want you to feel comfortable and happy. That's all."

"No, Florian," Daphne spoke up, with much determination. "I'm ready."

Before he knew it, she began to undress herself. Loosening up her buttons, within mere seconds, her dress slipped off her body and fell down onto the stone floor. Afterwards, she removed her lace corset and undergarments, until she was left standing stark naked in front of him with her long red hair covering her plump breasts.

"Florian, I want you," she demanded. "I want you to take me. Right here, right now."

"As you wish, my princess," he growled with hunger, as he swiftly scooped her up within his arms and pulled her body towards his chest.

Instantly, their lips locked in a passionate and heartfelt kiss. It was a kiss born out of extreme desperation and desire. Meanwhile, as their tongues glided against each other, Florian released his hold of Daphne, as he began to strip down.

Watching him remove his clothing, made her burn with excitement. Although she had seen him naked countless times before; however, this was the first time that she was going to be united with him, as man and wife. Therefore, upon seeing him remove his last article of clothing, *his breeches*, she suddenly gulped.

To her sinful pleasure, Florian's cock was *so* incredibly large and hard right now. Honestly, it was absolutely enormous. Just how was this union of theirs going to work, after all?

"Don't be shy," Florian grinned and winked at her. "I might be big, but you can take it, my love. It will fit perfectly inside that fine body of yours. You'll see."

Walking over to an empty chair, Florian sat himself down. Afterwards, he used his pointed index finger to help guide her towards him.

"Am I to sit on your lap?" she asked him in surprise.

"Yes," he answered with a devious smirk. "I call this act one. A prelude to what's to come, later on tonight."

Following her husband's instructions, Daphne walked over towards him and slowly, sat herself down above his lap. With their naked bodies stacked up against one another, she could already feel his bulging cock pressing against her wet behind. Surprisingly, it felt both comforting and stimulating.

"Relax," he whispered into her ear, as he gently bit down and nibbled on her flesh. "I need to warm you up, first."

"Alright," she hesitantly replied, not entirely sure as to where exactly this position was going to lead them.

Either way, Daphne trusted Florian with her whole heart. Plus, if this was something that he wanted them to do, then his eager student was up for the challenge.

"Now, start by sliding up and down my body. Rocking ever-so-gently," he instructed her.

Quietly, Daphne nodded. Following his words, she began to move, working her way up and down him. Meanwhile, as she slid downwards and upwards against his lap, she closed her eyes and allowed her naked flesh to grow accustomed to the warmth and feel of his muscular body that rested underneath hers.

To her surprise, Daphne was enjoying this new form of friction. Already, her body was awakening. Additionally, as she moved against him, her breasts began to swell, while her body grew moist.

"That's it," he encouraged her. "You're doing good, my love. Keep it up."

Suddenly, without any warning, Florian slid his fingers against her womb. Rubbing his hand against her folds, he felt her wetness seeping from out of there. By now, Daphne's womb was dripping fluid and was completely soaking wet. It was a glorious sight, similar to golden honey dripping from out of a honeycomb.

"Perfect," he proudly smiled to himself. Thrilled by the fact that *he*, and *he alone*, possessed the sole power to excite her.

A second later, Florian wrapped his arms around Daphne's waist and held her tightly in place.

"You're wet already, my love," he whispered into her ear.

"Is that a good thing?" she asked him, innocently.

"Yes, it is," he grinned.

"And now," he explained, "I'm going to slip my fingers inside of you. I need to stretch you up a bit, before we go any further. Will this be alright with you?"

"Yes," she released a deep breath, already anticipating his next move.

At this moment, she was both nervous and excited about having any part of him inside of her.

"Very well," he bit down against her earlobe. "Let's give it a go."

Just as he promised, Florian slipped two fingers inside of her drenched womb.

"And now, my fairest Daphne, *ride me*," he commanded.

Following her natural instincts, Daphne began to move against him. With his fingers thrusting deep within and stretching her womb from the inside, she rocked herself back and forth, rolling her hips alongside him, as she rode his fingers into oblivion.

Meanwhile, as she whimpered along the way, Florian moved his second hand away from her breasts and began to play with his enlarged and throbbing cock. And as he thrusted his fingers inside of her, he used his second hand to pump his erect cock, up and down in repetitive movements.

"Aaaahhhh…," Daphne moaned again, in heavenly bliss.

"That's right, keep going," he encouraged her. "That's a good girl. Don't be shy. It's just me. Ride it out."

Happily, she rode him, as he continued to pump his cock to the side, releasing his juice against the arm of the chair. However, by watching him pleasure himself from the corner of her eye, Daphne also felt obligated to assist him, too. And so, reaching over, she grabbed a hold of his hardened length within the tight grasp of her hand.

"Please allow me," she told him.

Instantly, Florian nodded and gave Daphne permission to stroke him. And as his fingers continued to thrust deeper into her body, she stroked his thick cock, from the tip and all the way down to its head.

Back and forth, she pumped his hardened cock, faster and faster, each time. Meanwhile, he continued to plunge his fingers into her womb, traveling deeper and hitting her harder with each consecutive thrust.

"God, *yes*, Daphne!" he exclaimed, as he closed his eyes with great pleasure.

"This feels amazing!" she moaned. "I love making love to you!"

A second later, Florian stopped himself and removed his fingers from out of her womb. Afterwards, he pulled her hands away from his cock.

"This act is just the appetizer," he told her. "Now, Daphne, my love, it's time to move on to the main course."

"The main course?" she turned around to face him from her behind. "What exactly do you mean? Is this not enough?"

"No," he laughed out loud, as his lapis blue eyes beamed with blissful joy.

"Until my cock is buried deep inside of your womb," he looked at her with a devious grin, "Then, this night won't end."

"Because, my fairest Daphne," he vowed, "I intend to *fuck you*, until you're left screaming nothing else but my damn name from that tongue of yours."

Instantly, Daphne shivered with excitement. Over the years, she had heard many wicked stories told by her elder sister and their female companions about the wildness of fucking a man. But, to finally experience it all for herself— that was truly a wonder. Needless to say, Daphne was eager to move forward with round two!

"Yes, please do," she smiled at him with approval.

"Do what exactly?" he teased her.

"*Fuck me*," she told him. "I want to feel your cock inside me. I want to know how it feels like for you to move within me. To actually scream your name against my lips."

"Then, you shall wait no longer. Not a second more," he promised her.

Much to her satisfaction, Florian arose from up their chair and eagerly carried her away with him and over to their bedroom. Once he crossed through the threshold, he gently placed his wife above the bedspread, as he crawled up beside her.

As soon as Daphne got comfortable lying down above the mattress, Florian slowly positioned his body above hers. With their bodies pressed down against one another, skin-to-skin, their combined scents of spring florals and warm cedar woods intermixed with one another, creating a wonderous smell consisting of lilies, honey and laurel leaves.

Finally, as their eyes locked in together, Florian bent down and kissed her tender lips. And this time around, their kiss was much more passionate and intense than ever before. Consumed with lustrous desire, their tongues ferociously danced and glided against one another, with their shared saliva dripping down their chins. By now, their lips were swollen and bright red.

Meanwhile, Florian's curious hands began to wander across Daphne's body. Eventually, he reached her glorious breasts and decided to give it a full pinch. Pulling his mouth away from hers, he proceeded to slowly lick her hardened and pink nipple. Afterwards, he began to suck it, while he squeezed her other breast. Instantly, Daphne moaned from pure pleasure.

"Aaaahhhhh…," she roared, as her hands tugged against his golden locks of hair.

Witnessing her excitement, Florian confidently continued to lick and suck on her nipple some more, before moving on to her other breast.

Meanwhile, he nudged himself in between her legs. Using his knees, he gently spread her thighs wide open, leaving an invitation for himself.

By the time he finally got Daphne into his desired position, he reached down and touched her private parts. And to his great delight, she was absolutely drenched.

"Splendid," he grinned with a satisfied expression, as he pulled himself away from her breasts. "You're ready for me, after all."

"Do as you will, Florian," she surrendered. "I'm ready."

"As you wish, my princess," he proudly smiled.

At long last, she was finally *his*.

Slowly, Florian brought his cock up towards her entrance. Gradually, he worked his way to nudge himself right in, breaking through her inner walls. Instantly, Daphne took in a deep breath, as she felt him enter inside of her.

"I'm going to go in slowly," he gently brushed her red hair aside and whispered into her ear. "It might hurt at first, but you will get used to it. But most importantly, *you will enjoy it*, too. That much I can guarantee, my love."

Following his lead, Daphne nodded and welcomed Florian inside her, as he strove to bury his cock, deep within her womb. Inch by inch, he pushed inside of her, slowing working his way into filling her up whole. Eventually, by the time he consumed her up entirely, Daphne had all but lost herself in the making.

Feeling his hardened length resting inside of her, she released another moan, reflecting her blissful pleasure. Overall, this was a milestone experience for her. There was nothing to compare the joining of their bodies to anything else.

The warm feel of his body pressed against hers was so intense. It was thrilling. It was exciting. It was pleasurable. It was heavenly. But above all else, his cock was rudely awakening all of her previously sleeping nerves and setting them on fire!

"Look at you, my love. I'm rather impressed," he complemented her with much pride. "You took me in without a fuss, just like a good girl."

"Is this it?" she asked him, innocently.

"Not quite," he chuckled.

"No, my fairest Daphne," he continued on, "In a second, I'm about to move within you. And as I move, you must move with me, too. Just slide up and down, as we work to achieve a rhythm. Do you think that you can do that?"

"Yes, I think I can."

"Good. Now, move with me, *now*."

And just like that, Florian proceeded to withdrawal and then, swaying his hips forward, he plunged himself back into her womb. Simultaneously, Daphne followed his lead and moved alongside with him. Thrust after thrust, Florian buried his hot cock inside of her, branding his name all over her body, claiming her as his very own.

Meanwhile, Daphne held tightly against his shoulders, as she clawed against his skin with her sharpened nails. And as he plunged his dick inside of her, she rolled her head back and closed her eyes shut, rigorously moving her hips as she embraced the feel of her husband-now-turned-lover within her hot body, losing her sweet innocence in the making. After tonight, she was no longer a maiden, but a true wife.

"God, this feels so good!" she moaned.

"That's right Daphne," Florian whispered. "Keep taking in my cock, like a good little princess. And I won't stop. At least, not until you cry my name aloud."

"Aaahhhh…," she cried.

"Daphne, that's not my name," he reminded her.

By now, Florian was slamming hard against her at full speed. With each new thrust, the prince was practically pounding against the soft flesh of his princess, with his balls slapping against her, while his hands squeezed against her ass. And with each new thrust, Daphne welcomed her husband's cock deeper inside of her.

"Harder," she pleaded. "Please, Florian. I want to feel you, *even deeper.*"

"As you wish," he wickedly grinned from ear-to-ear.

Following her command, Florian worked up his speed and pounded into her body even *faster*, *harder* and *deeper* than ever before. By the time they both reached their climaxes, Daphne screamed his name aloud from kingdom come.

"FLORIAN!!!" Daphne yelled with all her might.

A few minutes later, the young couple found themselves both breathless and exhausted from their union.

"That was amazing!" Daphne happily acknowledged, as she rested naked beside her husband in bed.

"This is only but our first night together," he reminded her. "We'll have plenty more opportunities to experience, once we return back home."

"Promise?" she stared into his lapis blue eyes.

"I promise," he answered her, with a bright smile. "But while we're here, let's enjoy another picnic by the lake tomorrow. Just you and me."

"A romantic date by the lake?" Daphne asked.

"Yes, a romantic date with just me and my bride," Florian promised, as he reached over and pulled his princess over to his chest.

And for the remainder of their stay, Florian and Daphne enjoyed their well over-due honeymoon together, nestled away in a small cottage that was located deep within the western woods.

# Chapter 15

## *Confessions of an Emerald Princess*

After spending the remainder of their weekend together in the woods, come Monday morning at the break of dawn, Florian and Daphne traveled home by carriage to the eastern kingdom.

Upon their arrival, their honeymoon stage was far from over. Instead, after graduating from their once marriage of convenience to a genuine union, the emerald prince and emerald princess spent their spare times making passionate love with one another, curiously exploring their hidden desires brought straight to life.

By day, Florian attended his daily meetings with his advisors and military officials at court, while Daphne was preoccupied with entertaining her ladies-in-waiting, along with the rest of her team of palace courtiers. While their lives were busy at court during the day; however, come nightfall, the happy couple were left alone to privately enjoy each other's companies into the late hours of the evening.

Since their arrival to the imperial palace, the crown prince and crown princess made love in practically every square inch of their shared bedchamber. From the bed to the floor, to the chairs to the walls, to the bathtub and table, there were no spaces left that they hadn't yet *blessed* with their erotic union.

And by now, the crown prince had taught his wife just about every possible sexual position imaginable. Daphne, the once innocent and shy virgin, no longer existed. By now, she was a full-fledged married woman, who was well versed in the art of sex as instructed by her adoring husband.

"Come tomorrow," Florian whispered into her ear, as he rigorously pumped in and out of his wife's stretched womb, ingraining his cock further inside of her and all the while, had her body pinned up and against the wall, with her legs wrapped around his hips.

Meanwhile, the portraits on the walls began to shake by their rigorous movements, until they eventually, all came crashing down onto the floor. Within seconds, the glass from the picture frames broke into pieces, with shattered fragments spread across everywhere.

Ignoring the mess that they had just recently made, Florian continued to thrust into Daphne's body, as he casually announced, "I plan to take you into town."

And as he whispered those very words, he also groaned at the same exact time.

"To town?" Daphne struggled to ask, as she desperately sought to formulate her spoken words, just as Florian rapidly moved inside of her.

Sex with him was never easy. He was *always* wild, when it came to her. A stark contrast to his usual calm, polished and poised self, which he often presented publicly at court.

However, whenever it came to the matter concerning the affairs of their bedchamber, Florian was far from a graceful gentleman. Instead, he was a real beast. A barbarian. A hungry wolf, who was ready to devour her at any given moment.

"Yes, to town," he answered with a strong and merciless *thrust*, savagely inserting himself even harder and deeper inside of her womb.

"Aaaaahhhh…," she moaned, as she closed her eyes and sought her balance.

"My fairest Daphne, if you're enjoying this now," Florian remarked with a deep grin, while also equally admiring the wet juice dripping down his wife's legs. Wickedly, he took immense pleasure by the sight of his own seed, leaking from out of her precious womb. "Then, you're truly in for a real surprise, come tomorrow. Because my love, I intend to spoil you rotten."

"Spoil me rotten?" she opened her eyes to gaze at him.

"Yes, spoil you rotten," he smiled, as he squeezed her buttock tightly with his hands.

Afterwards, Florian leaned forward and gave Daphne one last and final hard thrust, giving her the epic climax of a lifetime.

"But first, let's get cleaned up and bathe together," he bent down to kiss her forehead, as he finally withdrew his cock and brought her over to lean against his chest.

"But what's so special about tomorrow?" Daphne asked him, as she lifted her chin up to stare into his lapis blue eyes.

"You'll see," he smiled at her, lovingly. "Now, let's bathe and get ready for bed."

In the end, Daphne couldn't help but feel grateful for marrying her emerald prince. And as this emerald princess was coming to learn, Florian was filled with endless surprises. Indeed, she had no other choice, but to confess to herself that Florian really was the perfect husband for her. A real match made in heaven.

As promised, the following morning, Florian escorted Daphne on a date to tour the capital's town square. Apart from their previous road trip to the western kingdom, today's trip marked the first time that the crown princess had visited their kingdom from outside of the palace's walls. Much to her satisfaction, their eastern land was just as lovely as she had previously imagined it would be.

Peeking out through her carriage's window, Daphne observed the magical scenery that flourished around her. The site was a whimsical view of an enchanting land that represented the heart of spring in full bloom. As the land of eternal spring, the eastern kingdom lived up to its namesake and was surrounded by lush greenery, found all throughout.

From the fresh evergreens sprouting above the mossy green lawns to the rolling emerald green hills basking underneath the bright citrine sun and clear blue sky; to the bold yellow daffodils and crimson red tulips in bloom; to the lilac irises and white snowdrops blossoming across the open and wide fields; to the cherry and plum trees generously spread throughout this great territory and accompanied by humming birds and bees freely soaring high above the sky— in summary, the Kingdom of the East was just like a piece of heaven.

Certainly, it was unlike any of the previous places that Daphne had ever had the chance to visit to before. Truly, this world was serene and surreal. An enchanting fairy tale come straight to life.

Meanwhile, as the carriage continued to venture down the dusty countryside pathway, Daphne admired the fresh water streams and stone cottages that were nestled alongside the dirt road.

Through her window, she saw endless rows of water wheels next to the rivers and streams and windmills on land, across the orange poppy fields. And near each major windmill rested residential cottages.

These humble hovels were mostly medium in size and closely resembled her granny's cottage back in her sister's kingdom. Like Ruby's estate, they too were built with grey stones, covered with thatched straw roofs and surrounded by small herb gardens.

Once they reached the end of the country road, the royals entered into the main city and thereupon, their pathway was then converted into an urban style red brick road. As Daphne continued to gaze outside of her window, she noticed several tall buildings, with respective shops located within its structures.

From bakeries to banks, to clothing and hat boutiques, to fresh vegetable markets to bookshops— overall, the town square was filled with endless shops found on all corners. Furthermore, the crowded square was occupied by hundreds of people from all ages, gathered together and walking down the streets of the capital.

Glancing across the metropolitan square, Daphne was reminded of her own homeland. Just like the bustling streets of London, the capital city was just as equally busy.

Overall, the town square's appearance was impressive. All of the surrounding buildings appeared to be newly painted, while the streets were sparkling clean, without a single trace of dust or dirt.

Furthermore, in the center of the square stood a white marbled fountain that resembled an elegant swan sculpture. Not only was fresh water flowing through the swan's beak, but the rims encircling the fountain were also decorated with pink waterlilies all around, too.

Suddenly, the carriage came to an abrupt halt. Staring outside of her window, Daphne noticed that they were now currently parked right across from that fountain.

"We're here," Florian announced, as he tapped against his window with his cane to alert the coachman to open their carriage's door.

"Is this town square?" she asked him, as she quickly secured the back hooks to her pearl studded earrings and then proceeded to tie the lime green satin ribbon to her floral straw bonnet around her neck, which just-so-happened to match her lime green eyelet daydress that she wore for the special occasion.

"Indeed," he replied, as he fluttered his honey blonde eyelashes and dusted off his crisp royal navy-blue petticoat. A coat, which not only fitted his muscular chest to absolute perfection, but also resembled the color of his own lapis blue eyes.

Today, the emerald prince was dressed exceptionally well. Wearing a cream ruffled silk blouse, midnight black trousers with matching leather boots and a pair of sparkling silver cufflinks, the crown prince appeared as flawless as ever.

With a quick tousle of his curly golden blonde hair with his hands, Florian swiftly rose up from his seat and eagerly hopped out of their carriage's door.

"Come, Daphne," he directed, as he extended his hand over to hers. "I've got much to show you. Are you ready for today's tour?"

Delighted by his gentlemanly offer, Daphne put on her ivory laced gloves, grabbed her carnation baby pink parasol and graciously accepted his hand. With their arms interlinked, she followed him out of their carriage to welcome their next grand adventure.

"**P**rincess Daphne, you look absolutely stunning in this pink raspberry chiffon empire style gown!" Miss Iris Cedar gushed with great pride.

As the first stop on their journey into town, Florian escorted Daphne into a ladies' dressing boutique. Even though she already owned an endless supply of formal evening gowns and daytime tea dresses back at the imperial palace, the crown prince was still insistent that they visit the kingdom's most famous and highly-sought after fashion boutique in town that was exclusive for all young noblewomen and formally known as, *Dolls by Miss Iris.*

After trying on just about a dozen or so gowns, all ranging in various styles, colors, and materials, Daphne finally discovered an outfit that suited her figure the best. In fact, not only did she believe that this current pink raspberry empire style gown was the *only* selection suited best for her fair complexion and hourglass figure, but Florian and Iris also agreed, too.

As it turned out, empire dresses fit her body like a glove. Not only did it highlight her busty chest, but it also drew a close attention to her attractive petite waistline, as well. A standard silhouette, which also complemented both her sister and mother, respectively.

Striving to please her husband, Daphne modeled all of her prospective gowns on the runway to a sole audience of one: *the crown prince.* In the end, he, like her, thought that her current attire suited her best of all.

"I agree, this gown does look exceptionally lovely," Florian complemented his bride, with a great sense of admiration.

While seated down on a mustard yellow velvet chair with his legs crossed and smoking a cigar, the emerald prince watched his wife standing still on the stage from across the room. Blowing thick clouds of smoke rings into the air, he puffed on his cigar as he gave an approving nod over towards Iris' direction.

"I especially like the satin white bows around her chest and the extra layers of ruffles around her waist," he addressed the shop owner. "Her gown certainly makes an alluring statement. Her remarkable beauty is truly unparallel."

"Indeed, my prince," Iris agreed. "If Your Highnesses are interested, then we do have several more shades available in this particular design."

"Miss Cedar, do you happen to have green or lavender in this pattern?" asked Daphne, this time around. "Apart from pink, the colors green and lavender are my favorite shades, too."

"As a matter of fact, we do," Iris answered the crown princess. "Shall I bring them out, so that you can try them on, too?"

"Miss Cedar, that won't be necessary," Florian boldly interrupted them, as he emptied his cigar butt into the crystal ashtray. "I already trust that these gowns will look exquisite on my princess. No need for any further action. We'll take them all, as is."

"Very well," Iris happily replied, grateful to have made her best sale of the month thus far. "In that case, I'll go ahead and pack them as soon as I undress—"

"Again, Miss Cedar, that won't be necessary," Florian ordered.

Rising up from his chair, the crown prince directed his full attention over to Iris and instructed her, "Miss Cedar, if you could be so kind as to prepare our packages at your store front, then I shall take it upon myself to personally attend to the princess. Can you please give us a few extra minutes of privacy?"

"Oh!" exclaimed Iris, as she turned bright red by his surprising request.

In all of her many years spent working at her shop, this was the first time that a gentleman— let alone *the crown prince*— personally asked to attend to a lady in her boutique. However, given the crown prince's eagerness, Iris would never dare to deny such a bold request from a paying customer. Let alone, royalty.

"Actually, my packaging boxes are across the street at my neighbor's shop, the seamstress," Iris began to explain. "It will only take me a few minutes or so to fetch the boxes."

"Perfect," Florian replied, with a wicked grin. "That will give the princess and I ample time to prepare."

"Very well," Iris spoke, as she gave the crown prince a bow. "I'll be back shortly."

"Please, take your time," he said with a wink.

Finally, as soon the doors to the shop closed, the crown prince turned his attention over to his wife and said, "Come now, Daphne, let's get on with this quickly."

"Aaaahhhh…," Daphne screamed at the top of her lungs, as Florian slid his thick and hardened cock into her womb, plunging it deep from behind her.

As soon as Iris exited the boutique and without a moment's delay, the crown prince eagerly dragged his wife into the dressing room. Upon entering the premise, he immediately had her front body pinned against the wall with her back facing him, and his knee wedged in between her thighs.

Eagerly, Florian lifted Daphne's pink gown upwards, passed her hips. Leaving her white silk stockings and garter belts intact, he pulled down her undergarments, until they were left dangling in between her knees and exposing her plump and bare buttock for his pleasurable viewing.

But apart from her exquisitely curved ass, the crown prince also admired the long traces of his love marks left upon her, which stretched from the back of her neck and all the way down to her behind.

Pleased by the glorious and sexy vision in front of him, Florian snickered to himself, as he unhooked the buckle to his belt and pulled his hardened cock from out of his breeches. Once his cock was freed from its cage, the crown prince was no longer a gentleman. Instead, his gentlemanly persona was now replaced by a wild beast, ready to devour his prey without any rational thought.

Meanwhile, Daphne took in a deep breath in anticipation, as the prince finally plunged his erect cock deep inside of her, taking her full force from the behind.

"This shall be a new position for us, my love," he whispered into her ear, as he bit down onto it. "Furthermore, given that we're pressed for time, I can't promise to go gentle, either."

"Just take me," she pleaded, already enjoying the sensation of having his dick buried deep within her.

"Very well, this might be quick, but I promise to make it memorable," he vowed.

With Daphne's arms raised upwards and her hands pressed against the wall, Florian proceeded to pound into her soft flesh, with his cock pushing faster and harder within her. Inch by inch, he filled her womb with himself, until she was left screaming as he claimed her… over… and… over… again…

Thrust… withdrawal… thrust… Florian increased his rhythm by each passing second, as his cock rapidly moved inside of her. With his fist tugging at her long red hair and his other hand resting alongside her hip, the crown prince leaned down against his wife's body as he had his way with her.

"God, Daphne, you feel so good!" he groaned, as he closed his eyes shut in pleasure. "Fucking you is the highlight of my day!"

"Aaaahhhh…," Daphne moaned once more, as his cock rubbed against that special spot, hidden deep within her womb.

"Come for me," he roared. "Scream my name, as my cock claims that little wet pussy of yours."

Considering the limited amount of time that they had left, Daphne and Florian were relentless in their lovemaking. Even going as so far as continuing their shameful union, out publicly in the boutique's dressing room. After all, any second now, Iris could return back into the shop and catch them straight in the act!

"What about Iris?" Daphne struggled to gather her words, in between her moans and his groans.

"Don't worry about her," he told her, as he continued to move within her. "Your focus should be on *me*. Like I said before, I want to hear you cry my name out loud, first."

Desperate to hear her call for him, Florian continued to pump inside of Daphne from her behind, eagerly waiting for her release. And as his wife's wet juice leaked down in between her thighs, the crown prince grew even more motivated than ever to make her finally come.

Pushing speed, Florian was merciless as he pounded into Daphne's swollen flesh, leaving wet stains soiled along his wife's new dress. *Thrust. Deeper. Harder. Again. And. Again.* He continued to pound into her behind, like there was no tomorrow.

Finally, after much consistent effort, Daphne finally gave in.

"FLORIAN!!!" she yelled at the top of her lungs, as she finally turned around and collapsed towards his chest.

By now, both husband and wife were breathing heavily and sweating profusely.

"I'm a complete mess," the princess admitted in shame, blushing in the shade of deep red, out of sheer embarrassment.

"Nonsense," Florian grinned. "You look fresh and desirable."

"Yeah, freshly fucked," she laughed on.

"Hey," he spoke, as he lifted her chin up to meet his gaze. "Like I said before, I'm here to help clean you up, and I intend to keep my promise."

Without speaking another word, Florian promptly pulled up his trousers, buckled his belt and then, he proceeded to wipe Daphne down with a handkerchief.

After removing the rest of her gown, he redressed her in her previous lime green attire and then, tied the satin ribbon to her straw bonnet. Picking up her pink parasol, he escorted her back over into the waiting area.

"Don't worry about the gown, I'll ask for another," he told her, fully acknowledging the unfortunate mess that they had recently just made.

"No, don't," Daphne insisted. "I rather not have Iris be stuck with a soiled gown. I'll just keep it and have it cleaned back at the palace."

"Very well, as you wish, my princess," Florian accepted her request.

A few minutes later, the crown prince and crown princess finally exited *Dolls by Miss Iris*, ready to tour the rest of the town, along with a trail of shopping boxes in hand.

After spending the past two hours touring the capital, Daphne was all but exhausted. By this point, Florian had dragged her into practically every store imaginable.

As a result, he bought her several more dozens of pairs of shoes, ranging in all shades and styles. Additionally, apart from shoes, he also purchased her with other gifts in the forms of the most recent on trend hats, gloves, fans and purses.

However, if that wasn't enough, then Florian also escorted her into all of the best bakeries and dessert shops in town, and treated her to an endless feast of sweet treats.

From lemon sugar cookies to plum pies, to candy apple lollipops to chocolate brownies, to almond scones to blueberry muffins, to strawberry and cream tarts to warm cinnamon spiced cocoa, and everything else under the sun, the crown princess tried them all. And if she was hungry before their travels, then by now, she no longer knew the definition of hunger anymore!

Afterwards, the loving couple took a stroll at a nearby park. From what she observed, everyone in the kingdom seemed to be rather happy. Between the walking men and women, everyone appeared finely dressed and covered in smiles.

Perhaps, poverty wasn't an issue in this world, Daphne thought to herself. Indeed, Florian and his father, King Titus, appeared to resemble kind and righteous rulers who took great care of their citizens, regardless of their social classes and backgrounds.

Meanwhile, the children around them also seemed to be cheerful, too. Many of whom, appeared to be surrounded by their loving family members, as well. Walking by one of them, Daphne stared at the traveling balloon salesman, who was currently gifting a child with a free balloon.

Happily, she smiled to herself. In a world filled with laughter, free balloons and happy children, this was the ideal place where she wanted to call home.

"Are you enjoying the day thus far, my love?" Florian asked.

"Yes, my love," Daphne replied, with a bright smile as the sun shined across her face. "Today has been a real dream come true."

"By the way, would you care for a balloon?" he asked her, noticing her joyful expression as she watched a young child happily play with a red balloon from afar.

"No, I don't need a balloon," she said. "I'm just admiring the child holding it."

"Ah, I see," he acknowledged, as he adjusted his latest shiny new top hat above his head.

Another accessory that he had recently purchased for himself at the last shop that they had visited together, before strolling into the park.

"Do you have a soft spot for them? Balloons or children?" he asked her, with a raised brow.

"Both, perhaps," she sighed. "Balloons represents freedom and children the future. Maybe, one day, I can have both."

"You'll always have your freedom," he told her. "As your husband, I'll never get in your way. At least, not unless, you want me to."

"Yes, I know," she acknowledged, as she grabbed a hold of his hand and placed it within hers. "It's why I love you. Ever since we married, you've been nothing but a wonderful mate. Truly, I am lucky. You certainly spoil me rotten."

"And that's my job," he proudly stated, with a warm smile. "An honor that I keep close and dear to my heart."

Standing still, he leaned against her ear and whispered, "As for the children part, I'm sure that I can make that happen, too. Of course, whenever you're ready."

Instantly, Daphne blushed from embarrassment. After all, they were standing in the middle of a public park and surrounded by folks with listening ears.

"You know, in my family," she began, as she tried to regain her composure, "The brides are known to birth their children rather early. Would it bother you so much, if we had children born so soon into our union?"

Gazing straight into her emerald green eyes, Florian beamingly smiled from ear-to-ear and said, "Daphne, a child with you would be a dream come true for me. I could only be so lucky."

"Oh, Florian," she happily uttered, as she leaned in towards him and placed a gentle kiss alongside his tender lips.

"Come now, Daphne," Florian spoke in all seriousness, as he grabbed a tight hold of his cane, with its silver handle ironically shaped like a frog.

Adjusting his silver cufflinks alongside his petticoat, he said, "Don't go all emotional on me, right now. After all, we've got one last stop to make. I saved the best for last."

With their hands interlinked, Florian dragged Daphne to yet another shopping spree excursion. Meanwhile, from the corner of her eye, the emerald princess couldn't help but notice a peculiar black raven who was flying nearby.

Based on its traveling route and sudden appearance, the princess could swear that this strange looking bird was following them.

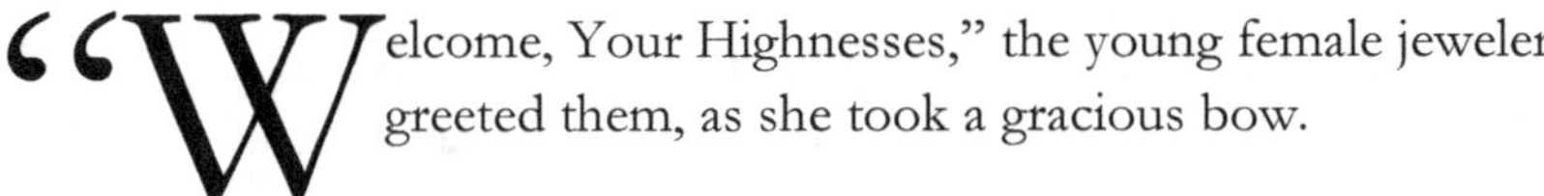

"Welcome, Your Highnesses," the young female jeweler greeted them, as she took a gracious bow.

Dressed in a canary yellow satin dress with her black hair swept aside and placed into a long and tight ponytail, this young entrepreneur was actively eager to please her new customers, the crown prince and crown princess.

"Daphne, this is Miss Jerrica Goldenshine," Florian introduced them. "She's the shop owner to this establishment. Miss Goldenshine owns some of the best sets of jewelry in town."

"Your Highness," Jerrica respectfully interrupted the crown prince. "I believe that the crown princess and I have already met back at the palace. It was during her formal tiara fitting, I believe."

"Yes, that's correct," Daphne smiled on, in agreement. "It was a pleasure then, as it is a pleasure now, Miss Goldenshine."

"Is that so? In that case, when will the emerald and diamond tiara be ready?" Florian inquired, as he invited himself over the center of the room and took a seat on the unoccupied red velvet sofa.

"Within a fortnight," replied Jerrica. "In the meantime, shall I show the crown princess the latest sets of jewels that I've recently acquired in my collection?"

"Yes, please do," Florian nodded in approval, as he reached into his pocket and took out a new cigar.

With his legs crossed, cane pushed aside and his top hat and gloves removed, he carelessly waved and signaled for them to carry on.

Following the crown prince's wishes, Jerrica quickly escorted the crown princess over to the front glass counter. Meanwhile, she also instructed Annette, her younger blonde apprentice, to serve the royal guests with a pot of hibiscus herbal tea, along with a side of lavender and honey biscuits.

Finishing his cigar, Florian poured himself a cup of tea, while Jerrica proceeded to showcase all of the lovely jewels that were housed within her boutique. From sparkling diamond earrings to shiny pearl rings, to ruby bracelets to amethyst tiaras, to golden chains to silver wristlets, Daphne was dazzled by all of the latest collections of jewelry associated with the most recent high fashion of the day.

"Your Highness, is there anything in particular that catches your eye?" Jerrica asked the crown princess.

"I must say," Daphne began, "Miss Goldenshine, they truly are all so incredibly lovely."

"Yes, they are," Jerrica agreed. "But, my princess, might I make a suggestion?"

"But of course," the princess replied.

Opening her desk drawer, Jerrica pulled out a set of two golden rings. The first ring contained an emerald oval-shaped stone, which was surrounded by miniature white diamonds that encircled it. Meanwhile, the second ring was identical to the same style as the first ring; however, this version was replaced by a sapphire blue stone in lieu of the emerald.

"I noticed that Your Highnesses have been wearing the traditional brass golden wedding rings," Jerrica remarked.

"Although it's a traditional custom for eastern royals, as well as for normal eastern citizens alike to wear such bands," she continued on, "But I do believe that the royal crown prince and crown princess should have something extra special and more refined."

"Special? More refined?" Daphne repeated.

"Yes," Jerrica confirmed, as she handed the rings over to the princess. "The emerald stone in this ring resembles your eyes, my princess. And the sapphire blue stone represents the prince. This way, you'll always have a piece of each other."

"So, the sapphire stone ring is for me? And the emerald stone version for my husband?"

"Precisely," Jerrica nodded.

"Aww, I do like that," Daphne was truly touched by the thoughtful sentiment.

Placing the sapphire ring around her finger, Daphne lifted her hand up into the air and gazed at her husband's face from afar. Indeed, this stone truly did resemble his dreamy lapis blue eyes.

Listening to their conversation with eagle ears, Florian abruptly arose up from his chair and came to his wife's side.

"It's remarkable," he observed, as he placed the second ring alongside his finger.

"It really does match your shade of eyes," he acknowledged. "However, this is only a false imitation of my beloved."

Without any warning, Florian swiftly pulled Daphne to his chest, bent down and placed a heartfelt kiss alongside her lips.

Embarrassed by their public display of affection, the princess abruptly pulled herself away from the prince's embrace. They might have been a married couple, but she still felt nervous about publicly showcasing their love in front of strangers.

"A bit too much?" he teased her.

Instantly, Daphne blushed bright red out of sheer embarrassment.

"It's quite alright," Jerrica chimed in. "Annette and I are used to it. Most of our newlyweds or engaged couples usually can't keep their hands off from one another."

"Oh," the princess remarked.

"You see, Daphne, I'm not such a bad guy, after all," he grinned at her.

"I'll tell you what," he continued on, "In honor of my beloved bride, I shall buy all of the jewelry in this entire boutique."

"What???!!!" Daphne cried, in shock. "Florian, you can't honestly be serious???"

"Oh, but I am," he replied, with much confidence. "Before I married you, did I not previously mention that I intended to adorn you with rubies and pearls? Daphne, I meant what I said, word for word. And today, I'm keeping true to my promise to you, as a man of honor. What can I say, I'm a prince who's madly in love."

"But really, Florian, it's simply too much!" Daphne exclaimed.

Ignoring his wife's pleas, the crown prince turned his attention over to Jerrica and instructed her, "Miss Goldenshine, please have everything delivered to the imperial palace by the end of this month, along with the promised emerald tiara."

"Yes, Your Highness. It shall be my honor," Jerrica bowed in respect.

Meanwhile, as the crown prince and crown princess embraced each other with another passionate and heartfelt kiss, a raven was busy watching the happy couple from outside of the shop's window.

Alas, the shop owner and her apprentice were not the only witnesses who were privy to the prince's absolute devotion to his new bride. Unfortunately, there was also another.

# Chapter 16

## *An Emerald Witch*

"This cannot be!!!" Esmeralda shouted out in despair, as she threw a glass decanter against the stone wall of her bedchamber.

"How can Florian be in love with her? That foreign wench!" she screamed with rage. "Are you sure what you witnessed to be true?"

"Indeed, it is the truth," spoke the black feathered bird, ironically named, Raven.

"Whether or not you accept it," Raven continued on, "But, either way, the crown prince's love remains to be true. From what I've witnessed first-hand, Prince Florian is besotted with his new bride, Princess Daphne. His devotion to her is unparallel."

"Don't you dare say *her name* aloud in front of me!!!" shouted the angered lady, as she aggressively pulled at her long black hair— which by now, tragically, resembled an entangled bird's nest.

"He was supposed to love *me*," she reflected in pure agony. "I was his fiancé! I was meant to be his one true love!"

"Well, love doesn't work that way," Raven carefully pointed out. "You cannot force such heartfelt emotions onto another. It must come willingly. That's why they call it *true love.*"

"Oh, shut up, you stupid bird!" Esmeralda yelled at him, as she threw a crystal vase towards his direction.

Fleeing for his safety, the bird instantly flew up towards the dangling chandelier, which hung high above the ceiling and by doing so, he luckily avoided the assault.

Wanting to avoid another potential catastrophe, a second later, Raven exited out of the castle through an open window, leaving Esmeralda alone to wallow in her own misery and tears.

Right now, at this very moment, this wasn't how her life was supposed to be. She was meant to be the emerald princess. It's why she was named Esmeralda in the first place.

At birth, their mothers had carefully planned their futures leading up to their eventual marriage. From the time Esmeralda spoke her first set of words, she was already referring to Florian as her fiancé. But sadly, after a lifetime of waiting for her promised groom, as it came to turn out, it was all for *nothing.*

In the end, he didn't pick her. Instead, he married another. And worst of all, he actually *loved his bride.* She, the other woman.

Again, this ending wasn't how it was supposed to be! This wasn't *her happily ever after!*

Crown Prince Florian Apollo of the East was meant to love *her, not* some other commoner! A so-called-lady from another realm!

In fact, Esmeralda spent her entire life trying her best to win Florian's affection and woo him over. To gain his attention. Favor. Respect. Friendship. *Love.*

But apparently, everything that Esmeralda did over these past several years (no decades!) really was all for *nothing.* By now, she foolishly presumed that after spending an extended period of time together in holy matrimony, the crown prince and crown princess would eventually grow to dislike one another and seek a divorce. That their honeymoon stage would now be officially over and the reality of their mismatched union would finally be acknowledged by the duo.

After all, he was the crown prince and she a commoner, plus a foreigner. Surely, they were incompatible with one another. Unlike the current crown princess, Esmeralda was Florian's true equal in every possible sense. Respectable families. Similar social circles. Wealth. Fame. Prestige. Intelligence. Indeed, she had high hopes!

Sooner or later, Esmeralda was convinced that Florian would come to see the error of his ways and thereupon, have his marriage annulled. Worst case scenario, divorced.

In her heart, Esmeralda remained hopeful that eventually, Florian would face the fact that his union with the so-called *Princess Daphne* stemmed from pure lust and nothing more. After all, Florian and Esmeralda never consummated their relationship.

Surely, he'd been sexually frustrated over the years. Chasity was a difficult virtue to maintain— especially, for a man. Naturally, their lack of intimacy must have been the sole culprit that pushed Florian into Daphne's accepting arms. Either way, that foreign wench must have seduced him!

Regardless, eventually, the prince would grow tired of his bride. It was an inevitable fact. Hopefully, by then, he'd come to long for their lost friendship. After all, they had been friends for almost all of their entire lives.

As a result of their early betrothal, Florian and Esmeralda grew up alongside with each other. They attended the same prestigious schools, were assigned to the same classrooms, shared many of the same mutual friends, ran in the same social circles and often spent holidays vacationing together, alongside with their parents.

Already, from the outside view, it seemed almost predictable and logical that the two were destined to wed. The future crown prince and crown princess of the east. The emerald prince and emerald princess.

In fact, their mothers wished for this outcome. The late Queen

Ophelia and the Marchioness of Clover longed for their children to be united in blissful matrimony. And as the future princess, starting at an early age, Esmeralda was groomed to become one. Sequestered away from the rest of the other children her own age, Esmeralda was personally trained by her mother and the late queen to become the future royal crown princess. A queen-in-waiting.

As a result of her mother's and the late queen's persistence, Esmeralda religiously attended all of her rigorous lessons. Lessons including: social etiquettes to dancing; speaking, reading and writing in Latin and Greek to hunting and sparring; painting to playing the piano forte; singing opera to mastering astrology; and even, conquering equestrian to archery, to name a few.

Therefore, being the only child of the Marquis and Marchioness of Clover, young Esmeralda worked very hard with her studies to make both her family and her future in-laws proud of her long-list of accomplishments.

Meanwhile, as Esmeralda slaved away with her studies; Florian, on the other hand, never did. While the crown prince regularly attended his own studies; however, he rarely seemed as focused nor as determined as her. Instead, the young prince prioritized his social life, often wandering off to partake on grand and jolly adventures with his good friend, Prince Maximus of the West. In fact, during their youth, the two princes were often inseparable.

As another member of nobility, Esmeralda was never jealous of any of the prince's other friends. After all, in the past, they were *all male*. Plus, everyone else within the Great Kingdom already knew about their engagement.

Furthermore, given Esmeralda's feisty reputation, no female would ever dare to cross her by flirting with her man. She'd kill them. Therefore, it was safe to say that Esmeralda never once feared about the possibility of another woman coming along to steal her betrothed. Hence, her mind was always at ease.

But apart from her duty as his fiancé, Esmeralda genuinely loved the prince. He was her first love. Her only love. In fact, her first kiss was with him.

At the age of sixteen, Esmeralda forcibly kissed him and foolishly confessed her romantic feelings. According to her teenaged heartfelt confession, she told him that to her, she didn't view their engagement as being limited to another political or forced family arrangement. Instead, *she loved him.*

From his bright blonde and curly locks of hair, dreamy lapis blue eyes, and muscular body, Florian was the apple of her eyes. One way or another, she was highly attracted to her fiancé.

But apart from his physical being, Esmeralda also adored his sweet personality, as well. From his kindness, sharp wit, eloquent speech, loyalty to his friends and his overall devotion to the welfare of his kingdom, Esmeralda loved every inch of him.

However, instead of relishing on her words and their first kiss, Florian was quick to push her away. Indeed, he did not reciprocate her love. Instead, he had a confession of his own.

With a somber expression, the emerald prince gently admitted to her that he considered her to be nothing more than a good childhood friend. Regardless of their mothers' wishes, he already knew that they could never be nothing more than *just friends.*

Even as a teenager, Florian's mind and heart were already well decided. He could never love her. Never be forced to be with her. Let alone, *marry her.*

After that disastrous kiss and heartbreaking confession, Esmeralda brushed his cold words aside. He's just too young, she convinced herself. He will change. He will mature. He'll eventually fall for me. For the sake of our families, *he has to.*

But unfortunately, for her, he didn't. Staying true to his word, over the years, Florian maintained a cordial relationship with her at a safe distance. Never one to hold her hand for an extra second longer, nor go above and beyond to win her favor. A friend, but never, a love interest.

While the kingdom saw them as a pair fated for matrimony; in reality, Florian made it perfectly clear to her from behind the scenes that their time together was a ticking clock. One way or another, he was going to end their betrothal. It was only a matter of time. And whatever the emerald prince wants, he always gets it in the end. Alas, Esmeralda's feelings for the prince were nothing more than unrequited love.

Heartbroken and outraged, Esmeralda was desperate to win the love and affection of her beloved prince. A man that she had so long admired and placed above on a high pedestal. Therefore, after his confession about his intentions to end their union, she decided to do everything in her power to reverse his emotions and win his favor.

Although many throughout the land despised the former Queen Vera of the West— a witch who was disposed of from off the throne; Esmeralda, in contrast, secretly admired her from afar.

Apart from her reign of terror, Esmeralda personally admired the late evil queen's relentless determination to conquer the western kingdom and usurp the throne for herself. One way or another, Queen Vera got what she wanted. And to get it, she used magic.

And so, Esmeralda desired to follow in Vera's footsteps. She, too, wanted to learn the art of magic. *Black magic.* To become a powerful witch, like the late queen. Someone, whom even Florian could respect.

Perhaps, if she could become a powerful and skillful witch, then she could gain his attention. And thus, woo him over into finally accepting her and most importantly, *loving her.*

Even though her parents frowned upon her devotion to the occult; in the end, Esmeralda of Clover was a rich and spoiled daughter. If she desired to become a witch, then her father was determined to make his only daughter happy by hiring a team of highly prestigious sorcerers to personally teach her. To learn from the very best.

Meanwhile, as her tutors taught her the simple art of white magic, Esmeralda was convinced that this soft version of magic was still not enough. White magic alone could never change the prince's poor opinion of her. Let alone, impress him.

Instead, she needed to follow in Vera's direct footsteps. Therefore, she secretly stole their forbidden dark grimoire and during the nightfall, she privately taught herself black magic inside the privacy of her bedchamber.

As the years grew by, Esmeralda's short hair grew into long strands of dark black hair, while her body blossomed with a full chest, along with a perfect hourglass figure. Meanwhile, her plain clothes were replaced with more black, tight-fitting and revealing gowns, which showcased her chest and voluptuous shape.

Even though many throughout their land grew to admire the attractive Esmeralda; sadly, her beloved Florian, on the other hand, never bothered to bat an eyelash towards her direction.

Tragically, Esmeralda's attempts to win the crown prince's affection were proving to be useless. Even when they reached into their adulthoods, Florian still refused to participate in any sort of romantic relations with her.

In fact, legally, they were already at the ideal age for marriage. Had Florian desired to wed her, then they could have moved forward with their union. Esmeralda could have already been a bride. A newly crowned princess. A real queen-in-waiting.

But instead, Florian prolonged their engagement for as long as possible. Going against his own mother's wishes, he avoided the topic of marriage regularly. However, regardless of his objections, Esmeralda knew that one day eventually, they'd come to marry. And once they married, then it was only a matter of time before he fell in love with her. *He had to.*

Unfortunately, that fate never came to be. Unexpectedly, Queen Ophelia passed away, leaving her family and their kingdom devastated. And while the world remained in mourning for their beloved queen, Florian took it upon himself to announce to his father and her parents his wish to end their engagement.

"For years I have held my tongue out of honor," he said on that fateful day at his mother's funeral. "But out of respect to my late mother, as well as to my own good conscience, I must request an end to my engagement to Lady Esmeralda of Clover. In truth, I consider the young lady to be a dear and sweet childhood friend. But unfortunately, that is the end of the road for us. As a man, I cannot give Lady Esmeralda what she desires. And she deserves to marry a man who will love her, through and through. Therefore, I must withdraw my legal status as her fiancé."

Those cold, bitter and heartless words were like a sharpened dagger, plunged straight through her shattered heart. Although Esmeralda knew as much, but to actually hear him declare his true feelings out in public and in front of everyone, was a devastating blow.

However, ending a royal engagement was not so simple. Even though Florian didn't love her; however, royal duties prevented him from obtaining his request. Instead, even the crown prince couldn't be released from their engagement, regardless if he loved her or not.

And so, their engagement continued on. Even though they kept up with their public appearances; but apart from social events, Esmeralda hardly saw him. It wasn't until he suddenly appeared at her castle on a surprise visit that she came face-to-face with her old childhood friend, after a long period of absence.

Foolishly, Esmeralda believed that his visit was to finally declare his love for her. That, after all this time apart, he finally came to recognize the reality that she'd make a fine wife and crown princess to him. But sadly, that was not the case.

Instead, he tricked her. Stole her grimoire and traveled through her magic mirror. Rescuing a damsel in distress, secretly marrying her and then, crowning the wench as the new emerald princess. And thus, officially ending their engagement.

Proclaiming Esmeralda as a dark witch alone wasn't enough to break their engagement. After all, her parents were wealthy and highly respected nobles at court. With one word from her father, then several investors could easily withdrawal all of their funds from the king's central bank.

Instead, Florian also needed a replacement. A security net to soften the blow of their breakup in the eyes of the public. After all, the public was more likely to accept the romantic fairy tale story about a crown prince traveling to a foreign realm and falling madly in love with a local fair maiden, instead of the truth that he actually abandoned his fiancé of thirty plus years for another younger woman. And sure enough, he did all of this and behind her back, too.

In truth, Esmeralda believed his recent marriage to be sham. A way to his escape his original marriage to her. After all, the new princess was a redhead, a foreigner, and wasn't classically trained in royal protocols, unlike her. Princess Daphne wasn't his type. Surely, Florian didn't marry her of all people, out of true love?

For the past several weeks, Esmeralda entrusted her flying companion, Raven, to spy on the royal couple. Since the crown prince and crown princess were often seen apart at court, Esmeralda was certain that this was a good sign. An indication that Florian was not truly in love with the new princess.

But now, hearing the news directly from Raven that Prince Florian and Princess Daphne actually seemed to be happy on their most recent outing into town… that they appeared to have a wonderful marriage… this really was the worst sort of news imaginable! A true horror!

Again, by now, Esmeralda expected them to divorce. She had hoped that he would have succumb to his senses. But sadly, tonight, the young witch finally realized that much to her own dismay, Florian might actually be *in love* with his wife, after all.

But this shall not do! One way or another, Esmeralda was determined to get involved in their relationship and break them up for good!

All these years, Esmeralda ironically became a witch to earn Florian's love. As children, he never noticed her. Foolishly, she believed that if she immersed herself in the art of magic, that somehow, he'd come to admire her... and eventually *love her*.

Persistently, Esmeralda tried and experimented with various types of love spells and potions. However, she learned early on that love was the one thing that couldn't be tampered with. One could project lust, but not love. There was a significant *difference*.

Love was something that could only be organically born, not created or bought. Therefore, she could only make Florian *lust* for her, but not *love* her.

However, now, after everything that had recently transpired, Esmeralda was willing to use the one thing that she never thought that she'd be forced to resort to: *a love potion*. In the end, if using a love potion on Florian was the means to drive a wedge in between himself and his happy bride, then so be it!

Finally, with that solid determination and newfound confidence, Esmeralda wiped her tears away and got straight back to work.

# Chapter 17

## *The Arrival of Spring*

"Spring is soon approaching us," King Titus beamingly announced at breakfast with his son and daughter-in-law by his side, along with his palace courtiers.

"Shall I schedule a meeting to discuss this occasion further?" Atticus asked.

"Nonsense," the king huffed in annoyance by the mere suggestion. "Why schedule a meeting, when we can simply discuss it here, over breakfast?"

"Well, Your Highness, if you insist, then I suppose…"

"We'll need to pay special attention to the gardens, and have all the trees finely chopped and the bushes perfectly manicured," King Titus instructed his aid, with a careless wave of his hand. "The roses and tulips shall be plucked and converted into elegant garlands and bouquets, while the fairy lights must be adorned on every tree and archway…"

"Yes, my king," Atticus agreed, as he hurriedly removed his quill, inkpot and notepad from his breast pocket and jotted down everything that the king had instructed down onto paper.

"And make sure that the invitations are sent all throughout the four kingdoms, as this year will be extra special," the king ordered.

Turning his attention over to his relatives, the king proudly beamed at his son and daughter-in-law and said, "After all, we finally have an emerald princess, now."

"Your Highness, very well," Atticus bowed down to his king. "As you wish."

Meanwhile, as the king spoke in great detail to his trusted advisor, dictating every last request concerning the arrival of spring, Daphne secretly whispered over into her husband's ear to inquire about the origins to the king's unexpected excitement.

"But isn't each day spring in this kingdom?" she asked the prince.

"Indeed, it is," Florian replied, as he took a sip of his juice. "However, what my father is referring to pertains to our famous Midsummer Night's Dream Gala."

"What's that?" Daphne curiously pressed on.

"It's an enchanting ball that we famously throw each year on the twenty-first of March," he explained. "According to tradition, it marks the official arrival of spring."

"I still don't understand," Daphne remarked in confusion. "This is the spring kingdom. Shouldn't it be called at the very least the Mid*spring* Night's Dream Gala? After all, this is the land of eternal spring, not summer."

"What can I say, my love," he shrugged. "My late mother was a fan of Shakespeare."

"Shakespeare? You know about him, here?" asked Daphne in sheer surprise.

Never in a million years, did she imagine that the famous authors of her homeland, would also be recognized here in this foreign kingdom, as well.

"But of course," Florian grinned, as he reached over to grab a piece of toast. "We know all of the great authors from your land. Shakespeare. Brontë. Dickens. Chaucer. Plato. And even, Austen. I could simply go on and on. You know, you and your sister aren't the first travelers to visit our lands from Earth."

"Amazing," Daphne admired. "So, does this mean that I can still read Jane Austen's books from the palace's library?"

"Indeed, you can," replied the crown prince. "Anytime, during your leisure."

Not getting too carried away with herself or getting overly excited about reading another beloved Austen book again— an option that Daphne had sadly thought was once lost to her the moment that she crossed over into this strange new world— she decided to remain on topic to the pending conversation held at hand.

"Florian, the twenty-first of March corresponds to Earth's spring equinox," she pointed out. "Meanwhile, each day is spring in the Kingdom of the East. Therefore, why a special annual celebration?"

"My fairest Daphne," Florian began, "But if spring was to have a birthday, then the twenty-first of March would be that special day. And yes, it's the same day equivalent to the spring season found within your homeland of England. Therefore, each year, we host an extravagant ball to usher in the blossoming of our beloved flowers. Lastly, in case you're curious, there are a few special flowers that only blooms on that particular day, too."

"Which sorts of flowers?" Daphne curiously inquired, as she took a sip of her raspberry infused orange juice.

With a happy and wide grin, Florian leaned in towards his wife's ear and whispered, "My darling, if you must know, then why don't I just show you, instead?"

Meanwhile, as King Titus was busy chatting away with Atticus, Florian and Daphne excused themselves from the breakfast table and headed out into the gardens for a morning stroll.

"**O**n this very laurel tree, worshipers across the land will present the Goddess Persephone with an egg," Florian carefully explained, as he stood in front of a tall and shady laurel tree, which grew within the heart of the imperial palace's main royal garden.

"An egg that they personally hand-painted to represent their wishes," he emphasized, with a wave of his hand. "Once a year on the twenty-first of March, it is believed that anyone who places a decorative egg underneath this very blessed laurel tree, then the Goddess Persephone will grant their wishes under the blue moon."

"Why this particular tree?" the crown princess inquired, as she stared up to gaze at this majestic and legendary tree, with the sun shining brightly against its evergreen colored leaves.

"Because it's believed that the Goddess Persephone's first-born son was born right underneath this very tree on the twenty-first of March. Therefore, it's blessed."

"So, in your land, the Goddess Persephone represents the goddess of spring?" asked Daphne, as she actively listened on to his charming tale.

"Indeed," the crown prince agreed. "According to our history, the Goddess Persephone was the founder of our spring kingdom. The first Queen of the East and the mother to the original emerald prince. Her son succeeded her, after her accession back into the heavens. And our family, House East, are her direct descendants."

"How very interesting," Daphne acknowledged in fascination. "Therefore, you and your family are directly descended from the gods? Is that the case for all of the other kingdoms, too?"

"Yes, and no," Florian replied. "We might be descended from *a god*, but we are very much *human*. After all, all of the previous kings took mortal wives and so, we've outbred any godly blood that we might have once possessed from centuries ago."

"As for the other kingdoms," the crown prince clarified, "It's true, each kingdom is descended from a god, as well."

"Which ones?" she asked.

"Well, in the case of your sister's family, House West," he explained, "The western royals are descended from the Goddess Karpo, Mother of Harvest."

"And then, there's the Kingdom of the North," Florian continued on, "The northern royals of the winter kingdom are descended from the Goddess Boreas, Mother of the Northern Wind."

Plucking a laurel leaf from off the tree and handing it over to his wife, the prince added, "Finally, there's the southern kingdom and they're descended from Auxo, Mother of Fertility. As you might have already guessed, each kingdom worships their founding queens as their local celebrated god of their regions."

"I see, so the Goddess Persephone is only recognized in this kingdom, but not in the others?" Daphne inquired, as she took a sniff of the delightful scent of the laurel leaf, which was currently resting within the palm of her hand.

"Not quite," replied the prince. "While our goddess is recognized throughout the Great Kingdom; however, she's worshiped only within our land by us locals."

"How very interesting," the princess acknowledged. "I must confess, I did not learn about this important part of our kingdom's history during my lessons with Lavinia and Hyacinth."

"They probably didn't want to overwhelm you," he concluded. "There's a lot for you to learn. Naturally, it's going to take you some extra time to absorb it all. But I must also acknowledge that you've adjusted here so incredibly well. Much better than I ever would, had the roles been in reverse."

"Is that a complement coming from my beloved prince?" Daphne teased him, as she moved to embrace him, while standing underneath the shaded tree.

"Indeed, it is," he smiled at her, as he wrapped his arms around her waist.

With much affection, the prince slowly bent down and placed a heartfelt kiss alongside her lips.

"Come now," he eagerly addressed her, as he grabbed a hold of her hand. "There's more to visit. Places that I eagerly want to personally show you, myself."

And just like that, the crown prince and crown princess were off to explore the rest of the gardens.

"So, this is the magical flower, which only blooms underneath a blue moon that's held during the Midsummer Night's Dream Gala?" Daphne asked, as she held on to the premature green bulb within the tight grasp of her hand.

"Yes, it's true," Florian concurred. "It's called the emerald lily and it only blossoms but once a year."

"How enchanting," she murmured to herself.

"This flower is only found within our kingdom," he further explained. "It's a flower not even found within your world, either."

"It's truly one of a kind," the princess sighed.

"According to legend, a blossoming emerald lily is supposed to help guide a person to their heart's greatest desire," the emerald prince further commented. "To lead them to their one true love."

"Is that really true?" she stared directly into his lapis blue eyes.

"It is, but in our case," Florian beamingly grinned, as he pulled her away from the plant at current discussion. "We don't need a blooming flower to prove what we already both know."

Suddenly, the emerald prince placed his wife's hand over his chest, right above his beating heart.

"Can you feel it?" he asked her, narrowing his eyes.

"Daphne, can you *feel* how mad you make me?" he whispered into her ear.

Slowly, he brought her hand down and placed it gently above his groin.

"My love, can you feel just how much you *excite me*, whenever I'm near you?" he took in a deep breath and got a whiff of her hair; which at this moment, smelled like a fresh bouquet of lilies.

Sensing his wild desire, Daphne was ready to surrender to the overwhelming mutual passion that was currently engulfing them. Already, she, too, was growing wet down below.

And now, being together alone, within the private seclusion of the imperial palace's main royal garden, the princess was ready to take control of this situation and seduce her husband.

"Then, let me embrace you," she pleaded, as she slipped her hand inside of his trousers, making her way down to touch his cock.

"Daphne…," he cried, as he closed his eyes shut.

"Please, Florian, allow me," she begged, as she began to rub against his dick.

Giving into the moment, Florian nodded his head in agreement.

With his permission, she moved to unbuckle his belt and swiftly, pulled his trousers down. Reaching into his breeches, the princess gently removed his cock into full view.

At first glance, Daphne couldn't help but happily grin. Her husband's package was truly a sight to behold. His length, thickness and hardness were difficult to ignore. Overcome by her own greedy urges, Daphne kneeled down before him and brought her mouth over to his dick.

"Daphne…," Florian whispered, as he grabbed a fistful worth of her red locks of hair within his hand.

"Shush," she told him. "Let me pleasure you."

Following her instincts, Daphne took one long lick of his cock, starting from his tip and all the way up towards his base. Instantly, Florian flinched, as he further dug his fingers through her flaming red head of hair.

Pleased by his reaction, the princess ambitiously continued to push forward. Using her hands, she held his base, as she proceeded to suck his cock, until she swallowed it whole within her mouth, hitting the back of her throat.

Meanwhile, her hands continued to rub against his base, back and forth, as she proceeded to lick and suck him dry with great force.

"Fuck," cried the prince with tears streaming down his cheeks, due to the extreme pleasure that he was currently experiencing.

And as his wife continued to lick and suck him whole, the prince was eager to surrender his entire body over to his lover.

"Daphne, I need to feel myself *inside* of you… *now*!"

Without a further delay, Daphne pushed Florian down onto the mossy grass lawn, as she climbed up on top of him.

"Are you sure?" he asked her, knowing that this was a brand-new position for them to explore as a couple.

"I am," she boldly replied.

Ignoring the need to discard the rest of their garments, Daphne simply removed only her underwear, leaving the rest of her stockings, garter belts and gown intact on her body, as she proceeded to straddle her husband.

Once comfortably seated on top, the princess slowly lowered herself down, until she slid his cock deep inside of her womb. And almost instantly, upon direct contact, they both released a loud moan.

"Aaaaahhhh…," the couple happily roared.

Determined to please her husband, Daphne began to rock back and forth, as she rode her husband with full force, with the sounds of slapping skin echoing across the garden.

At first, she tried to steady herself on top; however, once she felt more relaxed and comfortable, she increased her speed and decided to go full on wild.

Back and forth, Daphne rocked against Florian's cock, with each swing digging deeper and deeper into her body, penetrating all of her sensitive nerves.

"Daphne!" he cried, as his wife continued to move faster and faster, swinging her hips with as much force as she possibly could.

Meanwhile, Florian reached over and pulled her down towards his chest. Afterwards, he decided to take full control and promptly, rolled her underneath him— a surprising move that not only caught her off guard, but also excited her, too.

Stretching her legs further apart and wrapping them around his waist, Florian moved his hips forward and slid his cock right through her wet opening, as he worked to untie the front corset of her dress.

Once her breasts were fully exposed, he bent down and began to lick and suck on her pink nipple. Instantly, she moaned with bliss.

"Aaaahhhh… Florian… this feels amazing!" she screamed with pleasure.

Her sincere happiness brought him immense pleasure. And so,

eager to further please her, Florian delved his cock even deeper into her, thrusting harder than ever before. Rocking his hips forward, as he mercilessly pounded her into oblivion. Claiming her as his own, over and over again…

"Oh God!!!" Daphne yelled, as she tugged against the back of his blouse.

"You're almost there," he told her. "Come for me."

Just as he desired, Daphne surrendered to his wishes. By now, her thighs were soaking wet, with her inner juice leaking down her legs. Meanwhile, as Florian thrusted into her… over and over… and over… again… Daphne closed her eyes shut and lost herself in the moment.

A few minutes later, she reached her climax and soon afterwards, he did, too. For a long while, the happy couple just rested there motionless on the ground, enjoying the beauty of the garden, as they snuggled together within each other's loving arms.

Afterwards, as Florian peacefully slept away, Daphne stared at him and happily smiled.

"What would it be like to have a child with you?" she quietly whispered out loud to herself.

"Would they have your nose or mine? Your sunshine blonde hair or my fiery red locks? Your lapis blue eyes or my emerald green ones?"

Finally, as Daphne pondered about these thoughts, she glanced over at the laurel tree and knew that come the twenty-first of March, she now had one important task to accomplish.

Hours later, as the crown prince and crown princess made their route back to the palace, they managed to bypass a maze of bushes. Curiously, Daphne stopped in front of it and asked Florian about its unique design.

"This is an unusual maze," she remarked, as she carefully observed the scene around her. "I've never seen one so large before."

"It's called, The Lover's Maze," he replied, hoping to extinguish her curiosity.

"Oh really? How interesting! Why is it called that?"

"Well, according to legend, if a lover can travel through this maze to reach the end and discover their mate on the other side," he began to explain, "Then, it means that their love is true and eternal. For if one can successfully pass through this complicated maze, then nothing else in this world is unattainable for the happy pair. In the end, their love will overcome all obstacles. Therefore, they will be united together, for all eternity."

"That's so romantic!" Daphne exclaimed. "Does it matter which pair enters into the maze?"

"Actually, it matters not," Florian answered. "Either the female or the male can venture through it. Though, in practice, it's generally the male who assumes the quest."

"And who built this maze to begin with?" she inquired.

"That, no one really knows for sure," he shrugged. "It's been there since the kingdom's founding. Perhaps, the Goddess Persephone created it to test the bride of her son."

"If that's true, then did the bride succeed?"

"She must have, for my bloodline exists," he grinned. "Had the bride not succeeded, then today, House East would not be seated on the throne."

"So, I see," she smiled on.

Linking his wife's arm within his, Florian turned to her and with a stern voice, he commanded, "Please, whatever you do, do not come here without me."

"Why? Is it dangerous to go through that maze alone?" she asked, cautiously.

"Let's just say that most people will never make it out… quite the same," he revealed. "If you were to get lost inside of there, then you might not ever return back to me as you are, right now. So, please, avoid this place at all costs."

Looking straight into his eyes, Daphne swore, "I promise, Florian. I will only come here, if you're here with me."

And with that vow, the royal couple proceeded to return back into the imperial palace.

# Chapter 18

## *A Midsummer Night's Dream*

"**G**oddess Persephone, please accept my prayers," Daphne softly chanted, as she kneeled down against the mossy green grass and bestowed a golden egg in front of the famous laurel tree, which grew within the heart of the imperial palace's main royal garden.

The golden egg was decorated with painted images of green laurel leaves and pink waterlilies that encircled its sphere. After spending the past few days delicately brushstroking the oval-shaped object with paint, the crown princess was ready to place her cherished egg underneath the legendary laurel tree as a sacrificial offering to the founding goddess in exchange for a wish.

After all, today was the twenty-first of March, the first day of spring. Naturally, this offering meant that Daphne's secret wish to the famous goddess was most likely to come true. Even though it was still early in the day; however, come nightfall, her wish was ultimately destined to happen, once the blue moon reached tonight's dark sky.

But the truth was, Daphne's wish was already *granted*… albeit, *early*. As of yesterday, she had met with the palace's physician and was delivered with the unexpected happy news.

After suffering from an overall poor appetite and consistent morning nausea for the past few weeks, as it turned out, the crown princess was expecting. In a few months' time, Daphne and Florian were going to become the proud new parents to a future prince or princess.

Ironically, their time spent at her family's cottage was indeed, a milestone event. For it was there, at that blessed site, that Daphne conceived their unborn child. And now, her ever-slightly growing belly finally made sense.

Although Daphne wanted to share this happy news with Florian immediately; however, tonight marked the upcoming spring festival. Come nightfall, the Midsummer Night's Dream Gala was going to be held at the imperial palace. And as such, the entire palace— along with the king, the crown prince and all of their fellow courtiers— were currently busy running around the palace, like madmen.

Therefore, given these circumstances, Daphne decided to withhold this joyful news temporarily— at least, until after tonight's festivities. After their upcoming celebrations, Florian was going to receive the happy news that he was about to become a new father.

At long last, Crown Prince Leopold and Prince Tristan were finally going to gain a new cousin!

At the stroke of eight o'clock in the evening, the Midsummer Night's Dream Gala officially came into session. An infamous spring ball to top them all. Throughout the imperial palace's royal gardens, thousands of fairy lights and garlands of freshly plucked florals were decorated everywhere, on all corners.

Every tree, plant and bush were adorned with either silk ribbons or silver bells, along with hundreds of beaded and illuminated lights— similar to the appearance of decorated Christmas trees found within Daphne's native homeland of England.

Meanwhile, the palace was surrounded by an array of endless flowers, all in bloom. From the front doors to the back doors, to the outside columns to the indoor columns, to the staircases' railings to the hanging chandeliers, floral decorations were all proudly out on display. Rich and vividly colored floral garlands, which came in a variety of shapes, shades and types, including: bubblegum pink carnations, white lilies, deep blue and violet irises, sunshine yellow roses, crimson red tulips and lilac hyacinths, to name a few.

Tonight, the eastern white imperial palace was a mecca for all gardeners and flower lovers, alike. A living and thriving museum, consisting of fresh blooming flowers, all meant to usher in the new spring season.

Furthermore, in honor of their Goddess Persephone, her statues were all out on public display. Similar to the stone statues of the Virgin Mary found in England, the eastern kingdom also showcased some of their local artwork depicting the spring goddess as an innocent and virginal fair maiden, wearing a plain white cloak with her face humbly gazing down below towards the ground, while carrying a bouquet of baby's breath and lilies of the valley flowers. Meanwhile, other statues on exhibit showed her as a young mother holding her newborn son, the first emerald prince and ruling king of the eastern throne.

Judging by the large turnout, it appeared that almost everyone who received an invitation to tonight's ball actually came. Apart from the dances, fine feasts and entertainment, many had also traveled far and wide in the form of a religious pilgrimage, determined to pay their respects to the Goddess Persephone tonight by her sacred laurel tree.

According to Lavinia, many guests had already left their eggs underneath the blessed site, in the hopes of their prayers and offerings to be granted this year under the blue moon. Furthermore, Lavinia's assistant, Hyacinth, gushed that many lovers were already busy touring the nearby maze, as well.

Even though Florian previously warned her not to venture near the path of the maze; however, at the same time, Daphne also couldn't help but wonder that if one day in the near future, he'd later decide to change his mind and take her there, himself. After all, if other couples participated in the maze event to prove their love for their partners, then why not them, too?

As the happy couples danced the night away at the ball, Daphne finally made her appearance as she descended down the grand staircase, dressed in an exquisite and form-fitting gown that was custom made just for her.

It was a sparkling ivory mermaid gown, which contained hundreds of freshwater pearls and marquise cut white diamonds, which were individually hand sewn onto its silk material. Additionally, the gown's sleeves were made out of a string of pearls, which elegantly hung off her shoulders like an extra set of jewelry.

Meanwhile, her decolletage was slightly exposed, revealing just the upper half of her bosom. Space enough to showcase her new emerald cut diamond necklace, which also matched her pair of diamond studded earrings. A new collection of jewelry, which she had most recently acquired from Jerrica's boutique, curtesy of Florian.

In honor of tonight's festivities, Daphne wore her long red hair down in loose curls and above her head, rested the Lover's Knot Tiara. The tiara was comprised of a hundred miniature pink pear-shaped freshwater pearls, along with matching pink diamonds, which encircled each individual set of pearl.

Although Daphne was recently bequeathed with several dozens of tiaras from her husband; however, in honor of the Midsummer Night's Dream Gala, she decided to wear this particular tiara, which was previously owned by her late mother-in-law.

According to her ladies-in-waiting, the Lover's Knot Tiara was a beloved piece of the late queen. Therefore, in honor of Florian's mother, Daphne decided to wear Queen Ophelia's famous tiara to tonight's ball.

Lastly, the crown princess wore a pair of glass slippers, a pair of white satin gloves and carried with her an ivory feathered fan. Just by gazing at her at first glance, it was clear to anyone who attended tonight's ball that Daphne was truly elegant and regal. A real princess come straight to life, plucked directly out from an enchanted fairy tale. From maiden to crown princess, tonight's ball was truly her *Cinderella's* magical moment.

As the emerald princess proceeded to take her first steps down the grand staircase, she was suddenly saddened by the thought that her sister and brother-in-law were not going to attend this grand party. Unfortunately, Violet was well into the advance stages of her pregnancy. Therefore, it was no longer safe for the queen to travel so far away from her home.

While Daphne sympathized with Violet's reasoning for missing tonight's ball due her medical condition; however, she still felt disappointed by the outcome. But in truth, the crown princess could also relate to her sister, as well.

After all, in a few months' time, she, too, was also going to find herself in a similar state. Soon enough, Daphne was going to become a mother this year and then, her entire life as she knew it was going to forever drastically change. Albeit, for the better.

Smilingly, a pregnant Daphne scanned across the ballroom and happily recognized a few familiar faces. There was, of course, Florian's sister and brother-in-law, the Duke and Duchess of Starlight, as well as Lord and Lady Bleeding Heart and Lord and Lady Cherry Blossom.

Furthermore, there were the northern and southern royals, as well as Lady Petunia Aster and her husband, Ivan. Additionally, since returning back to the eastern kingdom after visiting her sister's palace, Daphne had most recently enjoyed a session of high tea with Lady Petunia, who was already, becoming a fast and dear friend.

Up until now, the emerald princess did not catch sight of her husband anywhere near her vicinity; nor Esmeralda for that matter. However, whether or not Esmeralda came to the ball; either way, it no longer mattered.

At long last, Daphne finally made peace in her heart with regards to her husband's former fiancé. In the end, Florian chose *her* and not his childhood friend; therefore, she felt convinced that she no longer needed to worry about their future together, after all.

For the first time in ages, Esmeralda arrived to the annual Midsummer Night's Dream Gala with a sole mission: seduce the emerald prince. After years of attending this infamous ball, while also desperately trying to woo her beloved's fickle attention and affection in the past; this time around, our villainess was determined to succeed, once and for all.

If she couldn't have his heart, then she'd gladly settle with a blissful night spent in bed with him. Princess Daphne might have owned his heart, but one way or another, Esmeralda would steal his body. Claim his manhood as her own. Make love to him endlessly, like the world was ending. Ignite all of his hidden desires, by mercilessly *fucking him* over and over again. Doing all the naughty and forbidden sexual acts that his wife would never dare to do with him…

In the end, Esmeralda was going to conquer him. And once she had him nestled away within her loving arms, then she'd convince him to divorce his wretched whore of a wife and remarry her, instead. To make her the true emerald princess. A future queen-in-waiting, just like their mothers had always envisioned her to be, up until *his betrayal.*

But before this whimsical dream could finally become a reality, Esmeralda first needed to ensure that Florian took a sip of her magical love potion. For days, she secretly worked extra hard to brew this special drink, just for him. It was the very first time that she had ever concocted such a thing before. Therefore, she wasn't entirely sure as to how this love potion was going to affect him, overall.

According to her grimoire, the love potion was designed to ignite the hidden passions and repressed sexual desires onto the recipient. While the potion could never replace the act of true love that's organically formed within one's own heart out of their God-given free wills; instead, it held the potential power to create lustful madness to encourage a person to give in to their sexual desires with the first person standing before them— similar to a cupid's arrow of love.

And so, this new love potion was a gamble. As to how long the potion's effects would last, she really wasn't sure. In truth, the grimoire was quite vague.

Based on her research, Esmeralda just needed to ensure two things: 1) That Florian drank a liquid that contained at the very least, a single drop of the love potion and 2) That Esmeralda was standing right by his side as he drank it.

Otherwise, if he stood next to another woman as he sipped it, then his lust would be inadvertently directed towards that other person. Therefore, come heaven or hell, Florian absolutely needed to drink the love potion next to her, in order for all of her dreams to come true!

With her dark black hair wildly streaming down behind her back and wearing a black velvet form-fitting mermaid gown, with a plunging neckline extending down towards her belly and a slit showcasing her slender thighs— which by now, was practically her everyday uniform— Esmeralda double checked to ensure that her love potion was still safely secured against the black garter belt that was attached to her inner thigh.

Much to her pleasure, it was still resting there. Now, all she needed to do was to drop a single ounce of the potion into a drink and graciously offer it to Florian to gulp down. And then, just like magic, the deed was guaranteed to work! The crown prince was as good as hers!

Meanwhile, Esmeralda was currently standing all alone at the ball, without a chaperone, a partner or even, her own family members by her side. Even though her parents previously begged her to stay at home, Esmeralda simply refused to honor their request. Regardless of the cruel gossip and gruesome stares directed towards her by tonight's judgmental crowd, she still couldn't help but sigh underneath her breath.

By now, Esmeralda was used to it. One way or another, she was hated by *everyone*. All throughout the eastern kingdom, just about every citizen alike had despised her.

After all, she was the wicked former fiancé of the emerald prince. The woman, whom the crown prince, himself, had publicly snubbed in exchange for a foreign bride. In the eyes of their kingdom, Esmeralda was a wicked witch and unworthy of their beloved heir's love. *A true villainess.*

Even when she was still his fiancé, no one else around them ever seemed to care for her. Not to mention, at the academy, Esmeralda was always a loner. Excluded by society. Was it because she was too free willed or a bit of a rebel? That she wasn't the typical fairy tale princess, like the others? Or, that she was too clever and smart for her own good? After all, Esmeralda used to have the highest grades of her class back in the day.

And because of these reasons, she turned her back against the world… all except for Florian. In fact, long ago, the crown prince was her only friend in the entire world. That's why, when he finally decided to abandon her, it was *extra* devastating for her.

But Esmeralda was also a lover of history, and she was well accustomed to the legendary tale behind the former Queen Vera of the West. She, like her, was a wicked witch and once upon a time, was also gravely misunderstood by the public.

Perhaps, this is why Esmeralda came to admire Vera so greatly, for they were very much alike. Both were victims to a crown prince, who traded them in for a more popular bride. Sadly, in the end, women like her always seemed destined to remain alone.

However, Esmeralda refused to accept such a lonesome fate. As the Goddess Persephone as her witness, she was going to get her happily ever after! Come hell or high water, she was going to get Florian to drink that potion, if it was the last thing she did!

And now, standing in the middle of the ballroom, Esmeralda searched through a sea of endless people for a glimpse of her beloved prince.

"Just where in the devil is he?" she asked herself, with her hands resting alongside her hips.

After taking a few turns around the dancefloor, Daphne already felt tired and out of breath. Perhaps, it was due to the extra height found on the heels of her new glass slippers, or the fact that she was pregnant and feeling a bit weaker than usual.

Either way, the crown princess decided to take a seat in the back corner of the ballroom to rest. Luckily, for her, her personal knight, Atherton, was right there by her side.

"Atherton, do you mind fetching me a drink of lavender rose lemonade?" she asked him. "I'm afraid that all the exercise exerted from my last dance with Lord Puck has made me a bit parched."

"But of course," Atherton replied, with a bow.

Even dressed in a full set of armor, Daphne could always recognize

Atherton from afar due to his exceptionally tall height. Otherwise, it'd be almost impossible to tell him apart from all of the others knights wearing the same silver uniforms.

"Your Grace, I'll return in just a second," he told her.

Meanwhile, Daphne proceeded to fan herself with her feathered fan, as she waited for Atherton's arrival. Unfortunately, the ballroom was a bit too warm for her liking.

If given a chance, then the princess would have much rather have sat outside to enjoy the fresh air, instead of remaining inside of this stuffy ballroom, surrounded by a large crowd of people.

A few minutes later, Atherton returned back to Daphne's side and handed her a drink, along with an enclosed envelope.

"What's this?" she asked her knight, as she took a sip of her much-needed drink.

"It's from the crown prince," Atherton explained. "His assistant delivered it me, while I was preparing your lemonade at the buffet."

"Oh!" exclaimed Daphne, excitingly.

Whatever Florian's reasons were for drafting her a letter during the ball was most intriguing. Perhaps, this was the reason as to why she hadn't yet stumbled upon him at the party, thus far? Either way, Daphne's curiosity got the best of her.

Eagerly, the crown princess tore open the envelope and reached in for her letter. It read as follows:

*My fairest Daphne,*

*Tonight, under the moonlight, I intend to partake in the maze trail to proclaim my eternal love for my beloved emerald princess.*

*Please come and join me at the maze at once.*

*With Love,*

*Your Husband*

Without a further delay, Daphne promptly rose up from her seat and slammed her empty glass of lemonade down onto a nearby table.

"Atherton," she commanded, "Please escort me to the maze, immediately."

And so, with great haste, Atherton escorted the crown princess outside into the gardens, as Daphne quickly made her way to meet with her beloved crown prince.

"What is it, Esmeralda?" Florian asked her in great frustration, with his voice sounding as annoyed as ever. "Please, whatever it is, say it quickly and get to the point."

"I understand that you're busy," she began, nervously, "But for old times' sake, let us have a drink outside on the balcony? Underneath the moonlight?"

After encircling the ball for an entire hour, Esmeralda finally spotted the crown prince. Much to her delight, Florian wasn't by Princess Daphne's side. Instead, he was gathered around by his old mates and apparently, discussing business matters relating to the welfare of the kingdom.

"I don't have time for drinks," he barked, as he rubbed his forehead.

"Especially, with *you*."

His choice of words instantly wounded her. Already, his anger felt like a blow to her already crushed heart.

"Listen," she spoke directly, with much determination, "Our engagement ended so abruptly that I never got any closure from it. A drink with me is the least you can do."

"Esmeralda," he warned, "How much closure do you need? I've already made my intentions well known to you about ending our engagement *for years*. It's *you* who refused to accept it. Like I've always said, you cannot force love. However, if it's friendship that you wish for, then I'd like to offer us a truce."

"A truce?" she blinked in surprise. "You actually want to extend an olive branch with *me*?"

"Why not?" he grinned. "We were always friends before, were we not?"

"I suppose, but still. You were my fiancé."

"And now, I'm not," he reminded her.

Taking in a deep breath, he explained, "None of this is your fault. I never blamed you. If anything, I fault our mothers for pushing us into an early engagement that wasn't suited to either one of us. You're a bright, intelligent and a strong young woman. One day, I hope that you'll find that special person, who will set your heart aflame. Just like my own darling, Daphne."

*Daphne*, cursed be that name, Esmeralda thought to herself! If ever she hated a woman, then the emerald princess was that *loathed female*!

"Come now, let us enjoy a glass of lavender rose lemonade," Esmeralda pressed on. "A final drink to celebrate the end of our union and the beginning of your marriage to the princess."

"Very well, one drink," Florian finally agreed.

But as fate would have it, at the precise moment that the crown prince was about to take the tapered drink from off of Esmeralda's hands, Lord Puck unexpectedly arrived onto the scene.

"Lord Puck, what brings you here?" the prince asked the young lord.

Lord Demetrius Puck, the tall, dashing, chestnut brown-haired and brown-eyed eldest son of Count Lysander Puck. He was another young aristocrat, who grew up alongside Florian and Esmeralda at the academy. A rich heartthrob, whom many young debutantes of all classes flocked to. Or, at the very least, dreamt about flocking to.

In truth, Lord Puck was rich, handsome, single, but most important to note, *picky*. And it was because of his strong noble-like character and exceptionally high standards reserved for his perfect future bride, that, needless to say, resulted in leaving a long line of unsatisfied ladies behind him, all suffering from unrequited love and a broken heart.

"I must say, Florian, you've made a fine choice with regards to your bride," he complemented the crown prince.

"What makes you say that?" asked the prince.

"Well, I recently danced with the crown princess, myself. I must confess, she's as elegant as she is graceful. A fine future queen she shall be."

"Thank you," Florian gushed with pride. "By the way, where is my wife? I haven't seen her all night."

"Oh, I believe I saw her leaving the ball with her knight by her side. From what I overheard; she's heading towards the maze, as we speak."

"The Lover's Maze?" Florian's heart instantly dropped down to the pit of his stomach.

Why was Daphne headed there, he thought to himself. Previously, he had specifically warned her not to go out there and most importantly, *without him*.

Furthermore, given that tonight was the Midsummer Night's Dream Gala, then the maze was sure to be an obscene scene, filled with ungodly orgies. Lovers freely exploring their sexualities openly, without any fear nor shame.

"I must leave at once!" Florian suddenly proclaimed, as he immediately rushed out of the ballroom, running as fast as he possibly could out into the gardens.

Meanwhile, Esmeralda stood there, frozen and in shock with the realization that her plans had literally fallen into ruin within the blink of an eye. However, things were only about to get even worse for our villainess. For at that very second, Lord Puck quickly grabbed the second drink of lemonade off from Esmeralda's hands.

"Thank goodness, Esmeralda, you've got an extra spare drink," Lord Puck remarked. "I'm simply parched after all these dances."

Much to Esmeralda's horror, Lord Puck quickly gulped down the glass of lemonade. Within seconds, he managed to finish the entire drink, all in one session!

Oh no, she thought in panic. Unless she managed to find another lady to stand in her place, then she was ultimately going to fall victim to the effects of the love potion!

"Lord Puck?" she asked him, nervously.

Already, her heart was beating at an accelerated rate, for there was no other lady standing near her vicinity to switch places with.

For a long second, Lord Puck appeared to be standing quietly, with no expression found upon his sweet and handsome face. Looking as unaffected and as normal as possible.

Was it plausible that perhaps, her love potion had failed? Maybe, Lord Puck was somehow immune to her lust spell, after all?

But then, something drastically changed in his demeanor. No longer was he the dashing and proper gentleman; but instead, he now held the wild expression of a rake. A devious and seductive playboy, ready to claim his next female victim.

"Please," he spoke with a devilish grin, as he quickly grabbed a hold of her waist and pulled her over to his chest.

And then, whispering into her ear, he demanded, "Call me, Demetrius."

# Chapter 19

## *Lost in a Maze*

Underneath the moonlight, Daphne stood in the center of the night garden and waited for Florian's arrival. Much to her disappointment, the crown prince had not yet arrived. Based on the urgency of his letter, Daphne presumed that he would have been here already, waiting for her. But rather, the emerald prince was nowhere to be seen.

Instead, the garden was filled with lovers, all throughout. In fact, the maze was covered with hundreds of naked bodies, consisting of both men and women alike, all proclaiming their heartfelt emotions and expressing their love so freely, out in the open field. Tonight, shame nor modesty, were a part of their vocabularies.

Instead, men and women happily partook on their grand sexual affairs out in the garden, most explicitly. Many fucking away underneath the blue moon, while visiting the famous maze. Shockingly, several groups of men and women came together with multiple partners, all at the same time.

In reality, it was an adventurous orgy party in action. Even the wonderous romances that Daphne had previously read from the pages of her beloved romance novels couldn't ever dare compare to the obscene scenes taking place right now, before her eyes.

Although the princess had read many steamy love scenes from various romance novels pertaining to such infamous parties; however, she never expected to *witness* a real one taking place at the palace's grounds, with her as a bystander. In fact, Daphne and Atherton seemed to be the only ones left standing and still wearing their full sets of clothes!

"Is it always like this?" Daphne asked her knight.

"Only during the Midsummer Night's Dream Gala," he replied. "It's an excuse for these lovers to go wild."

The word *wild* was truly an understatement. Meanwhile, as the Goddess Persephone's laurel tree was filled with a crowd of young ladies presenting their decorative eggs in the hopes of being blessed with a child; the maze, on the other hand, was consumed with couples striving to *conceive* a babe at this going rate!

Perhaps, this was the *real reason* as to why Florian had warned her about visiting the maze without his presence. Had it not been for Atherton, then Daphne was surely to fall victim into becoming an active participant in this lustful gathering. In fact, along her journey, a few men had already tried to woo her. Luckily, Atherton quickly got in the way to protect her virtue.

But as Daphne glanced across the fairy lit night garden, she managed to recognize a few faces from the crowd. Much to her surprise, she caught sight of a few couples, whom she never would have guessed were sexual partners in the first place.

For one, there was Pascal, the court jester, who was clearly making love to Isabella, one the palace's musicians. Then, there were her own darling ladies-in-waiting: Marcia, April and May. And based on the looks of it, Marcia was sleeping with Caldwell, the palace's chef; while April and May were engaged in a rough threesome with a hunky knight.

In reality, it was an ungodly scene that Daphne preferred to avoid. Innocently, she had originally foolishly presumed that the maze was going to be filled with young lovers, all seeking to prove their eternal loves to their partners in the form of a harmless race. Instead, she was brutally wrong. In truth, there weren't any active participants involved in a race. Instead, they were all engaged in various sexual acts.

At practically all corners, naked men and women were either lounging away or drinking or fucking in every possible position imaginable. Some, were fucking against the bushes, while others hid underneath the trees. Others opted to rest openly against the mossy green grass, while enjoying the moonlight and sparkling stars shining high above them. And at every turn, clothes were scattered all throughout the premise, with moans and groans that could easily be heard loudly from all directions.

Overall, the maze wasn't just a contest location to prove one's love and loyalty to their partners through the means of an innocent game; instead, it was a public field dedicated for lovers to succumb to their forbidden desires through sexual acts performed underneath the blue moon. A night built on burning passions, hidden desires and lustful temptations.

Sensing Daphne's uneasy discomfort, Atherton asked, "Shall we return back to the ball, Your Grace?"

Even though the princess still preferred to wait outside for her husband's arrival; however, Atherton was right to ask her to leave. By now, Florian was already late. Furthermore, if she was to remain standing out here alone, then it was only going to be a matter of time before another man sought to approach her again, asking for sex. After all, the garden was practically a betrothal.

With a heavy heart, Daphne was prepared to admit defeat.

"You're right," she sighed. "Perhaps, we ought to return back to the ball, after all."

And just as she was about to reach for her knight's hand, someone else from behind managed to strike his head hard with a silver lance. Instantly, Atherton fell straight down onto the ground. Alas, her knight was lying on the grass, completely unconscious.

Out of fear, Daphne looked straight ahead and sure enough, there was a second knight standing right before her. Except he wasn't wearing the standard silver suit of armor. Instead, he was dressed wearing a black knight's armor. A uniform that once belonged to the late western evil queen, Vera.

"No!" she cried in horror.

Taking a step back, Daphne instantly fled from the scene. Unfortunately, for her, as she ran, she managed to run into the maze. Due to the lack of fairy lights placed within this area of the garden, the maze was almost entirely left in the dark. And so, as Daphne fled, she tried her best to follow the moonlight.

However, as she ran, she encountered several lovers along the way. Even within the darkened maze, lovers were still here, hiding away and fucking at all corners. Again, some drunkenly leaning against the bushes, while others were passed out on the dirt ground. But either way, Daphne tried her best to avoid them.

Luckily, for the princess, the maze was not as confusing as she initially thought it would be. Much to her delight, the path was actually rather straight forward. A few zigzags here, and a few turns there.

As long as one stayed true to the main path, then the exit was only a few short paces away. At long last, she was going to exit this maze and run straight back into the palace to search for her husband.

But unfortunately, for the emerald princess, that plan of hers was simply not going to be. Instead, at the end of the maze stood the black knight. And just like a pawn piece, Daphne was about to lose in this game of chess.

Meanwhile, as the black knight grabbed her from the behind, Daphne fought with all her might, kicking and screaming at her captor. But sadly, she was no match to her opponent. For at that moment, the black knight placed a wet handkerchief against her mouth. A cloth that was heavily covered in chloroform. Instantly, she fainted.

And as Daphne collapsed into her enemy's arms, she also managed to accidentally drop Florian's letter down onto the ground nearby, as well.

# Chapter 20

## *A Stolen Princess*

After the disastrous failure of her schemes during the Midsummer Night's Dream Gala, Esmeralda sat in her bedroom at Clover Castle and wallowed away in her misfortunes. First, Florian failed to drink her love potion. And second, the *wrong man* drank it, instead!

Unfortunately, for her, Lord Puck was the mistaken recipient of her well calculated lust spell! As much as Esmeralda worked hard to ensure that her original plan succeeded; but alas, in a twist of fate, Florian managed to walk away, leaving his companion, Lord Puck, to drink the tapered lemonade in his place!

But escaping the arms of Lord Demetrius Puck wasn't easy. No, it certainly wasn't! As it turned out, Esmeralda's love potion not only worked, but it seemed to work only *too well!*

As much as our villainess never once took previous notice of her fellow childhood companion, Demetrius; but after last night's unexpected turn of events, she was forced to acknowledge that the proud, respected and honorable nobleman was indeed, besotted with her. Albeit, *temporarily.*

And so, for once, Esmeralda decided to give in to her sexual desires. If she couldn't be with Florian, then she'd take Demetrius as a replacement. After all, it was the Midsummer Night's Dream Gala. An enchanting night where hundreds of lovers gave in to their ungodly desires during the full moon.

At least for one night out of the year, Esmeralda decided to let go of society's expectations of her as being a sheltered aristocrat's daughter. And to instead, join the rest of the carefree and merry lot of lovers.

Therefore, going against her own moral code of honor, Esmeralda slept with Demetrius and thus, lost her virginity to the handsome nobleman. And while she did not love him; she, did, however, enjoy the feel of his warm body pressed against hers, as he penetrated into her womb, over and over again.

With this newfound pleasure, Esmeralda realized just how wonderful sex really was. Indeed, it was blissful. Joyful. Exciting. Thrilling. A wonderous and magical world filled with endless mirth. And now that she had some first-hand experience in this erotic arena, this knowledge was only going to prove handy in the future, when she eventually slept with the man whom she truly loved.

Meanwhile, as they fucked underneath the moonlight like the rest of the hundreds of pairs of lovers, come the next morning, it seemed like the love spell had quickly worn out its magic.

With the setting of the blue moon and the rise of the bright morning sun, Demetrius awoke besides her and with one gaze into his brown eyes, Esmeralda quickly saw the look of regret lingering within them. Alas, the spell was broken and Demetrius was once again, Lord Puck.

"I apologize," is all he said, as he intentionally avoided eye contact with her and instead, lowered his gaze down towards the ground in shame.

"Don't," she stopped him, while keeping her chin held up high. Unashamed of what had recently transpired between them, just mere hours ago.

"Let us speak no more of this," she promptly told him. "Instead, we can simply blame it on the enchantment experienced during the Midsummer Night's Dream Gala."

"Very well," he sighed with relief, as he slowly bent down to kiss her hand. "A secret night of passion to be remembered only by us."

Without a further delay, a very naked Lord Puck arose up from off the ground and quickly put on his breeches, along with the rest of his previously disregarded clothes.

Meanwhile, Esmeralda stared at him from afar and admired his muscular body. As it turned out, Demetrius not only possessed an enormous cock, but surprisingly, the high nobleman was also quite the skilled lover, too. And if she was going to have a one-night stand with anyone other than the crown prince, then she was glad that it happened with him.

In the end, while her love potion with Florian might have miserably failed, it seemed that not everything else went against in her favor. One way or another, her black knight managed to kidnap the princess.

As it stood, Princess Daphne was currently being held hostage down below in her dungeon. It was a good thing that Esmeralda's parents decided to vacation in the neighboring kingdom after last night's ball. With her parents gone, she was free to move forward with her devious plans.

One way or another, she was going to win Florian's heart. And with Princess Daphne held captive in her castle, Esmeralda decided to finally wash up and pay a special visit with the stolen princess.

Ever-so-slowly, Daphne gradually adjusted her eyesight as she struggled to grow accustomed to the darkened cell that she was now residing in. At the moment, the back of her head was consumed with a sharp throbbing pain, as she recalled having been previously attacked by a black knight from the night before.

Remembering that black knights were once a part of the late evil queen's dark army, Daphne was afraid that her deceased great-aunt might have risen back from the grave.

Glancing across her enclosed space, Daphne quickly confirmed to herself that she was indeed, imprisoned. Kidnapped and held prisoner in what appeared to be a dirty and rotting dungeon.

Her environment was dark and chilly, with drips of contaminated water leaking into her cell from up above. Additionally, cobwebs were all around her, along with black spiders and other insects found only in wet and darkened spaces. A stark contrast to her old bedroom back at the imperial palace, which was bright, regal and most importantly, *clean*.

Attempting to scratch the itch lingering on her back, Daphne soon realized that her arms and legs were chained to a chair. Alas, lo and behold, she was a true prisoner. A captive held against her will. Would she survive to live to see another day? Be reunited with her beloved Florian? As it currently stood, no one was here to rescue her.

In the end, Daphne was all alone in a darkened cell, with only a single window that was covered with iron bars. It was a depressing view. This was not what she envisioned her life to be. And now, being chained against her will, there wasn't a single opportunity to escape. What was going to become of her? Or, best yet, of her unborn child?

"I suggest that you stop wiggling in your chair," spoke a female voice. "If you promise to behave, then I will remove those chains."

*That voice*, it sounded awfully *familiar*, Daphne thought to herself. Looking straight ahead, she could only see a glimpse of a dark shadow appear from afar. Based on its outline, it seemed to resemble that of a female's figure. Was it possible that Vera had somehow kidnapped her? And if so, then why?

"Who are you?" the crown princess asked. "Why have you taken me as a prisoner?"

Stepping into the light, Daphne instantly gasped. For as soon as she saw her long black hair and jade green eyes, the princess instantly knew the truth. At long last, her husband's former fiancé had trapped her. And now, it was a full-scale war.

"Esmeralda!" shouted Daphne, angrily. "What is the meaning of this? How dare you!"

"Relax, princess," Esmeralda spoke in annoyance, as she picked at her nails out of sheer boredom.

Apparently, an angered crown princess was nothing to take notice of, nor fear.

"I have no intentions of harming you, *unless necessary*," she told her. "I merely seek to temporarily remove you from out of the picture."

"What do you mean?" the princess cried.

"I just need you away, so that I can try to mend my fractured relationship with the prince. Remind him of what he lost," Esmeralda replied, with a careless wave of her hand.

"All of this can end right now, too," she further instructed. "As soon as you *divorce him*."

"I will never!" Daphne yelled, in defiance.

She might have been chained as a prisoner, but she simply refused to give in to her captor's demands!

"Why not?" asked the young noblewoman mockingly, as she leaned against the bars to Daphne's cell. "Just one letter and the deed is done. Ask for a divorce and then, I shall grant your freedom. A fair deal, is it not?"

"I am *married* to him! I will *not* divorce my husband!" she shouted with much pride.

"Suit yourself," Esmeralda huffed in disgust. "However, unless you decide to part ways with the prince, then I won't release you from this cell. And that, dear princess, is my final verdict."

"He'll come for me, just so you know," Daphne warned her. "I'm his wife.

He will find me, one way or another."

"Are you so sure about that?" Esmeralda teased her. "After all, it's noon and no one from the palace has yet to contact my castle. As far as they're concerned, it appears that you, Princess Daphne, have run away."

"Florian knows that I would never abandon him, *willingly*," the crown princess emphasized to her captor. "Soon enough, he will figure out your schemes and once he does, be ready for his fury."

Resting her hand against her forehead, Esmeralda sighed. After her wild episode last night, along with several glasses of wine, she was now suffering from a bad hangover.

"I'll tell you what, princess," she began, "I will give you the honor to inform the crown prince about the news of your disappearance, directly from yourself."

"What do you mean?" Daphne asked in confusion.

"In a moment, I will ask my knight to release your chains and provide you with some writing materials," Esmeralda instructed. "And with that, you shall draft a letter to your beloved crown prince. Break the news to him of your kidnapping or ask for a divorce. Either way, it really doesn't matter in the end. Because one way or another, I will win his heart again."

"Do you assume that by kidnapping *his wife*, it will somehow win over his favor?" Daphne questioned her.

"You might be his wife for *now*," Esmeralda challenged her, "But once I speak to him in private, then I'm certain that I can convince him otherwise. Your kidnapping is merely an excuse for him to come visit me back at my castle. In the end, *Princess Daphne*, you are only but a *pawn*."

"Then, we'll see about that," Daphne spoke up, with her chin held up high. "Fetch me a quill and paper, and I will gladly write a letter to *my husband*."

"Very well," Esmeralda grinned. "Iago, fetch some writing materials for the princess."

A few minutes later, the black knight, better known as Iago, who was just as remarkably tall as her own person knight, Atherton, promptly appeared in front of Daphne's cell. After freeing the princess from her chains, he guided her to a nearby desk located within the back of her cell. Afterwards, he placed a pad of paper, envelope and a pot of black ink and a feathered quill by her side.

Meanwhile, Esmeralda reached into her pocket and pulled out an hourglass. Flipping its ends, with its grains of sand slipping through its neck, the young witch placed the timer above an empty table located outside of Daphne's cell.

"Given my busy schedule, use this time wisely to draft your letter," Esmeralda told her, as Iago relocked the gates to her cell.

"Afterwards," she continued on, "Give the envelope to Raven, the black bird, over there, and he'll personally deliver it to the crown prince, directly."

Gazing straight across her prison's cell, Daphne caught a glimpse of the black bird, conveniently named, *Raven,* sitting on the ledge of her window.

A second later, Esmeralda and Iago were gone. Once again, Daphne was left alone in the dark with nothing else but a chair to sit upon, a desk to write her letter on and an eager raven resting outside of her window, ready to retrieve her letter like a traveling postman.

"Very well, if I must, then I must," Daphne muttered to herself.

Taking the feathered quill in her hand, the emerald princess plunged her writing utensil into a pot of heavy black ink and began drafting her letter. But rather than writing a letter about her abduction or requesting for a divorce; she, instead, wrote a poem.

A beautiful poem, which came straight from her soul. After all, in her heart, she already knew that the palace had spies located everywhere, hidden across the country. By now, Atherton and Florian must have already figured out that Esmeralda was the culprit behind her kidnapping.

Therefore, instead of having Florian worrying sick about her, Daphne decided to keep her head up and prove to him that her good spirits were still as high as ever. Plus, she also had one very important news to deliver to him, too.

In the end, Daphne drafted the following:

*My dearest Florian,*
*Treasure of my eyes,*
*Pearl of my heart,*
*With eyes as blue as the majestic sky,*
*And hair as bright as the glorious sun,*
*Whose heart I came to miraculously own,*
*How it came to be,*
*I still know not,*
*But either way, it matters not,*
*I might not have loved you at first sight,*
*But as I came to know you,*
*I found myself falling hard,*
*For the man who made all of my dreams come true,*
*Is now, the owner of my beating heart,*
*While we may be apart,*
*Please know that I have no regrets,*
*If given a second chance,*
*I'd make the same choice,*
*I'd still be your bride,*
*Whether you're a Prince or a Frog,*
*It matters not,*
*I love you either way,*
*You're still the owner of my beating heart,*
*Forever and ever,*
*And one day,*
*You'll come to see,*
*That our love brought forth a new life,*
*One that grows in my belly as I write,*
*I hope we will be reunited one day soon,*
*So that we can finally be,*
*A happy family,*
*Just you and I,*
*And the baby in me.*

Afterwards, Daphne signed the letter and sat in silence at the table. For a long while, she contemplated her options.

In most circumstances, she would have fought back and tried her best to physically escape from her entrapment. But unlike her elder sister, Violet, who was more fearless and active than her; Daphne, instead, was a clever thinker.

After spending years tucked away within the dusty old libraries of her family's estates, she was more comfortable with a book in hand than that of a sword. Therefore, Daphne was more accustomed to using her mind, in lieu of her physical strength. Although she was well versed in combat, she was also aware that such actions were also not practical in her current situation.

For one, she was a foreigner in this land. Plus, she was completely unaware of her surroundings. Even if she were able to miraculously escape from this prison's cell by breaking through this small window, then where would she flee to?

Currently, Daphne was entirely unfamiliar with this remote territory, which surrounded her enemy's estate. Heck, she didn't even know the name to this very castle, where she was being held captive in to begin with!

But most importantly, Daphne was pregnant. Therefore, any decisions that she made from here on out, was going to directly impact the welfare of her unborn child. Miraculously, if she were to somehow break through the bars of her window and attempt to climb down, then was it worth risking the possibility of her slipping and falling down in the process and subsequently, miscarrying her child? No, it wasn't.

As it stood, she really was a pawn, sadly. According to Esmeralda, Daphne was just the means to reach an end, so that her captor could finally get in touch with her husband, the crown prince. Therefore, her nemesis still needed her. And most importantly, alive, too.

For if she was killed, then there was no doubt in her mind, that Florian would avenge her death. All potential negotiations on her behalf would come to an abrupt halt by her unfortunate passing.

According to Daphne's calculations, she was *safe*. At least, for now. In the meantime, she just needed to remain patient and wait for Florian's arrival. Because one way or another, she knew that he'd find her. As far as she was concerned, her crown prince was most likely already on his way to rescue her.

With high hopes, Daphne placed the letter into the envelope and sealed it shut. Walking over to her window, she handed the envelope over to Raven. Meanwhile, as the black bird flew away, she took in a deep breath, sat back down, rubbed her belly and prayed for a miracle.

# Chapter 21

## *A Declaration of War*

Rage was not the best word to describe as to how Florian felt at this precise moment. Instead, the crown prince saw nothing but red, fire and fury all around him, as he forcefully pounded his heavy fists against the hardwood of his desk, located within his study.

"Unacceptable!" he yelled in anger at Daphne's personal knight, Atherton. "How could you have lost her!"

"I apologize, Your Grace," Atherton shamefully bowed his head, before his master.

"You were supposed to be her personal guard! Specifically handpicked from my own imperial army!" the emerald prince shouted loudly. "Not to mention, you're as big as a mountain! How could you have been brought down so easily!"

"The culprit came from my behind," explained the nervous knight. "He must have been as tall as I, in order to knock me down so hard."

As upset as Florian was, he wasn't entirely out of hope. Luckily, for him, the crown prince miraculously discovered a letter at the scene of the crime. A letter that he *supposedly* wrote addressed to his missing wife.

"How could she fall for such a ruse? Obviously, this letter was *not* written by *me*," the prince highlighted this key fact over to his knight.

"Well I'll admit, it was rather convincing at the time," Atherton noted. "Even the princess believed wholeheartedly that it was from you."

"I can't blame her," the prince sighed out of frustration. "After all, we've only been married for a few months. And before that, we were strangers. Therefore, Daphne couldn't possibly have been able to distinguish my unique signature and writing style apart from others within a short period of time."

"So, you didn't author this note? The letter summoning the princess to the maze?" asked Atherton, in astonishment.

"No, of course not," Florian replied directly, taken aback by his knight's inquiry suggesting that he'd even write such a wicked invitation.

"And if I were to summon Daphne over to the maze, then it wouldn't have taken place last night during the gala," he further emphasized. "I'd never want her to witness that ungodly view of wild fornication with her own pair of innocent eyes! I'm not that cruel and heartless!"

"Yes, it was a rather blasphemous scene last night," Atherton agreed. "In fact, even a few men tried to have their ways with the princess. But luckily, I was able to intervene in time. Or, at least, before the accident."

"This wasn't supposed to happen," Florian anguished, as he pinched the bridge of his nose. "I promised to *always* keep Daphne safe. Already, I have failed her."

"My Lord, it's not too late," Atherton encouraged him. "We can still save her. First, we must locate her whereabouts, then retrieve her."

"There's no need to hunt around for her whereabouts, I already know where she is."

"You do?" asked the knight in surprise.

"This letter says it all."

"Your Grace, I'm not understanding…"

Fortunately, for Florian, he already knew the culprit behind this false letter. Previously, he'd seen this particular writing style and signature written down onto paper, a thousand times over. At school. At church. At study sessions.

Unfortunately, his former fiancé neglected to conceal her very peculiar key strokes, using the fine sharpened tip of her feathered quill. After all, Esmeralda was the only person, whom he knew who seldom dotted her letter i's and curved her letter t's using a slanted font.

"*This letter*," Florian muttered angrily, as he crimpled up the note tightly with his clenched fist, "Is written by none other than Lady Esmeralda of Clover."

"The Marquis' daughter? But she's a part of nobility!" the knight exclaimed.

"Atherton, crimes can be committed by *anyone*," the prince was quick to point out. "Nobles or commoners, alike. Jealousy and hatred do not discriminate against any persons, regardless of their social statuses."

"Are you certain that Lady Esmeralda is responsible for Princess Daphne's kidnapping?" Atherton dared to pose the million-dollar question.

"Without a doubt," replied the crown prince, confidently. "With every fiber of my being, I know that she's directly responsible for my wife's disappearance. Moreover, I'm fully aware that she's deliberately withholding the princess from me intentionally, too. In fact, I'm certain that my precious Daphne is most likely lying-in a cold, dirty and darkened dungeon as we speak."

"But why would Lady Esmeralda do such a thing? After all, you are the crown prince. Our future king."

"To gain my attention," Florian sneered with great disdain. "And to think, last night I actually tried to offer her an olive branch of peace. How stupidly foolish I truly was."

In all of his many years spent in Esmeralda's company, Florian never imagined how low she would go. Even after delving into black magic and opting to remain as a loner, he still never imagined that she'd turn to the world of crime. To have the audacity to steal what belonged to *him. His darling bride.*

Not to mention, for several years, he made it *very clear* to her that he wished to dissolve their union. Offering her a lifetime of friendship, rather than condemning her to a loveless marriage. Friends above lovers.

And yet, Esmeralda still refused to accept the inevitable. And this time around, she finally went too far. At this point, there was no returning back. No path towards redemption. From this day forward, not only were they former mates, but now, they were also sworn enemies. Sadly, as a result of her vile actions, they could never be friends, ever again.

"But now that we know where the princess is, shall we go ahead and travel to Clover Castle and retrieve her?" asked Atherton, eager to take swift action and save his master.

In a perfect world, the knight's suggestion would have been the ideal plan. However, Florian's kingdom was far from perfect and an invasion into Clover Castle would only result in total disaster. As much as the crown prince wanted lasting peace to thrive within his humble nation, he was also faced with an unfortunate option.

"Atherton, I believe that such wicked actions can only result in one possible outcome," he calmly stated, as he reclined back into his chair. "After all, the Marquis and Marchioness of Clover are members of the aristocracy."

"My Lord, what precisely do you mean?" asked the curious knight.

With a devilish grin resting across the crown prince's handsome face, he simply replied, "Why, it's a declaration of war."

# Chapter 22

## *A Sprinkle of Magic Might Do the Trick...*

For the past twenty-four hours, Florian locked himself within his private study to strategically plan about his next step. At this point, war was the likeliest action to take. After all, the Clovers had unjustly stolen his bride. While the marquis and marchioness were hardly at fault; however, it was their only daughter— the black sheep of the clan— who ultimately tarnished their family's reputation.

Regardless, he'd never be able to forgive their daughter for committing such a grave sin. Oh how, his beloved Daphne must have been suffering down in that wretched dungeon at Clover Castle! Damn Esmeralda to hell for daring to take what *belonged to him,* in the first place!

While Florian always expected that his former fiancé was somehow fated to throw a tantrum as a result of the dissolution of their engagement; however, he never imagined that she'd go so far as to kidnap his new wife as a form of retaliation. To deviously execute a sinister plot to distract him by offering him a glass of lemonade, while her personal knight snuck in and stole the princess right from underneath his nose. But alas, the deed was done. And now, Florian needed to get his act together and rescue his darling wife.

However, sending a fleet of troops onto Clover territory would essential be an official act of war. Unfortunately, the Marquis of Clover owned a fair share of land within his eastern kingdom. Furthermore, their family produced the majority supply of clovers, which the kingdom exported throughout the continent to fund their nation's economy. To destroy a long-term relationship with a key political ally would ultimately prove to be disastrous on his part.

Plus, the continent was still recovering from the last war, which was previously ignited within the neighboring western kingdom. Under Queen Vera's infamous reign of terror, the former wicked witch turned evil queen had imprisoned, tortured and murdered thousands of innocent civilians, all in an effort to control dominion over their land as a brutal tyrant. Thus, as a result of that war, thousands had died, while hundreds of small rural villages were burned down into ashes.

Had it not been for Maximus' and Violet's bravery on defeating Queen Vera, then the war would not have ended. Most likely, that ungodly war would have eventually spilled over into the other neighboring kingdoms, including Florian's very own eastern territory. Had Vera lived to pursue her true ambitions— which was to conquer the rest of the continent to establish a global empire— then Florian would most likely *not* be the current crown prince and his father, King Titus, would have been executed at the guillotine.

After the war, it took several long years for the western kingdom to recover from that devastating reign. Three years to rebuild all of the damaged infrastructures, and five years to repopulate the previously abandoned villages— with some, never recovering at all. Plus, it took six years to regrow their local economy, as well as the economies of the neighboring kingdoms too, including Florian's own country. That's why trade between their nations were so vital.

Now, if Florian was to wage yet another war— let alone, a civil war— then not only would he be dragging his kingdom into ruin, but he'd also grow to become a hated crown prince by his own people, too. After all, there were still many nobles who were loyal to the Clover family. Plus, war was never really the proper route to success, either. One way or another, it was always an ugly option.

Furthermore, if he were to contact his brother-in-law and sister-in-law to tell them about Daphne's disappearance, then he already knew the outcome of that conversation. As a key western ally, Florian only knew too well that King Maximus and Queen Violet would desire a full-blown and epic war to rescue the queen's beloved younger sister. That was a given. However, the risk of innocent lives dying as collateral damage in the process also wasn't the path that he wanted to take, either.

Given these circumstances, the crown prince was convinced that there just had to be another way to rescue Daphne, without thrusting the kingdom into a mass civil war. One way or another, there had to be an alternative option to exercise, in order to keep his citizens safe and away from this potential mess. If only he could somehow sneak into Castle Clover and rescue Daphne, himself.

Suddenly, the lights went on inside of his head. Alas, Florian finally had his answer!

He knew the blueprint to Clover Castle like the back of his hand. Over the years, he spent countless afternoons in the company of his former fiancé at her family's estate. If he could travel back into the castle discretely, then he could sneak into the dungeon, himself.

But to do so, he'd need to take another form. A form so small, that he could easily squeeze through the iron bars of Daphne's cell, while stealing the prison's keys in the process to free her. And to enact this new brilliant plan of his, Florian needed access to two specific items: a grimoire and a magic mirror.

While he might have previously stolen Esmeralda's grimoire in the past; but unfortunately, the palace's traveling magic mirror was currently out on display in his father's throne room. Had King Titus discovered the truth about Daphne's disappearance and his quest to save her, then his father would no doubt, choose war. Therefore, using his father's magic mirror was not a feasible option.

Additionally, his late mother previously owned a second magic mirror of her own, which once hung in the late queen's bedchamber. However, after her death, her magic mirror had accidentally fallen and broken into pieces during its transit while moving into storage, proceeding the late queen's funeral.

Sadly, the nearest magic mirror was located in the neighboring western kingdom. But again, if he asked Maximus or Violet to borrow it, then they'd only grow suspicious for sure. No, he couldn't risk them finding out about their troubles. And apart from his in-laws, Florian didn't feel too comfortable asking the other local nobles, including the neighboring northern or southern kingdoms, either.

Instead, there was only one other person, whom Florian knew he could trust, without question. Someone who was practically family to him. Someone who was wise, reasonable, level-headed and most importantly, wouldn't jump for an all-out war. That person was none other than Daphne's own great-grandmother and good witch: Ruby, the Elder.

"Ruby is the key," Florian happily chanted to himself. "Perhaps, a sprinkle of magic might be the trick needed, after all."

Without a further delay, the crown prince drafted a quick note and attached it to his messenger pigeon. Afterwards, he threw on his red military and golden buttoned petticoat and quickly exited out the door.

Luckily, for him, his great-grandmother-in-law was conveniently residing within his kingdom, in a property located in the heart of town square. And so, with much haste, Florian rode directly on horseback, determined to save his bride, once and for all.

After traveling on horseback for the past hour, Florian finally arrived to Ruby's townhouse. It was a tall brick building that was situated right across from the central water fountain in town square.

Luckily, no one managed to recognize the crown prince on his journey. In a last-minute-decision, he decided to forgo his regal red military petticoat and instead, opted to wear a simple grey woolen cloak. With a dark and heavy hood covering his face and riding on a shire black horse, no one mistook him for royalty.

"I trust that you received my letter. As such, thank you for helping me out," Florian graciously addressed his great-grandmother-in-law.

"But of course," replied Ruby, as she greeted him at the door. "We're family now."

"Not to also mention," the old woman continued on, "I will do everything in my power to ensure that you bring my great-granddaughter home safely."

"I promise that I will," the prince vowed.

"Afterwards, my dear prince," Ruby warned, "You must see to it, that something like this *never* happens again. One way or another, Prince Florian, you've got to give that Clover girl some closure. Right now, she's still holding out on the hope that you'll abandon my great-granddaughter and return back to her side."

"For as long as I live, I vow that this situation will *never* happen, again," the crown prince reassured her.

"Luckily, I believe you," Ruby told him. "However, unless you make a clean cut with this woman, then it will only get worse later on in the future."

"I will," Florian promised her.

"Very well," Ruby sighed. "Shall we get on with our business?"

A few minutes later, the old witch and crown prince were standing inside of her home laboratory. A private study dedicated with shelves displaying an endless amount of potion bottles, books and figurines. A place that resembled a magical curiosity shop, hidden within the pages of a whimsical fairy tale.

Furthermore, the laboratory contained an oversized black cauldron, which was housed inside of a red brick fireplace. But most important of all, was the brass golden magic mirror, which was currently leaning against the opposite stone wall, adjacent to the cauldron.

Reverting her attention over to her grimoire, Ruby explained, "Now, my spell might work a bit differently from the last enchantment that you previously enacted."

"How so?" the prince curiously inquired.

"Well, each spell may vary," she began to answer, "Plus, every witch possesses their own unique style of magical, as well."

"Can you please elaborate further?" Florian pressed on.

"When you first transformed yourself into a frog," Ruby explained, "You were cursed to stay in that form, until my great-granddaughter kissed you, correct?"

"Yes, that's correct," the prince confirmed.

"Right. However, in my version of this shapeshifting spell," Ruby pointed out, "You won't need a kiss to return you back into your mortal form."

"I won't?" asked the crown prince, in surprise. "So, how will I be able to return back into my humanly self again?"

"This is called a time's spell," Ruby revealed. "Which means, my dear prince, that you'll have exactly twenty-four hours to rescue the princess.

Afterwards, you will return back into your humanly form, with or without a kiss."

"Fascinating," Florian acknowledged, with much intrigue. "So, no two witches or spells are quite the same?"

"Correct," she replied.

"And now," she continued on, "Once you're ready, I'll transform you back into a frog and send you off through my magic mirror. From there, your journey will take you to your heart's greatest desire— which, in this particular case, are the dungeons of Clover Castle."

"Ah, one last thing," Florian quickly grabbed a hold of Ruby's arm.

"Yes?" she asked him, with a raise of her brow.

"Can you please help me out with something?" he tested her. "Call it, a backup plan, in the event that anything should go wrong."

"But of course," replied Ruby. "What do you need?"

"I'd like to borrow a spell from your grimoire," he answered, with much determination.

"A spell?" Ruby's eyes widened. "Have you ever been trained in the art of magic before?"

"In a way, yes," he replied, with a sly grin. "After all, my former fiancé was a witch, and I spent countless hours in her company, while I watched her conduct her spells in action. Therefore, if given the right sort of spell, then I'm confident that I can execute it. Plus, it was me who originally turned myself into a frog the first time around, and not Esmeralda."

"You turned yourself into a frog?" asked Ruby in sheer surprise. "I had absolutely no idea. Previously, I'll admit, I always presumed that Esmeralda turned you into your previous green state, and not the other way around."

"I had my reasons," the crown prince revealed.

"Very well, which spell would you like to borrow?"

Grabbing the grimoire from off the table, Florian flipped through its pages, until he came across a curious enchantment that left even Ruby taken aback by the prince's unusual choice.

"Are you certain that you really want this particular spell?" she asked him, out of concern.

"One hundred percent," Florian boldly told her. "I know that this might seem risky, but please trust in me."

Whether or not Ruby approved of her great-grandson-in-law's decision to use a rather questionable and dangerous dark spell as a backup plan to his mission, really didn't matter in the end. One way another, the old witch was faced with a determined young prince, who was willing to move heaven and earth to save his wife from the clutches of hell.

"As the owner of this grimoire, you have my utmost blessing to use this enchantment freely, should you actually *need it*."

Finally, with her permission, Florian promptly ripped off that infamous page from the grimoire and carefully tucked it away within his pocket. Afterwards, he turned his attention over to Ruby and asked for the old witch to get on with the show.

And with the simple wave of her hand, Ruby chanted her magical words out into the open. Within seconds, a green cloud of smoke suddenly appeared from out-of-nowhere and lo and behold, Florian magically transformed into a small and slimy green amphibian.

"Remember," she reminded him, "You have exactly twenty-four hours to remain in this enchanted form. Afterwards, you'll return back into your old humanly self. So, whatever you need to do, please do it quickly."

"I promise… ribbit…," he spoke. "Now… ribbit… take me to the mirror… ribbit…"

Following the emerald prince's command, Ruby bent down and grabbed Florian, the Frog, from up off the floor. Walking over to the magic mirror, she placed the green frog back down onto the ground and wished him farewell.

A second later, Florian hopped through the magic mirror,
determined to rescue his beloved emerald princess, come hell or high water!

# Chapter 23

## *A Leap of Faith*

After sitting in a gloomy and darkened dungeon, Daphne was forced to come to terms and face her hidden fears. All of her life, she hated slimy bugs, tiny insects and every creepy crawler known to mankind. Yet, in the end, here she was, alone and living alongside with these legendary creatures of the night.

Since the moment she arrived to this prison, she encountered countless of spooky critters. From black rats to furry spiders, to fat flies to blue beetles, and then some. In the past, she might have fainted by the mere sight of them all. But now, Daphne had matured so much and was far stronger than ever before.

At long last, the crown princess was no longer bothered by them, like before. Which in truth, surprised even *her*. Slowly, but surely, upon her arrival to this new world, she had inadvertently grown accustomed to the sorts of things that she used to dread in the past. And what she once feared, she was no longer troubled so much by them anymore.

Once upon a time, Daphne hated frogs. Absolutely, detested them. However, in a twist of fate, as karma would have it, she actually ended up marrying one of them. Back then, she might have been a maiden who didn't care for frogs at the time; but now, that wasn't the case.

After falling madly in love with her husband, she no longer minded frogs. In fact, she actually *longed* to see one *again*. For in truth, those slimy green amphibians reminded her so much of her beloved Florian.

Their marriage might have started out as a marriage of convenience, but that was in the distant past. Through Florian's consistent acts of kindness, thoughtfulness, generosity and patience, Daphne came to fall deeply in love with her darling husband for the man that he was. Additionally, it was through that very act of true love, that she was able to conceive a child with him— he, the man of her dreams.

Oh, what Daphne would not give to see him again! At this point, she'd take any one of his many forms. Man or frog, it mattered not. For as long as she was with Florian, then that's all that counted to her in the end.

Suddenly, Daphne heard a noise. It was a loud and high-pitched sound. Based on its tone, it didn't seem to be another fly or a beetle. Or even, a rat for that matter. No, this sounded like a...

"Ribbit...," it croaked again.

Instantly, she recognized that distinctive sound. It was the same noise that she once heard, back at the pond by her family's estate. It could only belong to...

"Who goes there?" Daphne asked, as she quickly jumped up from her seat.

It was impossible for her mind to be playing a trick on her. Indeed, that noise had to be the croaking of a frog. But how was that possible? This prison had no bodies of water stored within it. Frogs weren't supposed to be lurking here within this desolate dungeon.

"Daphne... ribbit...," it spoke.

Unlike the first time, when she nervously heard a frog speak to her back in her homeland; this time around, she was not afraid. Instead, Daphne actually felt relieved. For if there was a frog following her, then it could only be one being: *Florian*.

"Florian? Are you here, my love?" she spoke out into the dark.

"Yes… ribbit… it is me…"

Spinning around her cell, she whispered aloud, "Where are you? My love, I can't see you anywhere."

"Come towards the front of your gate," he directed her.

Following his instructions, Daphne did just that. And lo and behold, there he was.

At first, she couldn't see him clearly in the dark, looming within the shadows. However, his glowing yellow eyes certainly caught her attention. And as she stood still from behind the bars to her cell, Florian quietly hopped his way towards her.

"How did you manage to sneak in?" she whispered to him. "Or better yet, how did you turn yourself back into a frog?"

"I don't have that much time… ribbit… but your great-grandmother… helped me…"

"Ruby, of course," Daphne happily noted. "At least we can always count on her. It's good to have at least one wise grandmother-like figure still living here with us in this realm."

"Indeed," he agreed. "But now… my love… ribbit… I must get you out of here… before it's… ribbit… too late…"

A second later, Florian reemerged in front of her prison's cell, with the light from her window, now shining down upon him. And as Daphne stared ahead, she was once more, reintroduced to her husband's current slimy and green form.

"It's good to see you again," she happily smiled at him. "Even in your green state, you're still as handsome as ever."

"Really? Has your love for me… ribbit… truly blinded you… my love… ribbit."

"Indeed, I believe it has," she gushed. "No longer am I fearful of you. I might have run away from you at first; but now, I'm running towards you.

Knowing you, has officially ended my lifelong fear of frogs. But most importantly, having loved you, what I once found ugly, now, I see nothing short but beauty. In fact, I can surprisingly admit that I actually *like* frogs now. No, in fact, I adore them. I adore them, because they remind me of *you*!"

"My darling… that is… ribbit… without a doubt… the sweetest thing that… ribbit… you've ever said to me…"

Picking him up from off the ground, Daphne looked straight into his bright yellow eyes and with happy tears she confessed, "Florian, I've missed you… oh so terribly…"

"I've missed you… ribbit… too…"

Without second guessing, Daphne leaned down and placed a gentle kiss alongside his slimy green head.

"Oh no!" she cried. "I've kissed you! You'll turn back into a man!"

"Actually, no," he revealed. "I'm under a time spell."

"What's that?" she asked, in confusion.

"It means that your kiss… will not… ribbit… change my shapeshifting status…."

"So, you'll remain as is, in this current green state? But for how long?"

"Twenty-four hours… and then… ribbit… I'll return to… my old self…"

"Did you turn yourself into a frog, in order to sneak into the castle and rescue me?" she asked, with the emerald prince still resting within the palm of her hand.

"Yes," he confirmed.

"But how can we escape from here?"

"I will steal the key… give it to you… ribbit… and then… we'll flee… besides… I know this castle better than… most… ribbit…"

"Brilliant!" Daphne exclaimed, happily.

"Now… my love… just put me down… ribbit… and I'll go fetch the key…"

"Oh, one last thing, my love," she stopped him. "Before anything else happens, I must ask you something. Did you receive my letter from Raven?"

"A letter… no… I only discovered that fake note… from the party…"

"So, you don't know the news, after all," she sighed to herself.

"What…news?" he asked.

With Florian still resting comfortably alongside her inner palm, Daphne brought him upwards to her face and with a warm smile, she told him, "Darling, I'm expecting a baby. In a few months' time, we'll become new proud parents."

In that instant, Florian almost lost it. For years, he admired his best friend and brother-in-law, Maximus, with his children, Leopold and Tristan. Even though Florian was thrilled when he officially became their uncle through his marriage to their aunt; however, secretly, the crown prince also wished for sons of his very own. Children born from his one true love, Daphne. And now, his long-held dream was finally about to come true.

"Daphne… this is wonderful news… ribbit…"

"So, you're looking forward to becoming a new father?"

"Of course… any child born from you… ribbit… is a blessing…"

"Do you think that we'll be good parents?" Daphne asked him. "I don't have much experience with children."

"Nonsense," Florian was quick to respond. "You're an… excellent aunt… ribbit… Lee and Tristan love… you dearly…"

"But what if we mess up? What if we're not ready?" she pressed on. "After all, we're still newlyweds. And I'm still adjusting to my new role as the crown princess. Are we really ready to become new parents?"

"My darling," Florian sought to comfort her, "Nothing in this universe… is set in stone… ribbit… take us… for example…"

"What do you mean?" she asked, with a raised brow.

"Once again… I'm cursed… as a slimly… green frog… while… ribbit… you're held captive… and yet… we're still fighting together… against all… obstacles… ribbit…"

"My love, you're right," Daphne agreed, as she bent down to place another kiss against his small slimly green head.

"The future will always… be a mystery… ribbit… but we must… take a leap of faith… we are good people… my love… ribbit… so we will be… good parents… too…"

"You're right, again," Daphne concurred. "If we can escape from the dungeon of our enemy, then we can also conquer parenthood, too!"

"Indeed… and now… my love… ribbit… let me down… and I will go fetch that key…"

"But how can you do so, when you have no human arms?" asked Daphne, in confusion.

However, a second later, the crown princess got her answer. As Florian jumped down onto the ground, he hopped right through the bars of her prison's cell and traveled away and over to the opposite wall. A place where a pair of shiny silver keys were hanging against a loose nail.

With one powerful leap, Florian hopped high above and successfully managed to pull the keys from right off the walls, while using his long and slimy tongue to snatch it. A few hops later, Florian returned back to Daphne's side and presented her with the set of keys.

Although the keys were covered in saliva, Daphne was still, nevertheless, grateful to have them. Determined to free themselves from their entrapment once and for all, the crown princess tested each set of keys, until she finally found the correct one. Turning it against its lock, she successfully managed to open the gates to her cell and proceeded to finally step out of her enclosed prison.

"Now... my love...," Florian instructed her, "We must move quickly... and discreetly... ribbit..."

Grabbing her husband from off the floor, Daphne rushed straight ahead and proceeded to travel down a darkened tunnel.

"Walk straight ahead... until you reach... an iron door... ribbit...," the prince told her. "Afterwards... we'll go down a flight... of stairs... and... ribbit... we'll reach... freedom..."

Following his command, the crown princess quietly tiptoed against the cold grey stone floor, trying her best to travel both as quickly and as quietly as possible.

"We're almost here," she whispered to her husband.

"Good... now... turn the knob... and open... the door..."

However, unfortunately, as Daphne proceeded to push the iron door open, she was met with the most unwelcomed greeter, standing on the other side.

"Going somewhere?" asked Esmeralda, as she stood in front of the fleeing couple.

"I want to go home!" the princess demanded, at long last.

Lo and behold, Daphne simply had enough of this torture! After spending several days sequestered in a rotting prison, this foul game orchestrated by her nemesis was long over-due for a conclusion! Indeed, the princess was furious!

But as Daphne sought to punch her enemy straight across her face, Iago managed to stop her in the process.

"Take her outside into the courtyard," Esmeralda ordered her black knight. "I'll deal with *him*, myself."

Meanwhile, as the crown princess was violently dragged away from the scene against her will, Florian was left alone on the stone floor to face the wrath of his former fiancé.

"Florian," Esmeralda said, with a sinister smile. "Finally, it's about time that you came."

# Chapter 24

## *A Lover's Cage*

Several hours later, Florian awoke to find himself lying in a miniature and circular golden barred cage. Specifically, a *bird cage*.

Unfortunately, the prince was not sure how long he was asleep in this caged prison, nor how he got inside of here in the first place. As far as he recalled, after Daphne was taken away, he came face-to-face with Esmeralda and then, afterwards, the rest of his memories went blank. One way or another, she must have either drugged him or smacked his head hard enough to leave him unconscious.

Glancing across his vicinity, Florian quickly soon realized that he was somewhere outdoors. With the sun shining high above his golden cage and the fresh floral scent surrounding him, he instantly recognized that he was outside in a garden. Specifically, in the courtyards of Clover Castle.

Judging by the position of the sun, Florian concluded that his enchanted spell was running short on time. In a matter of hours, he was going to transform back into his humanly form and if by chance, he remained entrapped within this tiny bird cage, then it could mean only one thing: *his death*.

For if the crown prince failed to escape from this miniature prison, then the bars to this golden cage was destined to crush him alive from within. Therefore, time was most certainly, *ticking*.

But the worst of Florian's fears were still yet to be realized. For as fearful as he was about his own fate, glancing straight ahead, he saw his beloved bride tied up to a chair, blindfolded. Alas, her arms and ankles were chained. Instantly, out of anguish, Florian's eyes grew tearful.

Witnessing Daphne held captive in such a cruel and merciless state, felt like his entire universe around him was slowly crushing down into pieces. One way or another, he had failed her. *Failed them.* No longer did he care about his own fate; but rather, the fates of his wife and unborn child. And unless Florian acted swiftly, then he and his family were *all doomed.*

"Daphne," he cried. "Dearest… can you hear me?"

"Florian… where are you?" she asked the air, uncertain as to the precise location of her beloved husband.

"I'm across… from you…. but I'm… ribbit… trapped in a… cage…."

"I can't see you," Daphne cried out in despair, as a tear streamed down her eye to reach the bottom of her flushed cheek.

"How long… have we been… ribbit…out here?" he asked, while struggling to keep his own tears at bay.

"I can't tell… but without any food… I'm afraid that I'm starting to feel weak," she confessed.

Damn Esmeralda to hell! By starving his wife, not only was her health currently at great risk, but also the health of their unborn child, too! At this rate, the princess stood a high chance of miscarrying their baby, all due to this long-list of unnecessary and excessive stress!

With the lack of adequate meals, proper sleep and most importantly, *rest*, the crown princess was suffering greatly. Enough was enough! Something needed to be done to end this ongoing misery! And quickly, too!

"I'm afraid that you won't be able to rescue your princess, after all," spoke a female voice from behind him.

"Esmeralda!" Florian shouted. "You've committed… a grave crime… ribbit… against your crown prince… and crown princess… release us at… ribbit.. once… and if you do… ribbit… then perhaps… I may take mercy upon… ribbit… your wretched soul!"

"Mercy on my soul?" the young witch laughingly mocked at him.

"You two might be the crown prince and crown princess for *now*," she emphasized, "But what good did these titles do? As it currently stands, you're *both* my prisoners."

"Have you no… shame… ribbit… have you lost… your mind completely?"

"Florian, this is all *your fault, not mine*!" Esmeralda shouted right back at him. "You picked her, *not me*! Whatever happens now is purely a consequence of *your bad decision*!"

"Esmeralda… you need to let go… ribbit… of this anger… of yours… it's not… ribbit… healthy," he reminded her.

Approaching his cage, Esmeralda bent down to face him and with a sneer, she told him, "Then, *divorce her*. Say the word and then, I'll set you both free."

"No! Don't!" Daphne shouted out loud this time, with her blindfold still covering her eyes.

The princess might not have been able to visually witness the harsh exchange shared between them, but she certainly heard it all.

"Come now… Esmeralda…," he carefully approached her. "Let us discuss… ribbit… this matter… calmly… as adults…"

"As adults?" Esmeralda repeated in disgust. "What's there to discuss? There's nothing else that I want more than for you to divorce this whore of yours!"

"Watch your tongue!" Florian roared, angrily.

But rather than debating with the crown prince, Esmeralda simply giggled instead.

"I can see that there's no reasoning with you, after all," the witch laughed on. "One way or another, the princess has bewitched you. As it currently stands, you will never divorce her out of your own free will."

"I'm glad that… you've only… ribbit… yet to realize… this…"

"I have," Esmeralda agreed. "However, I *don't* accept it."

"As the crown prince… you must… accept my marriage…"

"No!" Esmeralda screamed in protest, as she proceeded to kick the mud from off the ground and high up into the air; which in return, allowed particles of dirt to splatter across the field and subsequently, land near Daphne's direction.

"Daphne!" Florian exclaimed, as he watched the kicked soil splash across his wife's face.

"You are too cruel!" the crown prince shouted aloud in anger.

"Cruel? Cruel? You have *yet* to witness my true wrath!" the witch shouted right back at him.

At this point, neither party was willing to budge. While Florian refused to divorce his wife; Esmeralda, on the other hand, was determined to forcibly end his relationship with the crown princess, once and for all.

"If you want… a role at court… ribbit… I can give one to you…," the little green frog prince proposed. "You want to be the emerald princess… well… ribbit… I can make you a royal… I can arrange for you… ribbit… to marry another aristocrat… a duke… or even.. a foreign prince…"

"You still don't get it, do you?" she confronted him, boldly. "It wasn't just about being the emerald princess. It was about being with *you*! *I loved you*! And still do!"

"Esmeralda… you cannot force… ribbit… true love," he reminded her.

"I know," she sighed, with tears of her own. "I can't force true love, but I can *curse* your bride, instead!"

"Whatever you're thinking… ribbit… don't do it!" he begged.

"It's too late," Esmeralda scowled. "The deed is as good as done."

Turning her back against him, the young witch swiftly walked over towards Daphne's direction. With her ancient grimoire in hand, Esmeralda opened the pages to her book and suddenly began to chant a spell.

> *"Daphne, the Fair,*
> *A Maiden not of our world,*
> *With hair as red as fire,*
> *Unbeknownst to most,*
> *You somehow managed to capture,*
> *The heart of the Emerald Prince,*
> *And now, with a broken heart,*
> *I, Esmeralda of Clover,*
> *Hereby curse you,*
> *Princess Daphne of the East,*
> *To remain as your namesake,*
> *A laurel tree,*
> *For all eternity."*

"NOOOOOOOOOO!!!!!!!!" Florian desperately screamed out in pure agony.

Unfortunately, for the crown prince, it was too late. For as Esmeralda chanted her spell aloud into the world, Daphne was instantly transformed. Within seconds, her body stretched far and wide across, with her torso turning into a trunk, her legs into roots and her arms into branches.

Meanwhile, her signature colored hair was replaced by a set of flaming red leaves. Sadly, the once beautiful and fair maiden was no longer human. Instead, she had fully metamorphosized into a tall and luscious laurel tree.

"What have you done?" Florian croaked, with his eyes filled with endless tears.

"Go ahead and take your time to grieve," Esmeralda carefully instructed him in a low and calm voice, as she finally opened his cage's door to release him.

"And once you're done, then come back to me, so we can properly converse with clear and sensible minds," she further added. "Alas, from here on out, there should no longer be any more distractions."

Afterwards, Esmeralda disappeared into the howling wind. Meanwhile, Florian, still in his frog form, hopped over to his beloved Daphne's side and cried alongside her bark.

# Chapter 25

## *Daphne, the Laurel Tree*

By sunset, Florian had finally transformed back into his former humanly form. Meanwhile, as he was blessed to resume to his old shape unharmed; his wife, on the other hand, remained as she was before: a laurel tree.

"This isn't fair!" the crown prince cried aloud to himself.

In truth, *none* of this was fair. Unjustly, not only was his beloved wife otolon, but his unborn child, as well. To his own horror, they were abruptly taken from his side, far too early. Both mother and child were ruthlessly denied the proper chance to live their lives to their fullest. Tragically, all for the sake of a single woman, who was nothing more than a selfish brat. A vengeful witch. *A heartless villainess.*

For hours, Florian simply sat underneath Daphne's tree and cried an endless amount of tears. Heart-wrenching tears, representing their tragic love, as well as the lost future that they might have shared together with their unborn child.

Now, Florian would never experience the blissful joys of fatherhood. For without Daphne, he could *never* take another wife. In the end, she was his one and only true love. And come hell or high water, he'd continue to remain faithful to her, from now and until eternity.

For years, he had pined for her. Yearned for her, *oh, so desperately*! For seven long and agonizing years, Florian patiently waited for her. Plus, after countless of failed dinner arrangements, balls and dates, he finally gained the courage to search for her directly, himself. And, at long last, in the garden of her family's estate, he finally won her as his bride.

But now, it seemed as if all of his efforts to claim her really had all been for nothing. Within an instant, his dreams were crushed into pieces. One moment, his beloved Daphne was here, standing beside him; and the next moment, she was gone. Cursed as a laurel tree, *for all eternity*.

No, this wasn't fair! This tragic fate was far too cruel! There were so many more adventures that he wanted to share with her, along with their unborn child! But instead, his plans for their futures were all forsaken. Stolen from right underneath the rug, by none other than his own childhood friend!

"Curse be to all that is holy!" Florian slammed his clenched fist against the trunk of her tree.

"Daphne, can you hear me?" he asked aloud, with a hoarse voice.

Sadly, there was no direct answer to his question, other than the sound of pure silence. Even in her cursed form, Daphne was forbidden to communicate with him. Indeed, the woman that he once loved was truly *gone*.

"There must be a way to save you!" the crown prince angrily shouted out into the air.

After everything that they endured together as a couple, it was still too soon to give up on their love so easily. No, Florian refused to accept this tragic fate. Indeed, their romantic tale wasn't destined to end in such great tragedy. No, their love story was fated to be a *happily ever after*.

"I will save you, my love," he vowed. "Meanwhile, I shall seek your vengeance. By the blood of the Goddess Persephone, I will avenge you. My love, I'll restore you back to your mortal self again, and you will give birth to our first-born child. You and I will happily gaze into the eyes of our newborn child, together. Our heir. I promise to set everything right, once again."

Gathering a few twigs and plucking the red leaves from off her branches, Florian crafted a wreath made out of laurel leaves in memory of the late princess. With a heavy heart, a devastated emerald prince placed the new crown above Daphne's branches.

"The next time I return," he spoke, with much conviction, "I'll kiss you again back in your humanly form."

"But first, my love," he continued on, "As much as it pains me, but I must leave your side. Albeit, temporarily. After all, I must seduce and steal the heart of a witch."

With that vengeful vow, Florian quickly fled the courtyard and returned back into Clover Castle. And this time around, he was determined to execute the single most important mission of his life.

# Chapter 26

## *The Heart of a Witch*

"Are you done mourning for your beloved bride?" Esmeralda sneered.

The crown prince didn't need to announce his arrival. Even with her back turned against the door, she was instantly aware of his presence. Like a sixth sense, she could always detect him from afar.

From his signature scent of lilies and honey to the loud tapping sounds of the soles to his boots against the stone floor, Esmeralda remained ever alert to his arrival. After a lifetime of admiration for her unrequited lover, the young witch knew her former fiancé quite well— even if he, in return, failed to take a second glance at her. From a wallflower teenager to a scheming villainess, Esmeralda was always fated to remain *alone.*

"On the contrary," Florian replied, as he took a step into her laboratory. "One needs to care, in order to mourn."

"What???!!!" Esmeralda exclaimed at that shockingly unpredictable statement.

His choice of words certainly caught her attention. Rising up from her chair, Esmeralda promptly turned around to face him, directly. Furthermore, rather than witnessing a heartbroken prince; she instead, saw a man with a determined expression, resting along his handsome face.

With his lapis blue eyes shining brightly against the candlelight, the emerald prince displayed the widest grin. It was a grin not born out of grief, but of mischief. And for the first time in her entire life, he actually *winked at her*!

"Have you lost your mind?" she asked him point-blank.

Even though Esmeralda wanted nothing more than to be the sole object of his affection; however, him being so straight forward like this was also hard to swallow. Even, for her.

"Are you actually Prince Florian? The same man, who's standing before me?"

"Of course, I am," he answered nonchalant, while still maintaining his deep smile and calm composure.

A beat later, he took a step forward, moving towards her direction.

Taking a step back, she said, "The last time I saw you, you weren't only green, but you were also crying for that damn tree!"

"To be fair, *a lot* has changed between now and then," he promptly told her.

"So, what's changed?" Esmeralda gulped, as she leaned back against the edge of her desk.

"I realized that I was under a spell," he shrugged, carelessly. "What can I say, my love? Daphne enchanted me. I was her victim. And now with her gone, her love spell has faded. But this shouldn't come as such a surprise to either one of us. After all, she was the great-granddaughter of a powerful witch."

"Wait… did you just call me *your love*?" she blinked.

"Yes, I did," he proudly declared, as he took another step forward. "And I'll keep on saying that, until you finally get used to it."

"I don't understand," Esmeralda muttered, as she nervously gazed down onto the floor, unable to face him, directly.

"What's not to understand?" Florian asked, as he continued to walk towards her direction. "You love me and I love you. It's as simple as that."

"You love *me*?" she choked.

Only in her dreams, could she ever imagine him saying such heartfelt words. This all was only too good to be true!

In her heart, as much as Esmeralda wanted nothing more than to wrap her arms tightly around him and believe his confession wholeheartedly; however, her mind warned her that his confession wasn't genuine. Even before Princess Daphne's arrival, Florian still refused to acknowledge her. *Love her.*

But all facts aside, wasn't this unwavering attention stemming directly from the crown prince what Esmeralda always wanted from her former betrothed, all along? Regardless, whether or not any of his newfound emotions made any sense, she still wanted Florian's affection, all to herself. It's why she did what she did.

After all, Esmeralda was a criminal now. After kidnapping and cursing the princess, her reputation was forever tarnished. At this point, a guaranteed life-term in prison was in order. That is, unless, she could convince the crown prince, otherwise.

"Florian, why did you wait so long to confess your love for me?" she asked him, directly. "Before your marriage, you easily could have had me… and yet, you ran from me. Why such a sudden change of heart?"

"Perhaps, I've finally learned the error of my ways," the crown prince replied, now standing mere inches away from her.

Taking another step forward, Florian finally reached her side. Leaning down, he whispered into her ear, "And now, I'm ready to collect what's *mine.*"

Without any warning, the prince suddenly wrapped his arms around her waist and kissed her. It was a passionate kiss that was filled with tongue and teeth. Meanwhile, as Esmeralda closed her eyes shut, she reluctantly surrendered her strong will and gave in to this fierce new desire.

And as his tongue glided across her mouth, she happily sighed within his. Meanwhile, his right-hand traveled down towards the opening slit of her dress. Afterwards, he began to roughly massage her inner thighs.

"Have you ever been with a man before?" he groaned.

Suddenly, at that moment, Esmeralda felt a bit ashamed. For years, she had waited for him. Foolishly, saving her virginity for him— he, her fiancé. But after the last Midsummer Night's Dream Gala, she lost her virginity to Lord Puck. And now, she was no longer a true maiden.

"I've slept with a man before," she shamefully confessed to him, with her eyes gazing down onto the floor.

However, instead of anger, Florian casually laughed on. From the looks of it, he even seemed tickled by the mere thought of her past promiscuity.

"So much for saving yourself for me, huh?"

"Excuse me!" she exclaimed. "*You* went on to marry someone *else*. What was I to do? Silently wait around forever, while you worked up the courage to claim me as your mistress?"

"Touché," Florian chuckled.

"Well, so the damage is done," she went on, with her arms folded around her chest. "If me not being a virgin is something that displeases you, then let's just forget about this union, altogether."

"Not so fast," he caught her by the arm, just as she was about to walk away from him.

"I only asked," he continued, "Because I wanted to know if you can handle me, that's all."

"*Oh*," she remarked, in surprise.

Determined to move forward, Esmeralda leaned in and gave him another kiss. At this point, with her body pressed up against the end of her desk, Florian had already used his knees to stretch her inner thighs wide apart.

A second later, her undergarments were removed and flung across the floor. Soon thereafter, the crown prince began to rigorously play with her folds.

"Already, so wet," he bit down against her ear.

Instantly, leaving Esmeralda blushing in the shade of bright red.

"Are you going to put it in?" she asked him, with her head held up high.

"Such a wild one," he laughed on.

"Well, I just want to know ahead of time, so that I can be ready," she told him, confidently.

"Hmm…," he pondered aloud for a brief moment.

"What should I put inside of you first?" he asked her. "My fingers or my cock?"

Instantly, Esmeralda shuddered by that very thought. Fingers or cock… honestly, it didn't matter. As long as *he* was *inside* of her, then that's all she cared about.

"Your choice," she whispered into his ear and then, moved to lick the side of his face.

Chuckling aloud, he promptly replied, "So, I see. Well, perhaps, I'll start with your breasts, instead."

Grabbing her hand, he swiftly brought it over towards the first button of her dress. With a stern expression, he commanded, "Unbutton the top of your gown. I want to see them. *Right. Now.*"

Following the eager prince's demand, Esmeralda unbuttoned her dress to reveal her perfectly round, full and plump breasts.

"No bra," he wickedly grinned. "Plus, judging by the look of your hardened and pink nipples, I can tell that you're already excited."

"I suppose that I—"

But before Esmeralda could even finish her words, Florian instantly smothered her breasts with his head. Ever-so-seductively, he proceeded to lick her nipples with his tongue, before sucking them whole.

"Aaaaahhhh…," she moaned, as she tossed her head back.

"So, soft and perfect," he complemented her.

Acting upon her instincts, Esmeralda tugged at Florian's golden locks within the palms of her hands, as she encouraged him to devour her.

"My body is yours, take what you will," Esmeralda permitted.

"So, are you saying that I can take any part of your body and claim it as mine?" his blue eyes shimmering with mischief.

"Yes," she breathed.

"Including, your heart?" he asked, with a raised brow and a devious smirk gleaming across his face.

"Especially, my heart," she promised him. "It's *always* been yours. Do with it, as you wish."

And with those spoken words, Florian immediately ceased moving.

"Is something wrong?" Esmeralda asked him out of concern, now surprised by his sudden halt.

With a beaming smile filled with blissful mirth… an enchanting smile that even Esmeralda had never seen expressed upon his handsome face before, the crown prince proudly declared, "My Lady, I shall take your offer. Like you previously stated, *your heart now belongs to me.*"

Taking a step back, Florian proceeded to pull a piece of papyrus paper out from his pocket.

"What's that?" she inquired.

"A spell," he replied, with a stern and serious face. No longer was he the same playful lover from a second ago.

Laughing on, Esmeralda stared at her prince and said, "Florian, why are you playing with a random spell at a moment like this? Previously, I was under the presumption that I was going to get your cock rammed inside of me, not to listen to you chant some silly spell, instead."

"It's not a silly spell," Florian replied, as a-matter-of-fact. "As for my cock, it's remaining inside of my trousers, *where it belongs.*"

"What?" Esmeralda asked, now, in confusion. "I don't understand…"

But rather than answering her directly, Florian instead, gazed at Esmeralda's concerned face and proceeded to chant his spell aloud.

*"As the owner of Lady Esmeralda of Clover's beating heart,*
*I, Crown Prince Florian Apollo of the East,*
*Hereby, place upon you, fair lady,*
*An enchanted curse,*
*From hence, this day forward,*
*No longer shall your heart belong to you,*
*But rather,*
*It shall remain hidden away,*
*Within the chambers of this emerald chest,*
*And until the fateful day,*
*When you can earn the love of a righteous man,*
*Who will love you unconditionally,*
*Only then, shall your true love,*
*Be able to break into the chambers of this emerald chest,*
*And return your heart,*
*Back into your chest,*
*Furthermore, as both punishment and as a mercy to your parents,*
*I, hereby, banish you into exile,*
*Never again, can you enter into the Kingdom of the East,*

*the Land of Eternal Spring,*
*And instead, you are now cursed to wander the Great Kingdom,*
*As a heartless villainess,*
*Until you meet your true love,*
*One day in the future."*

Upon chanting this enchanted spell that Florian had previously borrowed from Ruby's grimoire, a gust of lime green clouds suddenly appeared within the room. Afterwards, a dark emerald green miniature wooden chest came from out-of-nowhere.

Its proportions were no larger than the size of two male palms put together. Additionally, on each of its sides were bronze brass latches, along with a single lock found within the center, resembling the form of a golden heart.

"What have you done!" Esmeralda frantically cried, as the green clouds surrounded and consumed her.

"I'm giving you a second chance to redeem yourself," the crown prince proclaimed.

"You've committed a grave crime," he explained to her. "Furthermore, out of pity for your parents, who were kind and good friends to my family, I've decided to send you off on your road to redemption."

Without uttering another word, Florian's spell quickly took into shape. Meanwhile, as the green clouds dispersed around the space and surrounded Esmeralda's vicinity, her heart was actually ripped out from her chest by an invisible force.

A second later, her lost heart was magically escorted across the room, until it finally found itself placed inside of the miniature emerald green chest. Afterwards, the chest closed and the golden heart-shaped lock eventually locked itself shut.

"My heart! It's gone!" she cried out in despair.

"Not forever," he reminded her. "Now, Esmeralda, you shall go out into the world and earn the love of another. Only then, can your heart be restored back to you."

"You should have killed me, instead!" the young witch yelled, as she covered her face in shame with her bare hands.

"It's too late," the crown prince responded, without a shred of regret. "It's time to accept your fate."

Walking over to her side, Florian swiftly lifted up Esmeralda from off the ground. Ignoring her wishes, he promptly carried her over to the opposite side of the room.

"What are you doing?" she demanded, as she attempted to kick and claw against his arms in protest.

"I'm sending you and the chest through the mirror."

"What? Why?" she gasped in horror.

Suddenly, the hopeless realization of her doomed fate finally hit Esmeralda and *hard*, too.

Alas, the crown prince was *not* joking. The damage was truly done. Plus, judging by his foul attitude, Florian was furious with rage. At long last, he was going to ruthlessly punish her for her gruesome crimes and get rid of her, too. In the end, not only was she cursed, but she really was going to be banished into exile, after all.

"Please, don't do this!" she begged, while kicking and screaming out loud. "You will come to later regret this vile deed!"

Attempting to convince him otherwise, the cursed witch desperately pleaded, "I don't need to find another! You're already my one true love!"

Ignoring her insincere speech, Florian proceeded to drag Esmeralda to the front of her magic mirror. Ironically, the very same magic mirror that he had previously used to travel into Daphne's world.

As the former betrothed couple gazed into the mirror, Esmeralda stared on at the magical object and pondered about how much her fate could have been different had only Florian chosen to love her and not Daphne. Meanwhile, Florian stared straight ahead and thought nothing else, but his final farewell to his former lover.

"Goodbye Esmeralda," he finally broke their prolonged silence. "Remember, you can only regain your lost heart, after you win the affection of a righteous man who's worthy of your love. Only then, can your true mate return your heart back into your possession. Until then, Lady Esmeralda of Clover, you are hereby banished into exile."

Without allowing her the chance to protest any further, Florian pushed Esmeralda and her accompanying chest through the magic mirror. And just like that, she was gone.

Afterwards, the crown prince walked over to his former fiancé's desk and opened her grimoire. Flipping through its pages, he finally came across the infamous shapeshifting curse, which the young witch had previously placed upon his wife.

Happily, much to Florian's utmost pleasure, there was indeed, a cure to Daphne's curse. And lo and behold, the cure to such a curse was none other than his wife's most favorite of fairy tales: *True Love's Kiss.*

# Chapter 27

## *True Love's Kiss*

In the beginning of our story, Daphne might have kissed Florian to break his curse as a frog; but now, he must do the same to break *her curse*. However, his kiss can't be any sort of a random kiss.

Although their first kiss didn't require true love… but merely, a simple peck bestowed upon his former emerald green form; however, this time around, their kiss requires something far more intimate. Something deeper in emotion. Meaningful. Heartfelt. A kiss rooted in *true love*.

After stealing Esmeralda's grimoire and reviewing the damning enchantment that cursed his beloved wife, Florian returned back to the courtyard and stood in front of the laurel tree that now encompassed Daphne's spirit.

Silently, Florian constructed a second laurel wreath and placed it above his head, like a royal crown. Bowing his face and prostrating down against the dirt ground, the crown prince kneeled before his crown princess as he began to speak to her directly.

"Daphne, my love," he spoke, with tears streaming down his cheeks,

"Please know, that I love you, unconditionally. No matter which forms you take, whether it be a fair maiden or a laurel tree… or even another inanimate object… I will always love you for *you*."

Rising up from the ground, Florian took two steps forward, until he reached the trunk of her tree.

"From the first moment I saw you, I fell madly in love," he confessed aloud. "At first glance, seeing you, it felt like the wind had knocked me right off from my feet. Meanwhile, as I foolishly sought to capture your wandering attention for seven long years as a royal crown prince, it was ironically, when I took the shape of a slimly green frog that I was finally able to gain your notice and eventually, win you over."

Suddenly, Florian laughed happy tears, as he recalled the first time Daphne had frantically fled his side, when he previously confronted her back at her family's garden.

"Whether I approached you as a man or as another being, you always accepted me for me," he proudly told her. "And I will forever appreciate that warm and welcoming heart of yours."

Resting his hands up against her tree trunk, Florian took in a sniff of the fresh petrichor aroma that surrounded her. It was both comforting and painful, all at the same exact time. Yet, another heart-wrenching reminder of what he had previously lost.

"Daphne," his voice, now cracked and filled with anguish. "I probably didn't say this enough when you were still around, but I love you… so… dearly. You are my first and last love. My one *true love*. I have never loved anyone but you before, nor will I ever love another after you. From here to eternity, I shall always faithfully remain by your side, in whichever form you take. For without you, my love, I, myself, cease to exist."

And now, with his lips hovering but mere inches away from her trunk, he whispered, "Come back to me, my love."

With a hopeful heart, Florian leaned in and placed a heartfelt kiss alongside Daphne's tree trunk. And as he did this, something wonderous and magical was instantly released into the air.

As the prince gazed ahead, he noticed the abrupt appearance of a red gust of smoke. Meanwhile, as that smoke began to dissipate, he soon acknowledged that he no longer felt the rims of a tree around him. Rather, it was the figure of a female, instead.

Suddenly, a flash of a bright and golden light appeared. A second later, he felt a gentle kiss come crash-landing against his own bare lips.

"I heard every word," Daphne told him, as she pulled away from their kiss.

"I love you," he told her again, as he promptly wrapped her tightly around his arms.

"And I love you, too," she said, with a warm smile. "From now, until eternity."

After their happy reunion, Florian proceeded to crown his bride with the laurel wreath that he had previously made in her memory.

"In honor of our love," he proudly announced, "I, Prince Florian of the East, hereby proclaim that the laurel wreath will forever symbolize my wife, Princess Daphne of the East, and the eternal love shared between us. With I, the emerald prince, having loved her, and only her."

With that heartfelt proclamation, Daphne kissed Florian like it was the end of the world. As for the Kingdom of the East, the Land of Eternal Spring, from that day forward, anyone who was seen publicly wearing a laurel wreath within their kingdom, then it was done in direct honor and respect for the emerald princess.

# Chapter 28

## *Happily Ever After*

The next morning, before returning back home to the imperial palace, Daphne and Florian decided to enjoy one last romantic adventure together. And so, in the courtyards of Clover Castle, underneath a yew tree, the emerald prince and emerald princess made passionate love in celebration over the defeat of their adversary and her curse.

"Florian, I love you," Daphne cried, as her front chest leaned against the yew tree, while Florian fucked her from her behind.

Sliding his hardened and erect cock inside of her, Florian proceeded to thrust into her womb fiercely, as he rammed his dick against her most sensitive of nerves.

"Oh, God!" she yelled loudly, as the prince tugged a hold of her red hair with one hand, while his other rested against the side of her slender hip.

Plunging his hips forward, the crown prince proceeded to pound inside of her, pumping as fast and as hard as he possibly could.

"Deeper," Daphne begged, as her fingernails clawed against the bark of the tree.

"Anything for you, my love," Florian replied as he kissed her back and further increased his speed, plunging even deeper into her womb and thus, sending shockwaves of pleasure from within her.

"Aaaahhhhh…," she happily moaned.

A second later, Florian pulled Daphne over to his chest and then, he carried her off and placed her above a bed of grass. Once she was comfortably resting against the ground, he climbed up on top of her and stretched her legs wide and far apart.

Afterwards, without warning, he plunged his dick deep inside of her, thrusting and slamming against her inner walls, claiming her as his own… over… and over… and over… again…

Minutes later, after they climaxed together, Florian finally collapsed over to his side. Pulling her over to his chest, the happy couple gazed up at the sky and fell fast asleep.

Hours later, Daphne awoke at sunset to find Florian seated underneath the yew tree, with a miniature lyre held tightly within his hand. As she arose to join his side, he began to play her a sweet melody.

"Where did you find that musical lyre?" she asked him, curiously.

With a bright smile, he replied, "I always keep a spare in my back pocket."

"Can that lyre really fit in your clothes?" Daphne pressed on.

As it currently stood, even as a miniature instrument, the lyre was still far too large to fit inside of any reasonably sized pocket attached to male garments designed for today's modern fashion.

"Consider it as magic," he laughed on.

"Magic? Since when have you used magic before?"

"Come now, Daphne," the crown prince replied, most seriously. "Surely, I, the emerald prince, am capable of performing simple magical enchantments. After all, it was *I*, who first turned myself into a frog, in order to meet with you. Furthermore, it was also *I* who cursed and banished Esmeralda, before rescuing you from that dreadful spell. As far as I'm concerned, your great-grandmother might have some competition, after all."

"That's right, you did do all of those things, didn't you?" Daphne suddenly came to acknowledge these truths about her husband with both pure admiration and bewilderment.

Perhaps, her crown prince was also a secret sorcerer in-training as well?

"And now, Daphne, my love," he spoke with much enthusiasm, "Are there any more remaining special wishes that you'd like for your husband to grant you?"

"Florian, you've already given me everything that I could ever have possibly hoped to wish for and then some," she admitted with great pride.

"Oh, is that so?" he repeated with a wild grin, pleased by her honest answer.

"Well…," she began to think aloud, "Perhaps there's still *one last wish*, after all."

"Anything," he vowed. "Say the word, and I'll make it happen."

Leaning against her husband's ear, she softly whispered, "I wish to have four children with you."

With a beaming smile that stemmed right from his own fluttering heart, Florian simply replied, "*Done.*"

Needless to say, Prince Florian did indeed, keep his promise to Princess Daphne. In the end, the crown prince granted his bride's last wish.

Just like the blooming flowers found within their majestic garden, the couple would go on to have four children together: their eldest and only son, Crown Prince Fabian; twin daughters, the Princesses Laurel and Lily; and their youngest daughter, Princess Freya.

And they lived *happily ever after…*

# Epilogue

## *A Few Weeks Later...*

After her long journey traveling through the countryside by carriage, Daphne finally arrived to the Kingdom of the West's imperial palace. After spending a few months apart, the eastern crown princess had at long last arrived to Violet's kingdom to congratulate her sister upon the recent birth of her third child. A daughter, named Princess Marigold. Daphne's very own first-born niece.

Meanwhile, as the palace was busy with the preparations associated with the upcoming ball that was going to be held in honor of the new princess, Daphne decided to let the queen rest for a bit more in her private bedchamber, as she made her way over into the nursery to visit the newborn child.

Much to Daphne's surprise, Princess Marigold's bedchamber was decorated from head-to-toe in the color of gold. From a golden crib to a golden armoire, to golden-shaded curtains to a golden hued carpet, the color gold was all around. But if that wasn't enough, the little girl's nursery was also adorned with freshly plucked marigold flowers, which hung in every possible direction and corner of the space.

From garlands made of marigolds dangling across the curtains and ceilings, to fresh bouquets placed within golden vases located on top of every table, the room was covered with the sweet aroma of freshly plucked flowers. Apparently, as Daphne soon came to learn from the child's nanny directly, since the baby's name includes the word *gold* within it, King Maximus has taken both a fancy and an obsession on gifting his only baby daughter with an endless supply of gold and marigold flowers in her honor.

Upon entering the nursery, Daphne attempted to take her first peek at the child, while she quietly slept within her golden crib. With the nanny resting on her rocking chair nearby, the crown princess bent down to admire her newborn niece. However, as fate would have it, a lit candle that was previously resting against a shelf above the crib, accidentally came crashing down, nearly burning Marigold's arm in the process.

"Oh dear!" Daphne cried, as she quickly sought to put out the fire with her handkerchief.

Afterwards, as Daphne and the nanny proceeded to check upon Marigold's injuries, to their sheer surprise, the child was miraculously left unharmed. However, with a flickering flame burning so bright, shouldn't the child have suffered from a minor burn or some sort of a scar, at the very least?

Instantly, without speaking another word, the nurse knew the truth. For a child left unharmed by fire could mean only one thing. *That child was blessed.* Protected from fire by the great fire god, himself.

"She's immune to fire," Daphne acknowledged. "But how can this be?"

"Our princess is blessed," spoke the nurse, with much enthusiasm. "The great fire god, himself, has claimed her."

"Claimed her? Whatever do you mean?" the crown princess asked the nurse directly.

Suddenly, Daphne recalled her dream from before, while her sister was still pregnant with Marigold. Back then, she dreamt of a princess who was surrounded by gold and fire.

Glancing across the room, it was clearly evident that the young princess represented the same gold found within her previous dream. And now, apparently, fire was also an element that couldn't harm her, either.

Slowly, her past vision about the child were starting to piece together.

"He will come for her one day," the nurse warned.

"Who?" asked Daphne.

"The fire god," she replied. "She's already protected by his spirit."

"Speak none of this to anyone," Daphne instructed. "I will inform the child's mother about what has just recently transpired here within this room, myself. And from there, it will be up to the queen to decide the fate of the young princess."

Meanwhile, Daphne and the nurse looked on at the child in pure bewilderment, as Princess Marigold awoke only to giggle at their presence. Completely unbothered by the mere fact alone, that only a minute ago, her life had been miraculously spared.

But little do they know… that this young girl will later grow up to not only be immune to fire… but that she will also capture the very heart of the great fire god too… but that's another tale… for perhaps, a later time…

# AFTERWORD

To all my readers, thank you for taking this wonderous journey with me through the Enchanted Forest.

And this saga continues on with our next heroine, Princess Marigold, in…

### *Marigold*

## ABOUT THE AUTHOR

Kristina Stangl is an American author. She was born and raised in San Francisco, California, USA. She holds a Master's degree in Public Administration, MPA; a Bachelor of Arts in International Relations, with a minor in Middle East and Islamic Studies from San Francisco State University; along with Teaching English as a Foreign Language (TEFL) credentials from the University of Toronto, Ontario Institute for Studies in Education. Before writing her first novel, Kristina previously worked in both the public and private sectors, having served in the United States federal government for nine years. In addition to writing, Kristina enjoys traveling across the globe and visiting famous and historical sites, which she documents on her social media accounts. To date, she has traveled to over thirteen countries, three continents, and speaks three languages. When Kristina is not traveling or writing, she's at home experimenting with baking new desserts, pies and other sweet treats.

www.ingramcontent.com/pod-product-compliance
Lightning Source LLC
Chambersburg PA
CBHW060342310726
48976CB00003B/685